SANTUARIO

SANTUARIO, BOOK 1

G.B. GORDON

Riptide Publishing
PO Box 6652
Hillsborough, NJ 08844
http://www.riptidepublishing.com

Cover Art by Reese Dante, http://reesedante.com
Editors: Carole-ann Galloway and Kristen Osborne
Layout: L.C. Chase, http://lcchase.com/design.htm

ISBN: 978-1-937551-65-0

First edition
September, 2012

Also available in ebook:
ISBN: 978-1-937551-64-3

SANTUARIO

SANTUARIO, BOOK 1

G.B. GORDON

This first one's for my parents, who taught me that tolerance is a virtue, and who lived by that premise, no matter how much I tested it.

TABLE OF CONTENTS

200 YEARS TOO LONG

Santuarian Bicentennial Has Citizens Questioning the Past

pas. Hentavik - Thousands took to the streets of Hentavik yesterday on the 200th anniversary of the Santuarian generation ship landing on Jarðvegur. Individual voices have always questioned the Þing's decision to segregate the newcomers on "Santuario" as its inhabitants call the island, but those voices have never been as numerous as they are today. People of all political convictions are ready to end the Santuarian isolation. "It's not like they're space aliens," one protester told the Herald. "They're human beings, like us. We have the same origins, even if they're thousands of years apart. This planet gave us a home when we first came here. And we turn around and assign them some uninhabited, hellishly hot rock in the South Sea? That's contemptible."

Sources tell the Herald that more than a few Þing representatives share that sentiment and are lobbying to extend a hand to our neighbors in the south. The time to close the most shameful chapter in our history might be finally here.

CHAPTER 1

Three hours after sunrise, the temperature in the Quonset hut that served as the comandatura had already reached sauna level. When Alex opened the door to his office, he walked into the usual wall of muggy, stale air. A glance at the dead ceiling fan, a shrug, a quick check of his in-basket. The arbitration decision on the fender bender at the bridge had come in; each of the boys would pay for his own damages. The second paper was a handwritten note: Elena was withdrawing her complaint against her husband. Again. With a sad shake of his head, Alex ripped the domestic disturbance report to shreds and dropped it in the bin. Routine. Except . . .

He paused, pulled a folder from between two memos and drew his brows together. Looking at both sides of the thin cardboard sleeve, he perched on a corner of his desk. The capitán didn't put together files, at least not for the one-page reports of thefts and cantina brawls that filled most of Alex's days. And the files he did assemble, for cases having to do with the familias or Securitas, rarely ended up on Alex's desk. Alex gingerly folded his too-tall frame into his chair and carefully centered the folder on his desk before opening it.

First page—morning rounds report. The rurale had found a body on the beach not too far from the slaughterhouse; male, about forty years old, dressed in nothing but canvas pants. The dead man had old scars on his back and fresh abrasions on both wrists, as well as a deep wound in his skull.

Alex scanned the rest and wondered why the Securitas hadn't cleaned up after themselves. Unidentified bodies didn't exist on Santuario, at least none with rope burns on their wrists. There were injured and missing persons, but no murder victims. Alex tried to remember the last time he'd heard of a death the policía had investigated. There'd been a knife fight in Rajon Five in which one of the combatants had been killed. That was it. He had never worked a homicide. Not in eleven years on the job. Why didn't the capitán take care of this himself? Staring at a point beyond the wall, Alex dropped the report back into the folder, dislodging a yellow sticky note:

RUKOW:

I'M TOO TIED DOWN WITH A SANTILLAS CASE TO MESS WITHA DEAD DRIFTER. YOU SPEAK SKANES, RIGHT? INFORM ICE. THEY'LL SEND SOMEONE TO TAKE CARE OF THIS. BE POLITE!

MENDEZ

Alex swore softly. Work with ICE and probably annoy the Securitas into the bargain; he was doubly fucked. The capitán had smoothly disentangled himself from the mess. A pox on him. Alex mentally reviewed what he remembered of homicide procedures from the academy and briefly entertained the thought of letting the file disappear or losing it. Unfortunately, there was still a body in the slaughterhouse waiting to be transferred to the morgue in Hentavik.

With an accusing look at the fan, he left his office and strolled past the clerk's desk to the open door.

"Sultry today," he ventured.

"Storm coming," the clerk, Kazatin, nodded.

Alex leaned against the doorframe and studied the sky. "The poor sod they found on the beach this morning doesn't give a shit anymore."

Kazatin drew his head between his shoulders. "Gijón found him. He was already packed with flies. Why'd they leave him there?"

The same question Alex was asking himself. Not a breath of wind stirred the palm fronds. "Anyone from here?"

Kazatin shook his head. "Gijón hasn't said anything."

Hands in his pockets, Alex pushed himself away from the doorframe. "I'll go have a look."

He headed east down the dirt track that followed the coastline between the beach and the trees, now and then winding through the palms or brush. If the dead guy was a Securitas victim, they had hardly forgotten him there. They didn't make mistakes like that. Which meant they'd left him there for the policía to find. On purpose. The thought made him want to puke. Of course, there was still a slight chance that it was someone else's shit entirely.

A jumble of concrete and old bricks, the slaughterhouse occupied a patch of sparse grass and weeds between the road and the beach. Rambling vines had long conquered the walls and aided the sun and wind in widening cracks and peeling paint.

Rather than walk all the way around the building to the front entrance, Alex cut across the loose sand to where the wire fence had rusted away, and slipped through the hole. There were no windows facing the rear of the building, just a gray metal door. In the yard, an old man was emptying a pail into the incinerator. Alex tried to ignore the increasing stink of decomposition.

"Hola Miguel, quetal!"

The old man turned and raised a hand.

"You got a cigarette?" Alex asked.

Miguel looked at him sideways with raised eyebrows.

"Don't worry, I'm not starting again." Alex pulled down the corners of his mouth and pointed his thumb over his shoulder at the door. "Gotta go in there."

Miguel nodded his understanding, handed over one of his hand-rolled cigarettes, and struck a match. Alex inhaled the smoke deeply. He'd pay for that cigarette. Miguel shook his head, but Alex just grimaced. With a mock salute, he turned and entered the rendering plant.

The foreman came over as soon as he saw the tan uniform in the dim light. "Ah, Teniente, please come in. He's in the fridge. When are you going to take him away?"

"Soon."

"Soon, soon. A body in the fridge is bad for business."

Alex shrugged. "Así es la vida."

The foreman snorted, but shut up and led the way across the plant's floor to the refrigerated warehouse. He had to bear down on the handle with the full weight of his skinny body to open the heavy metal door.

After the heat outside, the cool air felt pleasant, but when the door fell shut behind him, Alex shot a nervous glance over his shoulder.

"Don't worry, Teniente. It opens from the inside as well. Down the right aisle, all the way to the back," he said as he left.

Alex nodded and walked between the ceiling-high metal shelves to an aluminum table on wheels that had been pushed against the back wall. The man lay on his back. Alex had never seen him before. Which answered at least one of his questions. It was nobody from Peones. He was skinny and filthy and had bad teeth. Anywhere between 40 and 50, Alex guessed. The description fit a good many of the *djeti*, as the familias called anyone who didn't belong to them. Alex checked the abrasions on the wrists—rather unambiguous signs of forcible confinement. The head wound was deep; the skin around it had been neatly shaved and part of the skull plate removed. No fall or blunt force trauma, that one. It looked more like surgery. He squinted through the cigarette smoke. Hardly any blood, no other injuries he could see. So maybe not Securitas after all; they tended to be less circumspect with their victims. He wondered what the crime scene looked like.

Goose bumps on his arms reminded him to get out. He rubbed his hands across the skin, and with a last musing look at the body, turned and walked back to the door. A twinge of trepidation made him push down on the latch more forcefully than necessary, but the door opened without a problem. Humid heat smothered him like a wet towel. The door into the yard stood wide open; Miguel was nowhere to be seen. With a slight feeling of regret, Alex dropped the cigarette butt in the sand and ground it out with the toe of his boot.

Down on the beach, the waves had draped black seaweed on the sand, and bolts of lightning flashed on the horizon. Still, it would be evening before the cooling rain would reach the coast. Alex grinned without joy. At least this case would keep him from roof repair duties and having to dig houses out of the mud. Hands in his pockets, he stared across the gray surface of the water, his eyes searching the northern horizon as always, even though the mainland was much too far away to be seen from here. He couldn't imagine anyone wanting this murder solved. Or did Mendez? A drifter with a professional surgery wound. What a nice little puzzle. One that would give someone more than just a headache. Alex swore it wouldn't be him, but he couldn't help wondering who the guy had been and why he'd had to die.

"So contemplative, Rukow? Thinking about your case?"

Alex almost flinched. He turned slowly, carefully relaxing his facial muscles to achieve the vacant, indifferent expression he habitually showed to the world. He'd practiced that expression, rehearsed it for hours in front of a mirror until it revealed nothing of what he might think or feel. Survival training. "They don't pay me to think," he said.

Vilalba smiled. Alex was almost sure the other teniente had been posted in the small comandatura to watch someone. Vilalba didn't fit. The clerk, Kazatin, was barely smarter than a slice of bread, and Gijón, the young rurale, was a rookie. It made perfect sense for them to be stationed in the boonies. Alex had Luìz to thank for being stuck in Peones, the village he'd been born in, the village in which he would die. And he thought Mendez might have pissed someone off. But Vilalba was a hard-liner, had contacts, and wasn't stupid. He didn't belong here. Apart from which, Alex didn't like him. All good reasons to stay out of his way.

"'Taluego." Alex saluted carelessly, only lifting his hand halfway to his hat. Then, he turned deliberately and walked west along the beach and through a grove of palm trees. It was unnaturally silent under the canopy, the calm before the storm, like having water in both ears.

Angling back north after a few minutes, he saw the neon-yellow spray marks as soon as he stepped through the underbrush. Gijón had preserved the silhouette of his find exactly according to manual, and the lasting calm had kept it mainly intact. Alex would soon find the photos on his desk.

The victim had lain there as if thrown away. Trash, no good anymore, not even a danger. *Don't take people to heart so much. Don't let them get too close.* Good advice from a mother who'd been a bad example in that respect. Getting involved, helping, dying. An inevitable sequence of events he'd experienced firsthand. He should find it easier to follow her counsel.

He walked the beach in a grid and hoped not to find anything. The cigarette he'd smoked had his body screaming for more, and he cursed his weakness. Focus. Whoever had brought the body here had left no traces. Alex briefly removed his hat to wipe the sweat off his forehead and out of his eyes. He checked further toward the road—no tire marks, no drag marks, nothing. He decided he'd done his duty and started back toward the comandatura.

Kazatin brought leftover tea. Alex—feet on his desk, a mug on his chest, and a sandwich in hand—waited for the power to come back on. The weird pre-storm light and the unusual events of the morning conspired to create the feeling that he was an observer, one step removed from reality. He would wake up any moment now and realize he'd escaped Santuario long ago, that being stuck here was only a dream, that his father . . .

A familiar tightness closed his throat. Abruptly, spilling tea on his shirt, he took his feet off the desk, set the mug down, and got up. *Don't think.* Self-pity wouldn't get him out of here. For a moment, he stood, undecided, sandwich in hand. Then he wrapped it back up. He didn't feel like eating anymore. Where were those photos?

Slowly, the ceiling fan came back to life, interrupting his pacing. He automatically reached for the phone list. He had to call ICE, the mainland noseys. Shit! Wasn't life bad enough without crap like this? Reluctantly, he reached for the receiver. Maybe the power would go off again right away, or maybe there would be no connection.

Dial tone. That didn't sound like a reprieve. Drumming his fingers on the tabletop, he waited for the series of clicks that connected him to the Skanes system.

"Investigation Commission for the Executive, Reception. Who would you like to talk to?"

Alex had no clue, had never done anything like this before. But he'd prepared what he wanted to say in Skanes beforehand. "This is Santuario, Comandatura Policía, Rajon Three, Teniente Rukow. I need to report a murder."

"On Santuario? Uhm, one moment please." Unfamiliar music hummed through the line. Alex's foot began to tap to the rhythm.

Then a woman's voice, a name he didn't catch. Did they know who the dead person was, she wanted to know. Where and when had the body been found, how long had he been dead, what kind of injuries, and on and on. Laboriously, Alex stumbled his way through the answers in a language he'd once learned but never used.

"Very well, Teniente Rukow. We will send a coroner and a homicide investigator. Would you please pick them up at the airfield?"

"Sure. When?"

"Tomorrow morning, ten o'clock. Is that convenient?"

"No problem." Alex had no idea when Mendez would be back with the zorro, the light utility vehicle they all used. But he'd be damned if he'd show weakness to a stranger.

"And, Teniente Rukow, please envoy us your report and the crime scene photos today."

"Envoy?"

"Yes. Is that a problem? Do you have the address?"

Envoy. That meant a computer. Shit. "Yes, I have it. No, no problem." He politely said good-bye, then slammed down the receiver. Envoy! The comandatura didn't have a computer. He'd have to use the one in the Hotel Aldea, where the Securitas kept their whores and had installed a kind of office. Alex hated to go there, hat in hand, and beg to use their computer. He never knew who he'd encounter, could never be sure he'd get out in one piece. Even just to be noticed by someone who might later remember him wasn't good.

Kazatin chose that moment to bring him the missing photos. Alex's stomach turned to lead. He put on his "face" and shoved the photos into the file. "Thanks. Mendez back yet?"

"I haven't seen him today. He went to Tierraroja yesterday, because of the Santillas thing. Said it could be a few days."

"Shit! I need the zorro tomorrow morning."

Kazatin shrugged. "I'll tell him when I see him."

Alex didn't even bother with a comment, and Kazatin disappeared back to his desk. The report took barely more than a page and was typed up too quickly. No reason to linger. Alex got up heavily, played with the folder, then mentally kicked himself and grabbed his hat from the hook by the door. "I have to pay a visit to the Aldea," he informed

Kazatin. "I shouldn't be long," he stressed, but doubted that Kazatin would even notice if he never came back.

Dark clouds were piling up in the sky, and the air stood like warm water in a bathtub. He strolled up the road, stopped on the wooden bridge to spit in the creek and look at the mist-covered hills. It would be good to drop this whole miserable case into someone else's lap tomorrow. A Skanian's lap. He chewed on his lip. He wasn't nearly as curious as he'd been eleven years ago when, fresh out of school, he'd applied for that security job in the mines, but still, he couldn't help wondering who he'd meet tomorrow.

The mines, the only area on the mainland where the Skanians allowed anyone from here, the only way to leave Santuario. This island, this life. How naively he'd believed in the possibility. But of course Luìz had found out. And of course he'd made sure not only that the job application disappeared, but also that Alex would be stuck in Peones for the rest of his life. He'd been a fool to think learning the language would be his biggest problem.

How had Mendez found out he'd learned Skanes? Alex had scoured the library for information about the mainland, but hadn't found a lot beyond the language book. It was supposed to be a cold country, full of lakes and evergreen trees, with somewhat primitive inhabitants—huge and lumbering.

Alex had never seen a Skanian, but he doubted that the animal-like drawing in the ancient encyclopedia matched reality. He sighed deeply and pushed off the rail.

The Aldea was a decrepit building on the outskirts of Peones. All the curtains were drawn, but the door stood open. Alex slipped into the tiny, club-like entrance hall and waited for his eyes to adjust to the dim light within.

"Alex, what're you doing here?" Alessa sat on the reception desk, kicking her naked legs against the wood. Sixteen, with a clear Madonna face; Alex liked her.

"I need to use the computer."

"You'd better come back some other time. Leonid is upstairs."

Alex felt the blood leave his head. It took an effort to keep his mask in place. "Is he busy?"

"Julia's with him. But you never know how long he'll be."

Alex shook his head. "Gotta be today. Anyone in the parlor?" No need to specify that he didn't mean the girls.

"Two from Rajon Four want to share a girl, but I don't think it's because of the money." She wrinkled her nose.

Alex tried not to picture the details. "I'll manage. Your brother back on his feet?"

"Of course." She waved her hand dismissively. "Only the good die young."

He touched his hat in a friendly salute, took a deep breath, and stepped into the parlor.

A dark-haired Adonis lounged on the leather sofa, watching his friend dance with Lena to non-existent music. Alex tried to look as if he belonged. He made it three steps toward the office before the dancer noticed him and blocked his way. "Whoa, hold it, where's the fire?"

Alex glanced at his face—lean and unshaven with light-colored eyes—then the stripes on his shoulder. He made a placatory gesture and lowered his eyes. *Don't fight back.* He still had a chance to get out of this without raising any dust. "Don't let me disturb you, Sargente. I just need your computer for a few minutes, and then I'll be out of your hair."

The guy didn't budge, simply stared at Alex with narrowed eyes. "Ain't he cute, Kolya?" he asked without turning his head.

Kolya slowly studied Alex from head to foot. The way he lolled on the sofa could only be called lascivious. Full lips and cold, black eyes. "Mhmmm, uniforms should be outlawed. They only seduce decent boys like us." He talked with a slight accent, had probably grown up in one of the Rus-speaking tierras.

Alex deliberately relaxed his jaw muscles and waited. No sense in arguing. They would leave him alone when they tired of their game, not a second earlier.

Lena wrapped her arms around the lean one, who stank of sweat and booze. "Come on, dance with me." He ignored her at first, but when she tried to take his hand, he shoved her away hard.

With feline smoothness, Kolya came up from the sofa, positioned himself behind Alex, and shoved both hands in the back pockets of Alex's pants. Reflexively, Alex clenched his butt and straightened his shoulders. Mistake. Kolya kissed his neck, and Alex was unable to hide a shudder of revulsion. Lean Guy grinned.

"Madrios! You make me sick!" a voice rang out from the stairs. Alex's head whipped around, and the two Securitas stood at attention. Leonid! For a fraction of a second, Alex couldn't decide whether he was relieved or scared shitless, but then he shoved the thought aside and, using the reprieve, disappeared into the little office in two long strides.

The folder stuck to his hand. "You are lucky you don't serve in my rajon," Leonid's voice rumbled through the slightly open door. Fingers flying across the keyboard, Alex scanned the pictures and reports. *Scan in progress. Please wait.* "If I had trash like you two in my unit I'd rip your pansy asses open." Alex didn't doubt it for a second. He pictured Leonid prowling around the two, typed in the envoy address, nervously shifted his weight—*connecting*—threw a quick glance toward the door. "Dismissed! Now scram before I forget that I'm not your CO." *Connection established. Sending envoy.*

"Are you looking for your daddy?"

Alex whipped around. Leonid stood in the door—one hundred thirty kilos of contempt for humanity, arms as thick as Alex's thighs crossed over a heavily muscled chest.

"What do you want?" Alex barked at him. He felt sick, but he was in for a solid licking anyway. Better get it over with.

"What do *I* want?" Leonid raised one eyebrow, then took a sudden long step forward, crowding Alex, looking down on him. "You little gnat. As if you'd stand even the shadow of a chance."

Alex could smell the breath mints Leonid was addicted to. He tensed the muscles over his solar plexus in anticipation of a blow that didn't come, and was unprepared when Leonid's head rammed his forehead. He felt his eyebrow split, stumbled backward. He quickly measured the distance, trying to calculate whether he'd reach the door if he kicked Leonid in the balls. Leonid grinned, and Alex remembered having pulled that stunt at their last encounter. Leonid wasn't stupid enough to fall for the same trick twice. Accepting the inevitable, Alex grinned back in a show of bravado he knew he wouldn't be able to back up. He was waiting for the blow that would break his ribs when Leonid suddenly laughed. Without the scar across his cheek, he would have looked boyish. "Your father is wrong, gnat. You're no coward." Then he left. Incredulous, Alex straightened up and wiped the blood out of his eye. Behind him, the computer beeped. *Transfer complete. Sign out?*

As he walked back to his office, the scene played over and over in his mind, but he had no explanation for it. Luìz had found Leonid about a year ago. Blond, handsome despite the scar, a year or two younger than Alex, and the perfect Securitas officer, he was exactly the kind of son Luìz had always wanted. He'd made Leonid his special pet and loved to sic him on Alex for perceived infractions. Ever since then, Leonid had given Alex the impression that it was his personal goal to break every single bone in Alex's body at least once. This was certainly the first time he'd ever helped Alex, however unintentionally.

Thunderheads piling up in the sky blotted out the remaining light of the evening, and the storm had almost reached the island when Alex opened the door to the comandatura. Mendez still wasn't back. Alex would have liked to talk this weird case over with him. He liked the calm, somewhat distanced way with which the capitán approached problems. And he was the only one around with whom it was possible to have the occasional rational conversation.

Kazatin's desk was clean, and Gijón was holding the fort by folding paper planes. He looked up guiltily when Alex entered. "The sargente went home. He was sure nothing else would happen today."

Alex wearily waved the apology aside. Good thing he hadn't needed the help. Though he hadn't really counted on Kazatin to sound the alarm if he didn't return. The cavalry only existed in old stories. "You can go home, too," he told Gijón. "I'll lock up." Not that it would do much good if anyone really wanted to break in.

The young rurale breathed a sigh of relief and scrammed. Alex perched on the edge of his desk. Listening to the first few raindrops patter on the roof, he reviewed the day. Vilalba was watching either him or Mendez, he was almost sure of it. But for who? Luìz? Hardly. Luìz needed neither reason nor pretext to "discipline" Alex. Besides, he didn't team up with razor creases like Vilalba; not his style at all.

Vilalba was probably after Mendez and merely enjoyed sideswiping Alex now and then.

But those two goons from the bordello? That could've gotten nasty. You suffered the Securitas like a pest. You didn't fight them—not more than once, anyway. Had Leonid seen who the envoy was addressed to? Had the encounter at the Aldea been a setup, or did the Securitas have nothing to do with the corpse? In either case, an ICE investigator would spoil their mood. With that, the nausea was back. Suddenly, Alex knew it was only a matter of time until the Securitas dealt with him once and for all.

With a flash of lightning and an almost simultaneous crack of thunder, the storm broke loose. Rain drummed deafeningly on the corrugated tin roof, drowning out Alex's thoughts. He checked the windows, locked up, and watched the light show from the porch for a few minutes, then fingered the chin cord out of his hat and gave himself up to the elements.

Within seconds he was drenched. He crossed the yard on the double and loped up the road. Soon, the rising wind at his back forced him into a run. The few houses he passed on his way home were boarded up tight. Just after the bend, a loud crash made him flinch. Lightning had felled a tree and dropped it through the roof of Ria's house. A baby wailed in the darkness. Alex prayed Ria and her son were okay and went to check. Her husband had been disappeared last winter without ever having seen his son.

He hammered his fist against the door, though he felt a bit ridiculous considering the giant hole in the roof. She opened the door with the baby in her arms. Panic made way for relief in her eyes when she recognized him.

"Alex, gracias a Dios! I can use your help."

Over her shoulder, he could see the rain pouring through the ceiling. "I can try," he yelled against the storm. "But it doesn't look good."

For more than an hour, Alex tried to cover the hole in the roof while Ria moved her belongings and shoved furniture into other rooms. Then, with a loud crack, the storm tore the roof off completely. In the pelting rain, Ria snatched up a few things for the baby while Alex wrapped him in his jacket. A futile gesture, since they were all utterly soaked. Holding on to each other, they fought their way through the lightning-lit darkness. In some places, the road had turned to a knee-deep morass, and the rain fell so densely that Alex almost missed his own house.

A tree lay diagonally across his driveway, but the roof was whole. He forced the door open against the wind, shoved Ria through the gap ahead of him, and let the door crash closed behind the three of them. They stood dripping in the narrow hallway, dazed, wiping the rain out of their eyes, stretching their shoulders, savoring the relative calm. Around them, muddy water collected in a small pool.

Ria shivered. Alex moved the child to his left arm and gently turned her by the shoulder. "Come."

Wordlessly, Ria followed. Alex gave her the baby, went to find her some dry clothes, then walked her to the bathroom, talking quietly all the while.

"Here's the bath. Wash off the mud. I'll make us some tea," he said. "Take your time. It might take me a while to get the fire started in this weather."

In the hallway, he kicked off his muddy boots. His shirt and pants were no less filthy, so he stripped and left everything in a pile by the door.

There were some live embers left in the stove, which made starting the fire easier than he'd thought. He put the kettle on, washed at the kitchen sink, pulled on dry clothes, and did a quick round through the house, checking shutters and doors—all reasonably tight. Having poured the boiling water over the tea leaves, he grabbed a pillow and blanket to make himself a bed on the couch.

When Ria reappeared, Alex smiled at the way she was drowning in his clothes. She'd rolled up both sleeves and pant legs a good few inches.

"Tea should be ready." Alex waved her toward the kitchen. "Or do you want to put the little one to bed first? You take the bedroom, I'll stay here.

Ria just nodded, wrapped her son in the blanket Alex had given her, and disappeared into the bedroom. Alex poured the tea through a sieve into two mugs.

"He was asleep before I left," Ria said as she walked up behind him. He gave her a mug. "Thank you." She sank onto a chair and sipped carefully, eyes closed, both hands wrapped around the mug. "I'm exhausted. And it didn't even do any good."

"Don't think about it now. It'll look less desperate in the morning. Tomorrow we'll go look at the damage. So far we've always managed somehow, even if it looked hopeless at first." He was tired, too, and felt much less positive than he was trying to make her think, but Ria managed a smile.

"You're right." She finished her tea and set the mug on the drain board. "Tomorrow then, and thank you!" She kissed him on the cheek and left.

Alex stood there, clinging to his mug, felt his throat grow tight, and wished it had been more. He shook his head. Slowly he drained his mug, took his clothes off and tried to get as comfortable as possible on the short sofa. Wind and rain brawled about the house, and despite his tiredness, he tossed and turned for a long time.

He must have fallen asleep eventually; when Ria came to him, he started awake from a confused dream he couldn't remember. "What happened?"

"You yelled something. Did you have a bad dream?"

"Must have."

She gently straightened his blankets and smoothed his hair back. "That sofa is way too short for you. I've made a bed in your drawer for the baby. Come with me, you'll be much more comfortable in your own bed."

She left without waiting for an answer. Alex wasn't too sure he hadn't dreamed the whole thing. Slowly, he stood up, wrapped the blanket around his middle, and risked a peek into the bedroom. Ria, still in his too-big shirt, was sitting on one side of the bed, invitingly tapping the mattress with one hand.

"I . . . you don't have to . . ." he started.

"I know, but it's a bit spooky with the storm and in a strange house. And it's not exactly warm either. I could just use some company for one night. Do come."

With a last hesitant look at the peacefully sleeping baby, Alex closed the door and snuggled into bed with her. She was warm and his soap smelled different on her.

She loosened the blanket and nestled against his naked body. Alex closed his eyes, let his hand wander across her thigh, her butt, her waist, opened the buttons on her—his—shirt, felt her lips on his chest. Her hand softly traced the scars on his back. He removed her shirt, kissed her lips, throat, the tips of her breasts. Slowly feeling their way, they kissed and caressed, and held on to each other, each trying to escape their own storm-tossed loneliness.

She fell asleep in the crook of his elbow, one arm across his stomach. Alex had shoved his left hand like a pillow under his head, stared into the darkness, and tried not to think. He rarely spent the night in someone else's bed, and even more rarely shared his own. But every time he did, he had the feeling he was on the brink of finding what he was looking for, or at least of finding out what that was. And every time, he fought the disappointment afterward—that it was no different from taking things into his own hands in the shower. Why couldn't he just lose himself in a beautiful woman? And she was beautiful. Straddling him, eyes closed, head thrown back against the flashes of lightning, she had been a goddess from a different reality. And yet his vague longing remained unfulfilled. As always.

A tree burst in the storm. Alex's thoughts drifted back to the murder that had tugged at the rug under his feet. But then, that too was familiar. Turmoil had been part of his life for as long as he could remember.

He pulled on the tablecloth to reach the fruit bowl in the middle. Unfortunately, it slid toward him faster than he'd expected. It exploded into a thousand shards right in front of his feet, oranges bouncing through the kitchen like balls. Mama turned toward him, and Alex's lips quivered at the prospect of a scolding that never came. Instead, she stared past him at the door. A man Alex had never seen before stood there in a suit covered with green and brown blotches. Alex went to look at it more closely, and the man picked him up and studied him intently.

"Is that my son?"

Mama held her hands to her cheeks as if she had a toothache. "He is my *son, Luìz. You didn't care for over five years. Why now?"*

"You never told me you were pregnant when I left."

"It wouldn't have changed anything."

"Mila says he's my son. She also told me you quickly found a replacement for me. Where is he?"

Mama didn't answer.

"Where is the bastard?" the man yelled so loud that Alex started to cry. Mama took him in her arms and comforted him. The man turned on his heel and went to the bedroom, even though Papa had the nightshift and must not be disturbed.

"Luìz!" Mama called. "Leave us be. You don't want a family. Why come back now?"

"You are mine," the man called over his shoulder, then turned and pointed his finger at Alex. "And so is he." Then he disappeared into the bedroom. Mama cried and ran after him. Alex couldn't comfort her, and then there was blood everywhere and Papa didn't move.

"Don't worry," the man said. "I'll send someone to clean this mess up. We'll be a real family."

The storm had cleared the sky overnight, and the soggy earth steamed under the morning sun. Alex opened all the shutters and stood on the porch, trying to figure out how he'd get the tree out of his driveway. Despite the early hour, sweat was running down between his shoulder blades into the waistband of his pants. Since Rajon Three had only one service car and Mendez was usually the one driving it, Alex almost never used his driveway. Luìz was the only one who occasionally parked his zorro there. With a vicious grin, Alex decided to leave the tree. He toyed briefly with the idea of a morning swim, but he was already running late. Besides, after the storm, the water in the bay was probably anything but clear.

Ria blinked sleepily when he came in to get a fresh uniform shirt from his closet.

"There's bread and fruit in the kitchen," he whispered. "I've got to go, but I'll try to send you someone later to help with the damage. You take care of yourself."

"You too. Thank you. For everything."

"What are neighbors for?"

CHAPTER 2

"Halden, I'm sure reading the news can wait until after we're done eating. Bengt, dessert? Bengt! Are you mooning over that silly boyfriend of yours again?" Mamma rapped her knuckles on the table in front of him, startling him from his thoughts.

"I'm not mooning," Bengt protested. Mooning indeed. He was hardly a teenager. He looked at his aunt across the table for support, but Svenja only winked at him with a grin that made him growl. It was perfectly normal to be a bit preoccupied with the end of a relationship. You couldn't call that mooning.

"Dessert?" Mamma repeated, waving a plate of apple crumble under his nose.

"No thanks, really." Bengt patted his flat stomach. "Just tea for me, please."

"As if you needed to watch it," Freya grumbled next to him. "You're all muscle."

"Only because I watch it, little sister. We're fighting the same genetics here."

"Who're you calling little, bro," she challenged him with a smile, unfolding her tall frame from the chair.

Bengt just grinned. "Don't even try."

They'd all three of them inherited their father's height, but also his tendency toward bulk. So far, Halden was the only one of the siblings losing that particular fight.

"What's caught your attention so completely?" Bengt asked, trying to peer over the rim of Halden's newspage.

"Santuario," Halden said. "They're not letting up. Now the little buggers want representation for opening their borders."

Bengt nodded. "It's gonna be all over the evening news."

Halden's boys, who'd been quietly shoveling apple crumble a minute ago, broke out into a hot argument over who could claim the last piece.

Mamma's knuckles hit the table again. "Hey! Volume doesn't increase the truth of your arguments. You two are way too old to fight. Your brains are perfectly capable of reasoning. Use them."

"Sorry, Mormor," the twins said in unison, then put their heads together to negotiate, serious concentration settling over their five-year-old faces.

Bengt caught Halden's eyes, and they both smiled.

"The Santuarians have a point, you know." Svenja nodded toward the newspage. "I suppose you could make an argument for isolation when they first settled here, before they started working in the mines. But you can't have it both ways. If you want them to work for us, you have to acknowledge them."

Halden shook his head. "They should be grateful we gave them a place to stay. The second we let them step off the island, they'll make trouble."

"But they're already here. Working shit jobs. Without any rights or protection," Svenja countered.

Bengt held his peace. They both had a point. The islanders were extremely isolated in the South Sea, so not much was known about them, but everyone knew that they were ruled by an undemocratic lot. And the only Santuarians some Skanians came in contact with were the miners. Those were a rough bunch; Bengt didn't blame his countrymen for having reservations. Even the miners lived in an enclave, though. Their entry had been permitted, under strict conditions, because they were capable of dealing with the heat of mining kisa ore underground. Bengt and Svenja weren't the only ones who saw that as exploitation. While many Skanians hated the idea of opening the borders to a potentially dangerous culture, more and more were becoming increasingly uncomfortable with the status quo.

Their forefathers had probably hoped the problem would solve itself, that the colonists were too few to sustain a population and would eventually die out. Yet despite the hellish tropical climate in which they lived, their numbers had grown. And more than two hundred years after being stranded on Jarðvegur, they still posed a problem for the Skanians.

"We'll have island conditions here in no time," Halden growled.

Svenja stuck her chin out. "And what conditions would those be, exactly?"

Halden nodded toward Bengt. "Ask him," he said. "He's worked security in the mines. I'm sure he can tell you a story or two."

Bengt flinched, but was saved by his phone. He checked the number, then walked out onto the back deck. The late summer rain was still warm, and the garden smelled of leaves and earth. It was Sunne.

"Shit, Bengt, I'm really sorry for spoiling your Familyday," she said by way of greeting.

"No worries." If she was calling him at his mother's place on a Familyday afternoon, it had to be serious. Sunne didn't make waves about nothing. Two years younger than himself, she'd leapfrogged over him to make team lead and was running for the Þing in the coming elections. Bengt hadn't been surprised. He'd shot his own career in the foot before it'd even started. But Sunne was good. He'd vote for her. Her demands were always high, but most of all toward herself, a trait that ensured her almost boundless loyalty from her team at ICE.

"How's the family?" she asked.

"Excellent. Well, you know them."

He could hear her smile. "I infer from that cryptic answer that your brother's there?"

With a dismissive wave of the hand, he changed the topic. She hadn't called him to talk about Halden. "So, what is it?"

"I just received a funny call. Well, not funny really." She paused.

Bengt leaned against a post and watched the rain drop from the trees, giving her time to sort her thoughts and wondering, not for the first time, if she had any idea how hard he found it to curb his impatience.

"The matter is somewhat delicate, Bengt," she finally said. "Have you heard about the petition the islanders submitted?"

"That topic is hard to avoid these days. We were just talking about it over dessert. They want a seat in the Þing."

"One? There are several factions among them, each of which is demanding—demanding!—a seat. Squabbling over it. You'd think they'd jump on the offer of having the borders opened. Instead, they seem set on derailing the process." Again she paused. "I mean, most of our þingreps are in favor of eventually integrating Santuario. Proportionally, mind you. And this has been unofficially signaled to the Santuarian senate. They've been here long enough now and haven't threatened us in any way. Not that we give them much of a chance," she added.

"Cultural isolation was the only way to prepare an eventual integration with due diligence," Bengt said, quoting the Þing's favorite set phrase. "Yaddah yah."

Sunne laughed, but became serious again almost immediately. "We've had a somewhat troubling call from Santuario." She waited for his reaction, but he merely hummed for her to continue. "There's been a murder. The timing couldn't be worse. The opposition is just waiting for a juicy morsel to feed their counterattack. Keep this low profile. You'll have to figure out the details as you go."

"Excuse me? I can't go to Santuario."

"Caseload's light at the end of summer, and the team is perfectly capable of finishing up. You're the only one who speaks the language. I need you for this. You've worked with them before."

"And I suppose you forgot how that turned out?"

"I'm sorry, Bengt. It's got to be you. I've already booked your flight. You're leaving tomorrow morning."

Bengt barely managed to swallow the sarcastic comment on the tip of his tongue. Was she really that hard-pressed to find someone else, or was she trying to give him a second chance? Either way, it was a really bad decision to send him, but he could hardly say that. She might be a friend, but she was also his commanding officer. And she didn't make it sound as if the matter was open to discussion.

"I'd better get going then." He ended the call and firmly slammed a lid on memories he'd have much preferred to leave dead and buried. He went back to the dining room, paused in the door, and managed to catch Svenja's eyes. She quietly got up and followed him outside. Sharp as a blade, his aunt. She was closer to him in age than to her own sister and was his best friend.

"Work?" she asked as soon as they were out of earshot.

Bengt nodded. "I have to leave for a few days, possibly a couple of weeks."

"Right now?"

"Pretty much. Flight's in the wee hours, so I have some stuff to take care of."

"And you want me to make your excuses to escape the questions and the fussing?"

He grinned at her guiltily. "Would you mind?"

"What would you do without me? Can you tell me where you're going?"

"Just keep it to yourself, okay? Santuario."

"Shit."

"Pretty much."

He spent the rest of the evening in his office, dug out what he thought he might need from among his old notes, cleaned up his desk, and wrote a transfer report. Then he sat for a long time, just staring at the wall. He already hated every minute of this assignment.

Around midnight, he packed and met the ME at the airport. He'd worked with Kvulf on a case a couple of years back and found him somewhat aloof. That didn't seem to have changed. Immediately after boarding, the pathologist buried his nose in a journal about parasite infections, and ignored Bengt. Their common assignment was to inspect the body and prepare transport; then Kvulf would return with the body and send Bengt the autopsy report as soon as possible. He didn't seem to find that reason enough to strike up a friendship.

Bengt decided he didn't like him. But his unwillingness to communicate gave Bengt an opportunity to read the report Sunne had given him. It wasn't much. A few photos, a copy of the death certificate, an officially worded description of the dead man that managed perfectly to deprive the nameless victim of any individuality. A teniente, Alexander Rukow, had filled out a form with a typewriter whose e's drifted a millimeter too high and whose n's seemed to fall over sideways, so Bengt's eyes started to water after only a few lines.

Teniente Alexander Rukow was requesting that ICE take over the investigation under protection of the Policía de Santuario's sovereignty, because he didn't have the means to investigate the case to mutual satisfaction in an acceptable time frame. He was also applying for the services of a forensic laboratory and a pathologist.

Bengt grinned appreciatively. The wording skillfully glossed over the fact that Santuario's police force wasn't even authorized to deal with a homicide. Just like cases of smuggling and drug or human trafficking, murder fell under the jurisdiction of ICE. That was the price the colonists had had to pay for their sanctuary. But then, not much happened on the island, anyway. It was the mining crews that fueled the statistics.

Bengt sighed and forced himself to reread his old notes. After the incident in the mining camp, he'd buried them deeply in the file he'd dug back out last night. Back then, they hadn't helped him. But surely one couldn't compare the testosterone-laced atmosphere in a mining camp with the normal population of a mostly rural island. He read the marked passages in the dossier he'd been given twelve years ago:

> The Islanders, also Santuarians or Esprussians, exhibit a fascinating cultural diversity. [. . .] Because of their low physical strength, they prefer simple living quarters that can be constructed without much effort. They only work enough not to starve; stockpiling is largely unknown to them; nevertheless, they are not dependent on imports. In the financial sector, the bartering system is predominant, since that way they can avoid income tax and other fees. The ruling class is made up of so-called familias (which means clans); they are without a doubt the population group with the most business acumen and efficiency, and they command goods like education and culture, while the rest of the population remains largely in a state of cultural innocence (school attendance not being compulsory). [. . .]

The dossier had been ancient back then. The style seemed even more patronizing and unbearable now. And some of it was simply wrong. There were few more recent analyses, though. Sunne had compiled some more current statistics for him from an article she was working on for the Þing.

> For a population of about 4,000,000 Santuarians, there are 20 hospitals. Childhood mortality lies at about 10 percent. Medical training is only available at exclusive private schools. Nearly half of the population is functionally illiterate.

Sighing, Bengt shoved the dossiers back into his briefcase. He felt no better prepared now than he had twelve years ago. Less, in fact. He'd been so naive and arrogant. So young. And the situation had escalated. Santuarians were more fragile than Skanians and more volatile. Well, more than most Skanians.

Watch, learn, keep your pants on. Treat them like equal partners in these investigations and pay them the respect they're due. Important to stay open-minded. And keep his temper contained. Yeah, especially that.

Sunne had had a passport issued for him that temporarily appointed him "Commissioner on Special Duty with Plenipotentiary Powers," as well as forms for his expense account and a letter of credit. Bengt raised his eyebrows. So much for "bartering."

All official documents were issued in Skanes and Esprus. As he went over them, he remembered the melodic sounds of that language. He'd hoped to make friends with the miners, instead . . . the suffocating stench of iron. He rubbed his eyes.

"Hard night?" Kvulf asked.

Bengt itched to wipe the superiority off Kvulf's face, but merely shook his head. "Not an easy assignment," he said.

"Ah, well." The magazine went back up.

Asshole.

CHAPTER 3

The comandatura had weathered the storm relatively undamaged. Only the porch roof was missing. Alex unlocked the door and switched the fan on. No power. Well, he would've been surprised if there had been. When Kazatin came in, Alex sent him to Ria's house before the clerk could settle at his desk. At just after nine, the sound of a motor drew him toward the window. The zorro cut deep tracks into the soft soil, and the windshield was covered in mud around the arches the wipers had left. Mendez climbed out and stretched—a slender, quiet man, just the other side of fifty, with deep-set eyes that rarely betrayed anything.

Alex went to meet him. "Good thing you're here. I need the car. Have to pick up the ICE guys at the airfield in Cuevas."

Mendez greeted him with a careless wave, studied Alex's face, and nodded toward the split brow. "Do I want to know what you did yesterday?"

"Not really."

"Apart from that, things are okay?"

Alex shrugged. "Hard to say. The whole thing's pretty off-key. My report's on your desk. It'll be good to hand the case over."

Mendez followed him into the office. "Hand it over?"

"Well, to ICE. That's what they're sending their guys for."

"No, Rukow, whoever they're sending to investigate this case will need help. Those people don't know the first thing about Santuario." Mendez glanced through the papers on his desk, then looked up, his gaze holding Alex's. "I want you to keep a close eye on them. Don't leave them out of your sight. You'll have to watch out for them."

"Me?" Alex stared at the capitán, hardly trusting his ears. He couldn't even watch out for himself.

"Of course you. This is going to be ticklish, and you're good with people." Mendez fished out a report from among the papers Alex had handed in a couple of days ago. "Case in point," he said. "Andres managed to get his truck stolen in Cuevas, but instead of filing it directly with the local policía, he comes to you."

"Because he's known me since I was knee-high to a grasshopper."

Mendez shook his head. "Because he trusts you." Then he sat at his desk and got busy with the stack of papers in front of him. Dismissed.

Alex stood undecided for a moment, then took his hat and left.

He drove carefully, intent on avoiding obstacles and deep mud or pools of water. The bridge was gone; only the posts on either side had survived the storm. He backed up and steered the zorro through the crossing further upstream. Thankfully, the water was already receding. The small town of Cuevas hummed with activity. Trees were being moved out of the way, shutters repaired, shingles replaced. He reached the airfield just as the plane touched down. Leaning against the zorro, hat pulled low against the sun, he let his mind run through possible dialogues in Skanes, thought of the drawing in his encyclopedia of the hunchbacked, hairy beast, and stared intently at the plane. The asphalt reflected the heat and made the air shimmer.

The plane taxied to a stop, and the door opened. Two figures appeared. And stopped at the top of the stairs as if they'd walked into a wall. Barrel-chested, long hair tied in the back, they were definitely not hunchbacked. Their faces were shaved, and they wore long-sleeved, dark suits that made Alex cringe in the heat. They looked like boxers who'd taken a heavy hit, until the taller of the two came down the steps and held out his hand in a gesture that looked freshly learned. Alex took it and shook it briefly. Firm grip, but no crushing contest. The nails were cut short, the back of the hand covered in soft, blond fuzz.

"Teniente Alexander Rukow?" the Skanian asked in a deep, quiet voice. "I am Bengt, Commissioner on Special Duty." Alex was easily a head shorter than the massive Skanian and had to look up to welcome him. Bengt looked well-groomed and elegant, not in the least primitive. And way more normal than Alex had imagined after the picture in his book. A bit exotic maybe with his bright blue eyes, sand-colored hair, and high cheekbones. A strong jawline hinted at some steel behind that soft voice. But if it weren't for his size, he'd barely be noticed in Santuario. Except for the eyes. Eyes like that would be noticed anywhere.

"My colleague, Kvulf, medical examiner," the comisario said, introducing the other one, who was a few inches shorter and not quite as solid.

Alex shook his hand as well and threw a skeptical glance at the zorro's narrow seats. "There is maybe a problem," he said, hoping his Skanes was not as rusty as it felt.

"Will it hold?" Bengt asked.

"Yes."

"Then we'll try it," he said and squeezed himself into the back. His colleague had no choice but to fill the passenger seat. The suspension groaned painfully, and Alex hoped the roads had dried somewhat so they wouldn't get swallowed by the mud.

CHAPTER 4

The first impression Bengt had of Santuario was heat. An assault that burned the membranes in his nose and covered him in sweat before he'd even set one foot on the ground. Heat, and the smell of tar and burned rubber. For a moment, he stopped at the top of the gangway and squinted into the glaring sunlight. Next to him, the pathologist moaned. An open vehicle stood waiting on the tarmac. It was wider than high, which wasn't saying much, since the seats were on the same level as the big all-terrain tires. The driver seemed asleep, leaning against the side door, his face hidden by a wide-brimmed hat, but Bengt thought he'd been looking up at them earlier. Was that the löjtnant who'd typed the report? *Teniente*, he corrected himself silently. The sooner he started thinking in Esprus, the better.

Bengt slowly went down the steps without taking his eyes off the man. The sand-colored clothing was probably a uniform, sleeves rolled up neatly to just above the elbows. Long legs, narrow hips, shoulders like a swimmer. Bengt barely remembered the appropriate greeting in time to hold out his hand as he introduced himself. The Santuarian's grip was firm and brief, the muscles of his forearms sinewy under deeply tanned skin. Brown eyes regarded Bengt steadily from under the brim of his hat, the chin-cord of which ran loosely across a five o'clock shadow. He smelled of sweat and soap—and a mix of ocean and possibly herbs Bengt didn't know. His uniform looked rumpled and sweat-stained, and his pant legs were covered in mud. But despite these signs of negligence, he conveyed an inner tension Bengt couldn't put his finger on. Surprisingly, the man spoke Skanes. His language was a bit stilted, but grammatically correct, and his soft accent made Bengt's mother tongue sound enticingly exotic.

The vehicle proved to be as tight as Bengt had feared, which made the heat even worse. At this rate, he'd be wrung out before he'd even started to work. He claimed the back seat and carefully stretched his legs across the drive shaft as far as he could. Let Kvulf squeeze in the front.

The Santuarian drove past the squat airport building onto the road. The town looked like a single chaotic construction site. Everywhere people hammered and cleared away debris, carried boards and buckets, and called from one roof to the next. Loud music blared from a radio somewhere.

After only a few minutes, they'd left the town behind. Trees and thick underbrush lined the largely deserted road.

Now and then, a pedestrian stepped out of their way; once, a few chickens fled into the ditch. The stifling heat and the swaying vehicle soon had Bengt in a stupor.

A pothole slammed him awake again. The teniente had left the paved road and turned onto a dirt road where deep ruts and potholes shook the vehicle and its passengers like a fun fair ride. Bengt held onto the door and the back of his seat for dear life. The doctor had managed to wedge himself between the seat and dashboard. Only the Santuarian seemed unaffected; he let the steering wheel glide loosely through his hands, and his body swayed back and forth in his seat with the movements of the vehicle.

"Everything all right?" he asked Bengt over his shoulder in his lilting Skanes.

"Mhmm.

"We are almost there. Not long now."

A few tiny wooden houses came into view, and became a village that quickly disappeared behind them. The Santuarian steered the vehicle through a creek, water splashing high on both sides. A few minutes later, he stopped behind a Quonset hut, climbed out, and stretched his arms.

"I would like to introduce you to the capitán. Then we can walk across the beach to the . . ." He searched for the right word, and finally said in Esprus, "slaughterhouse."

Bengt peeled himself out of the vehicle with difficulty, grateful to be able to stretch his legs again, but unsure how much movement he could expect of himself in this heat. He felt sticky and light-headed. Tiredly, he wiped the sweat from his face. "Where are we?"

The Santuarian briefly took his hat off and ran a hand through damp black hair. Only now did Bengt notice the fresh scab over one eye.

"This," the teniente said with a wide gesture, "is the Comandatura Three. Welcome to Santuario."

Bengt had an uncomfortable feeling that he was being mocked, and gave the Santuarian a searching glance, but he'd already turned away to meet the man coming around the corner of the barracks.

Gray-haired, but not old, maybe fifty, alert eyes. He, too, wore his chin cord like a scar across his cheeks. When he saw them, he smiled and held out his arms.

"Welcome to Santuario," he said, echoing the words of the teniente in his own language.

Bengt had trouble quickly calling up enough Esprus to greet the capitán, who winked at him understandingly.

"If you need anything, please trust Teniente Rukow to take care of everything," the capitán assured him with a side glance at his subordinate, whose expression froze instantly.

Bengt clenched his teeth in an effort to overlook the exchange. He remembered this kind of impoliteness from the miners. The Esprussians didn't value openness. He'd known that, had expressly resolved to ignore it as a cultural idiosyncrasy, and yet . . . As the surge of blood in his ears mixed with the surf of the ocean, the events seemed more and more like a movie in which he was only a spectator.

Blood and scraps of meat rotted in the heat on the floor of the rendering plant, green flies shimmered in beams of sunlight, and the stench gave Bengt the final blow. Even the Santuarian covered his nose with his hand until they stepped inside the cold storage unit. Meat hung from hooks and lay unwrapped on metal shelves—the dead man on the wheeled table only one piece among many. Kvulf visibly pulled himself together to conduct a cursory examination. He talked into his voice recorder for a bit, then turned to the Santuarian.

"How long has the body been in cold storage?"

"Since yesterday morning," the teniente answered in his slightly halting Skanes.

"Incredibly precise information. At which time was he brought here?"

The teniente's cheek muscles jumped, but he merely shrugged. "The rurale found him. Maybe six. The exact time is written in the report. He was brought here as soon as possible. No more than an hour after."

The doctor rolled his eyes. "Am I supposed to roll dice for the time of death, or what?"

Bengt wondered how they'd be able to bring the body to the mainland in any reasonable condition, and was thankful that wouldn't be his problem.

"I'd like to go over the dump site," Kvulf finally said.

The Santuarian didn't move. "There is nothing anymore. The storm washed all out."

"What in the—" the pathologist started impatiently, but Bengt put a calming hand on his shoulder.

"Please," he said to the teniente.

The Santuarian turned without a word and left.

The doctor shook his head. "Is he retarded or just lazy?" He packed his bag. "I really don't envy you this assignment."

Bengt laughed mirthlessly. He certainly hadn't asked to be sent here and had no clue how he'd manage. What riled him was the vague feeling that they bothered the Santuarian as much as he did them, and Bengt couldn't for the life of him see why.

The teniente led them to the place where the body had been found, and Bengt marched up and down the deserted beach trying to get an impression, let the atmosphere speak to him. Finally, he gave up. He couldn't get a feel for this place, for this whole indescribable island—the heat, the filth, the people, the fact that no one even remotely cared enough to explain to him what he needed to know.

"Did you find anything that looked like a murder weapon?"

"No."

"Any possessions with the body?"

"No."

"Does anyone live around here?"

The Santurian lifted his thumb back over his shoulder to point in the direction of the village they had come through earlier. "In Peones."

Having just held back the doctor, Bengt now realized that he, too, was in danger of losing his patience. "Could you be any less chatty?" he asked, half joking, half exasperated.

"No."

Fine. Bengt turned abruptly and walked back toward the comandatura. *Don't lose control now.* Sloppy police work and arrogance was a hard-to-bear combination, but he had also felt the Santuarian's anger and had noticed his rigid stance. *Shit.* Something was decidedly wrong here.

The teniente led them back to the comandatura and swore when he noticed the capitán had gone with the zorro. It took Bengt a minute until he understood that "the zorro" was not a person, but the vehicle they had ridden in.

The Santuarian asked them inside and served them a lukewarm drink he called tea. Bengt wondered why people in this furnace didn't at least drink something cold, but the slightly tart drink quenched his thirst surprisingly well.

Only when he was finally in his hotel room that afternoon, standing in the shower with tepid water running over his head, did his thoughts begin to clear. He didn't towel off; just turned the A/C to "Max" and stretched out on the bed, relishing the cool air on his wet skin. His feet hung over the end of the bed. He braced himself for a few uncomfortable nights, and, sighing, mentally went over the events of the day for his report.

They had been stuck in the Quonset hut for over an hour. At some point, the fan on the ceiling had started moving, the power had come back on, and the teniente had phoned around for transport. In the end, though, it'd been the capitán after all who'd come back with the zorro. He'd apologized to the Skanians and exchanged a decidedly non-apologetic grin with his teniente.

Things couldn't go on like that. They were laughing at him. That not only undermined his authority, but also cast a bad light on the country he was, after all, representing in a way. Him of all people. He was painfully aware of the fact that he just couldn't function here. He desperately needed something to help him deal with the climate—

and more suitable clothes. With the decision to envoy his department immediately, he promptly fell into an exhausted sleep.

He woke up with a pounding headache, drenched in sweat. The morning sun blazed through the window, and the A/C had obviously capitulated under its cosmic attack. Groggily, he pushed himself upright and swayed to the only chair in the room, on and around which his luggage lay piled. He stood at the narrow desk under the window, swatted the brochure of the *Grand Hotel Cuevas del Yeso—all rooms air-conditioned* off the table, slid his netpad out of its cover, fumbled the plug into the adapter, and connected the device to the wall socket. The battery sign lit up when he switched the computer on. He swore tiredly, typed his SOS list and clicked send. The system hummed for a moment, but then informed him it hadn't found a connection. He stared unbelievingly at the screen, wanted to grind the netpad into the equally disobliging A/C or at least send it flying after the brochure. He clenched his teeth, his splayed fingers hovering inches above the screen; then he curled his hands into fists and resignedly closed his eyes. He should have guessed.

When the knock on the door sounded, he was in the shower. He grabbed the thin hotel bathrobe, which was, of course, several sizes too small, tossed it aside, and instead wrapped a towel around his hips while walking to the door. Teniente Alexander Rukow, freshly shaven, in a clean, if rumpled, shirt, hat pushed back to his neck. A thin film of sweat glistened at his throat; other than that, he didn't seem to feel the heat. He looked fit and well rested, which didn't improve Bengt's mood. On closer inspection, the scab over the teniente's eye turned out to be quite a split, which might have warranted a stitch or two. Without that, it was sure to leave a scar.

The Santuarian lifted an inquiring eyebrow, and Bengt took a step back.

"Please," Bengt cleared the chair and sat down on the bed, but the Santuarian went over to the window to draw the drapes against the sun. The relief was instant and remarkable. Despite, or maybe because of that, Bengt couldn't hold back a "Feel right at home."

The Santuarian ignored him.

"Did they say anything about a power outage downstairs?" Bengt asked.

Again, a grin flitted across the teniente's face, quickly suppressed, but unmistakable. Rising anger joined Bengt's bad mood.

The Santuarian shrugged. "You will maybe have power in the afternoon, rarely in the mornings."

"And what about the communications network?"

"There is a telephone in the lobby. Or you can have an international line through our office. Envoy only with special computer lines or satellite." The teniente's face lost every expression. "Only the Securitas has those lines. At least here. Tierraroja has its own access."

Bengt snorted. He grabbed the netpad off the table, added extra batteries and a sat-phone to his list, then printed it. The Santuarian leaned back and didn't take his eyes off him.

"I need a few things. Would you envoy this to my office?"

Long fingers drummed four, five beats on the desk, the hand covered in tiny scars from knuckles to wrist. Finally, the Santuarian took the list and read it. "It is not good enough to just telephone this through?"

Weird sentence structure, but the Santuarian probably didn't have a lot of opportunity to speak Skanes. "If it's not too much trouble," Bengt insisted, not quite managing to keep the irony from his voice, "I'd prefer an envoy."

The teniente looked at him, then immediately lowered his eyes back to the list. "No problem."

Bengt watched him closely. There'd been the briefest flash of anger, or maybe fear—there was definitely a problem. Why didn't he say what he thought? The conflicting signals made him nervous—the indifferent eyes, the tension in the shoulders, the restless vigilance in the hands. Did he know more about the case than he was sharing?

The Santuarian folded the list twice and shoved it in his shirt pocket. "I will be in touch."

Bengt frowned. "When?"

The teniente lifted hands and shoulders.

Again Bengt's temper rose. Couldn't the bastard just talk to him, at least make some polite conversation? Bengt stood up, wet, dressed only in a fucking towel, and tried hard not to shake the guy. The Santuarian, who barely came up to his chin, slid back toward the door. *Easy, Bengt. Dial it back a bit.* But then the bastard nonchalantly leaned his shoulders against the frame and shoved his thumbs in the waistband of his pants.

Insolent bastard, Bengt corrected himself. The corners of his mouth twitched appreciatively, but he was too mad to allow himself the grin. He took a deep breath. "What about the investigation?"

The teniente raised one eyebrow. Whoever had found it necessary to split that flexible brow had Bengt's spontaneous sympathy.

"Has the victim's description been relayed to the other departments?" He was too loud, felt light-headed, the room shrinking around him. He made a fist against his thigh. It annoyed him that no one had told him how the heat would affect his body, and even more, that he hadn't thought of it himself. Obviously, the teniente wasn't the only one capable of negligence.

"I will mention it."

"Shit, what in the world are you people even doing here? A man died two days ago. Maybe I should be happy that anyone even noticed."

The Santuarian lowered his eyes. But then that mobile brow rose in a mocking arch, and he let his gaze wander slowly up Bengt's betoweled body. He briefly held eye contact, lifted his hand to his forehead in a salute, then turned fluidly on his heels and left the room.

Arrogant asshole. Bengt slammed the door shut behind him, ripped the towel off his body, and balled it up in his hands. With a frown, he regarded the wet terrycloth, made a conscious effort to relax his muscles, and hung the towel on the rail in the bathroom. Granted, he might not be the most patient man in the world, but to let someone get under his skin that easily was inexcusable.

He should write his report. Sunne would want to know how it had worked out. Fuck! Nothing had worked out, nothing had been accomplished. The doctor was lucky, must already be back on the plane by now. Sunne would recognize from Bengt's SOS list that he had problems, but she could also expect those to disappear once he had his supplies.

Of course they would disappear. The exhaustion, this feeling of not being able to grasp anything, running up against walls, being the butt of some joke—it was the heat. Had to be.

He shook his head. He hadn't asked the right questions. It wasn't information about the case he was lacking, but about the world he had entered. He'd take the next occasion to ask this Teniente Alexander Rukow to explain some things to him. The thought of the expression his questions would elicit made him clench his teeth.

Maybe his mother was right and the breakup was still affecting him, even though he'd been the one to end it. But that was his personal problem and didn't have anything to do with the case. He'd better just ignore the teniente. After all, what had really happened? The Santuarian did as he was told and wasn't interfering; Bengt had worked with guys like that before. ICE had plenty of them. He'd get a grip on the teniente. He sighed and rubbed his face. Who was he kidding? He had about as good a grip on the man as on a wet bar of soap.

CHAPTER 5

Alex jumped when Bengt slammed the door on his heels. *Asqueroso.* Now he was not only playing babysitter for a Skanian with heatstroke, but he was also being forced to poke a hornet's nest. Well, at least the hornets wouldn't be giving him any lectures. He ran down the stairs, counting the steps to calm himself. Mendez had been right; letting this cop-of-the-year candidate run loose on Santuario would not only bury the investigation, but also one of the policía's finest. Yeah, right. It annoyed him that Bengt obviously thought him incompetent. Arrogant bastard. But it annoyed him even more that he gave a shit about what this poster boy thought. He shouldn't be giving a rat's ass. He pushed the lobby door open with such force that it banged against the wall. Bengt was right; he didn't even want to solve this murder. He really didn't need that particular headache.

"Teniente?"

Alex looked around at the usual bustle of guests, hookers, and hotel staff.

"Teniente Rukow?" The receptionist waved at him across the crowd.

Alex pushed his way over to the desk.

"A Capitán Mendez called for you. He asks that you call your office."

Alex had to wipe his suddenly sweaty palms on his pants before giving the man a tip. Mendez didn't chase him down by phone just because he forgot to turn the lights off.

He played with the coins in his pocket as he slowly made his way back through the crowd to a row of public phones on the opposite wall. No use chasing after bad news.

He got a dial tone on the first try, and Kazatin answered. Alex drummed a coin against the phone while the clerk went to fetch the capitán.

"How's your charge?" Mendez asked.

"Fried," Alex replied. He couldn't help feeling some uncharitable satisfaction about that. "Our climate doesn't agree with him," he explained. "He's ordered drugs."

"Then you'll have to continue on your own."

Alex opened his lips to protest.

"We have another body."

"Shit! Where?"

"In One."

"How's that our problem?"

"The same injuries, Rukow. I only found out about it because I'm still in contact with Tierraroja over the Santillas case, but I'd bet my life that the murders are connected. Drive down there and find out what you can. Don't let them shake you off."

Alex sighed. He didn't need an eager beaver reputation. "Sí, Capitán."

"And Rukow?" Mendez chuckled. "Do it now! One of the maids can make the cold compresses for your charge." The line went dead before Alex could answer.

Asqueroso. Cold compresses. As if. He wouldn't get that close to the Skanian. Groggy or not, there wasn't an ounce of fat on that huge body. Alex briefly entertained the thought of siccing Bengt on Leonid. He quite liked the idea. That would give Leonid the opportunity to taste defeat for once. Alex wasn't too sure if Bengt had the necessary killer instinct, though, and he'd probably get into trouble if he didn't return the Skanian unscratched. Although a moment ago the comisario had almost lost his temper and looked like he would have loved to clock Alex. Instead, he'd just pressed his fists to his thighs, which had extended the tattooed band around his bicep alarmingly. No, not a tattoo, it had looked more like a brand.

Alex put his hat back on. He'd better make sure the Skanian got his meds; after that, there would be no more visits to hotel rooms. His stomach ached at the mere thought of having to send that envoy. He could try to send it from Rajon One, but then the message would be delayed for some hours, and the Skanian had looked a bit peaky there. He'd better move his butt back to Peones and get it over with.

As it turned out, he didn't see anyone at the Hotel Aldea. The reception desk was deserted, and while Alex listened for sounds before opening the door to the salon, it too was empty. He sent his envoy without hassle and even received an answer right away that the package would be on the next flight and sent directly to the hotel. Impressed by so much efficiency, Alex hoped the package wouldn't take twice as long to cross town. Carefully, he deleted all envoys and the history. One could never be sure who was reading what.

He vaulted back into the zorro and left Peones, then drove southwest until Cuevas disappeared behind him as well. Here, the road turned due south into the heartland of the Tierra Andúja. Why was Mendez sending him there? He could hardly expect a commendation from that kind of initiative—more like the opposite. Or was he trying to impress the Skanian? Naw. Anyone else, maybe, but not Mendez.

Alex turned the radio on, fiddled with the dial until he found a station with music and let the Son rhythms relax his muscles. He wished he had a cigarette. Did the Skanian smoke? Hard to imagine Bengt with a coffin nail; didn't go with that chiseled, clean-shaven chin. Not that that had anything to do with the case.

He didn't know anyone in the Comandatura One, couldn't imagine anyone would even talk to him. Oh well, it'd work out somehow. He'd just have to play it cool.

Rajon One was more densely populated and urban than Three. After about an hour, the first houses appeared on either side, and as the dirt track turned back into paved road, suburbia gave way to small villas and business areas. Around noon, he reached the center of Tierraroja.

The Comandatura One was a low-slung, whitewashed building on a side road. Glass door open to the breeze, a rurale at his desk and a cabo in a neatly pressed uniform, who rose and saluted as Alex entered.

Alex pushed his hat back. "Descanse, Cabo. I'm here on behalf of Comandatura Three, Capitán Mendez. He has a comisario from ICE breathing down his neck who's interested in your dead body."

"The capitán is out for lunch. I don't think he will be back before three."

"He's taking it easy, and you have to hold the fort?"

The cabo shifted his shoulders uncomfortably. "How may I help you, Teniente?"

"As I said"—Alex rested his elbows on the narrow counter that divided the public entrance from the office space behind it, and read the name on the cabo's breast pocket—"Huelva, you have a body with a head injury and a shaved spot on his skull. I'd like to take a look at it."

"I'm sure the capitán will accompany you as soon as he's back."

Alex ignored him. "He didn't die where you found him, did he?"

Huelva spread his hands on the counter. "I'm sure I couldn't say."

"Never mind." Alex straightened. "Bodies are not really my thing anyway. I'd much prefer it if the ICE snoop took care of this himself. You have no idea what a pain in the ass it is to work with these guys. With a bit of luck, he'll ensconce himself here, and I'm rid of him."

The cabo played with a pen; his eyelids twitched.

"Of course, that's gonna be an amazing opportunity for your capitán," Alex continued. "Cultural exchange, comparative investigation methods, all that jazz. I'm sure he's already informed ICE of the murder."

Huelva dropped the pen and opened his mouth.

Alex perfunctorily touched the brim of his hat and walked to the door. "Please, give him my best regards."

"Teniente."

"No, no, really. I didn't feel like coming here in the first place."

"He didn't die where he was found."

A smile tugged at the corners of Alex's mouth, but he put his face on before he turned back. "Thought as much. I'm sure that'll be of great interest to our man from the mainland when he arrives."

Huelva stepped through the opening in the counter. "Teniente, don't you want to . . . I mean, I could drive you. It's not far. Just a few streets down. Please, Teniente."

"Vale. If it means that much to you." He followed the cabo to his car. "Has he been identified yet?"

"Some bum. One of the whores from the zonas recognized his picture, but nobody seems to miss him."

Tierraroja boasted a real morgue in which smoking was prohibited. The dead man had been younger than the first, but the head injury seemed identical. He also had abrasions on his wrists that spoke of restraints, and no other injuries as far as Alex could see. "ICE will send a pathologist. Dr. Kvulf probably; he already knows the case."

The cabo rolled his eyes.

"Precisely. You should send a photo and description to the other rajones. ICE loves envoys. You'll get ours as well. They want us to coordinate our investigations."

Huelva nodded resignedly. "Wouldn't you like to wait for the capitán after all?" he asked when they arrived back at the comandatura. "Our coffee is not too bad, or there's a nice café across the road."

"I'm afraid I still have quite a drive ahead of me. 'Taluego."

Just outside the city limits, he noticed that the zorro's fuel cell was close to empty. Shit! Go back? But he didn't know anyone here. No one would change a battery for a stranger. He had no choice but to take his chances. He drove as economically as he knew how, but the way back seemed thrice as long. By the time he finally reached Peones, the charge bar was a tiny sliver on the display.

The comandatura had heated up to its usual temperature. Gijón sweated quietly at his desk. Alex took his hat off and wiped the sweat out of his eyes. "The zorro's battery is dead. Mendez in his office?"

The boy jumped to attention. "I'll take care of it immediately, Teniente. Yes, he's in his office. Teniente Vilalba is with him."

Alex grimaced at the name, but then a thought crossed his mind, unique in its brilliance, that lightened his mood considerably. Why shouldn't Vilalba actually be good for something once in a while? Alex went to fetch the murder file from his desk before turning to Mendez's office. The door stood ajar, so he knocked on the frame before entering.

"Excellent timing, Rukow. We were just talking about you." Vilalba's tone insinuated that it hadn't been good, but Mendez merely nodded at Alex. "What did you find?"

"Another homeless guy. The only one who recognized him was a whore from the zonas. This one was a bit younger, maybe thirty. The same head injury, ligature marks on his wrists, nothing else. He didn't die where he was found. That's it. We'll get the photos and report and anything else they have."

Vilalba gave an exaggerated performance of being impressed. Alex badly wanted to smash his face into the desk.

"Good work, Rukow." Mendez got up. "Now we should send our files around quickly as well."

"Absolutely," Alex agreed deadpan. "Unfortunately, I have to be back at the hotel to pick up the comisario. But I'm sure," he slapped the file against Vilalba's chest and grinned wolfishly, "the teniente would love to do that."

Mendez smiled. "Indeed. Why don't you attend to that, Vilalba." He turned back to Alex. "You think Bengt is back on his feet?"

Alex checked his watch. Almost six. "I hope so. We have a lot of pavement to pound tonight."

Bengt was seated on one of the leather sofas in the lobby, reading the paper. He'd switched the towel for a pair of light linen pants and a short-sleeved shirt that covered the brand around his upper arm. He looked relaxed and sophisticated. Alex's brain conjured up the picture Bengt had presented that morning, dark shadows under his eyes, taut as a bowstring, chin thrust out aggressively. Every muscle so precisely defined, droplets of water in the tiny hairs on his chest and arms . . . He shook his head. Obviously the comisario was back in business. Alex sat down across from him, which made Bengt lower the paper.

"Teniente Alexander Rukow. I've been waiting for you. As you can see," he pointed to his clothes, "I received my emergency package. Many thanks."

Alex nodded, trying to switch his brain to Skanes, as Bengt continued. "I bought a newspaper to get reacquainted with your language and maybe pick up the odd piece of information. I think we should switch to Esprus from now on?"

Again, Alex just nodded. Something more than the Skanian's clothes had changed, a shift Alex couldn't quite put his finger on.

Bengt folded his paper. "Did you have a successful day, Teniente Alexander Rukow?" He spoke with a hard accent, but fluently.

"Depends on how you look at it. There's been another body. In Rajon One. And, guess what, they noticed right away." He should really play it cooler than that, but it felt too good to throw the Skanian's earlier words back in his teeth.

Bengt flinched, hesitated for a moment, then seemed to come to a decision. "I owe you an apology. I had been so firmly resolved not to lose my temper. No, sorry, that sounds terribly prejudiced again. Just, please forgive me. We had a bad start. Could we blame it on the heat and start over? Please?"

Alex swallowed. That was unexpected. He hated to be put on the defensive like that and would have loved to say no, but the Skanian's openness disarmed him completely.

He nodded and gave Bengt a brief summary of the day. "We'll have to knock on a lot of doors, especially in the zonas, the red-light district. Likeliest place for a drifter to hang out." He handed Bengt the new photos, and his hand strayed to his breast pocket before he remembered there were no cigarettes there. He caught the movement and massaged his neck instead.

"Tired?"

"Tedious driving. It's a damned boring road." What did the Skanian care if he was tired?

Bengt studied him for a moment. "Have you eaten anything?"

"At some point. Sure." He snapped his fingers. "I remember. Breakfast."

"That's not enough. Aren't you hungry?"

"Haven't had time to think about it." *Shit.* What the hell was going on here? Was this revenge for the babysitting this morning?

Bengt got up. "Let's try the restaurant. Maybe you can explain some things to me over dinner."

Alex had no choice but to follow. The thought that the Skanian was mothering him made him supremely uncomfortable.

When the waiter had cleaned away their dishes, Bengt leaned back, opened the file he'd brought, and played with the photo of the body from the beach. "Teniente Alexander Rukow . . ."

Alex couldn't help but grin at the Skanian's valiant effort to be as polite as possible, and Bengt caught it immediately. "Shit, I knew that was wrong. But it's not Señor when there's a rank, is it? Or is it Teniente Alexander? No, wait; I have to use the second name, don't I?"

Alex laughed. "Okay, stop, please. You'll put a knot in your brain. And in mine, too." He held out his hand. "Just 'Alex' will be fine." What the hell was he doing?

The Skanian shook his hand and shrugged with mock regret. "I only have the one name, Bengt."

Again, Alex had to laugh. "I think we'll manage. What did you want to know? More about the guy in the picture? I'm afraid I've told you all I know."

"More about you Esprussians."

"Esprussians?"

"Is that the wrong term?"

"I've never heard the word. Esprus is a language, or rather, a mix of languages. If I remember my history correctly, the colonists who originally crashed here were a mix of cultures whose main dialects found their way into the usual Standard. There's no people called Esprussians. Although," he looked around, "it's a good description of the mishmash that descended from the colonists."

"It's a beautiful language. Like music."

"Where did you learn it? You're much better than I am in Skanes." No reason not to be polite. While the Skanian was direct to the point of rudeness, Alex wasn't sure that he was doing it on purpose.

A shadow crossed Bengt's face. "I worked security in the mines for two years." He winked at Alex. "If one of my expressions occasionally slips in style, I mean no offense."

"I'll take none."

"So the original cultures are not distinguishable anymore?"

Alex shook his head. "Not really. The family names haven't been any indication in a long time, except maybe those of the familias. You can sometimes hear in which tierra someone grew up, but that's pretty much it. In two of the five tierras, they speak more Rus than Espan, especially in colloquial speech, but even that seems to melt together more and more with every generation."

"The tierras are administrative districts?"

"Sort of. More large land holdings, really. A tierra belongs to the familia, and thc word of thc patrón—or his whim—is law."

Bengt snorted incredulously. "How can someone's whim be law?"

"You'll see."

"Why wouldn't you do something to change that?"

"Easier said than done."

Bengt didn't seem convinced, but Alex didn't want to start another fight. They'd probably get back to that sooner or later anyway.

"Within a tierra, you have the rajones, between five and seven per tierra," he continued.

Bengt stuck to his guns. "But there's a senate."

Alex rolled his eyes. "If you want. The patrones occasionally meet for dinner and call that the Senado. That's where they focus on their rivalries. The only goal they have in common is to uphold the status quo, and that," he pressed his lips together, "they manage very effectively."

"You've got to be joking. Although that explains some of what I've heard." He looked at Alex, stopped himself short and smiled half in apology, half in embarrassment. "Thank you for the background info. So, where do we start?"

Alex checked his watch. "Best start in Peones while it's still daylight. It's way too early for the zonas in Cuevas."

The waiter came with their check, which Bengt paid before he drained his glass and stood up. "Peones it is. Who do you want to question first?"

"Dunno. I'll have to see who's there." Alex led the way through the lobby.

"Who is where?"

"We'll leave the zorro at the bridge." Alex fished the car keys out of his pocket. "And start with a leisurely stroll around the plaza. We'll run with what we find."

They climbed into the zorro, which leaned precariously to Bengt's side. The Skanian was busy stowing his legs. "But don't you want to show them the photo? Ask if anyone knows our victim?"

"Yeah, maybe. Later. I don't know yet. Depends on what they have to say, how they react . . ." He'd hardly burst into the crowd Securitas-style. *Madrios!*

A light breeze from the sea relieved the humidity, and most of the villagers were enjoying the evening outside, standing or sitting in small groups about the plaza, chatting and laughing. Music sounded across the road. Alex held Bengt back. "Why don't you stay in the background a bit? I don't want you to scare anyone."

Bengt threw him an accusing look, but didn't protest, falling back as Alex stepped into the open from between two houses and walked toward Andrés and his cronies. The ancianos had pushed their chairs against a wall for a quiet smoke.

"Hola!" Damn, this would be a lot more unobtrusive if he could just have a cigarette. He leaned against one of the porch posts and watched the younger crowd playing the ancient game—pass each other, eye contact, smile, move on, next round. His foot started to beat the rhythm of the music of its own accord. They would dance tonight; it was in the air. He wished he could stay. Out of the corner of his eye, he saw Bengt shift his weight from one foot to the other. *Patience, big guy.*

Andrés dropped his cigarette butt and leaned back. "Are you coming to dance?"

Alex shook his head regretfully. "Next time."

"Your mother would have come to dance."

Alex shoved his hands in his pockets. "Yeah, I know."

The old man nodded and fell silent. Alex leaned his head back against the post and relaxed his shoulders. He knew that Andrés knew he wanted something, but he refused to let Bengt's impatience push him into making the first move. With a man, moreover, who was twice his age and to whom he owed the courtesy of letting him choose his own timing.

Andrés's curiosity delivered him soon enough. "Did you know him, Sasha?"

Alex breathed a sigh of relief. "Naw, no one from here."

Again they fell silent. At any other time, Alex could have played this game all night without giving it another thought. But Bengt radiated impatience so intensely that it tingled on his skin.

"Might be one of us knows him anyway," Andrés finally said.

This was going better than Alex had hoped. Despite the stranger hovering in the shade only a few steps away. Or maybe because of him. "Might be," he replied.

A small smile played across Andrés's face. "If only you had a picture . . ."

"Yeah, well, I just happen to have one in my pocket." Alex gave him the photo and stepped back to where Bengt was waiting as the men passed it around.

"What the blazes . . .?" Bengt hissed.

"Relax."

Bengt rolled his eyes, but shut up. After a while he nodded toward Andrés. "He called you Sasha?"

"None of your business."

"Excuse me." Bengt sounded offended. "I'm just trying to figure out all these names."

Madrios, couldn't the Skanian stop asking questions for five minutes? "These people have known me all my life. It's a pet name. Forget it."

"What's the big deal?" Bengt asked, surprised. "Why the sudden stonewalling?"

"Just leave it, okay? Drop it." At that point the old man came back with the picture, and Alex was grateful for the excuse to turn away.

Andrés shook his head. "Nobody's seen him, Sasha. He hasn't been around."

"Thanks anyway." He had expected that; had the man been hanging around here when he was alive, Alex would probably have seen him himself. He pocketed the photo, raised his hand in a goodbye gesture, and walked back to the car. He didn't give a shit whether Bengt was coming or planning to grow roots where he stood. He dropped into the driver's seat, stuck the picture behind the visor, and stared into the dead face. *Tell me who you are.*

Bengt waited at the passenger door until Alex finally looked at him. "I made a mistake. I didn't mean to give offense. I'm really sorry." He obviously had no clue in what way he had stepped on Alex's toes.

Madonna. This was going to be fun. "Just get in."

Alex took a detour by his house. "I need to lose the uniform. Back in a sec." Inside, he quickly checked the shutters, pulled a pair of black pants and a shirt out of the closet. No time to shave; he dragged wet fingers through his hair and was back outside within five minutes.

The drive to Cuevas was a silent one. Alex parked the car behind Bengt's hotel and led the way through side roads into the zonas. "Let's start with a drink."

"On duty?"

Sweet Lady, give me patience. "Listen, you're conspicuous enough. We really don't have to waltz into the next cantina and order milk, do we?"

Bengt's cheek muscles jumped, but he held his peace.

"Vale, look, I'm not suggesting we get wasted. You don't have to drink it. But at least order something."

They hit five cantinas before they got the first hint. Alex was holding onto his beer at the bar, while Bengt was leaning against the back wall, watching the suerte players, to their obvious discomfort.

Alex waited until the mesonero was close enough to listen. "I think m'brother goddit," he mumbled into his beer.

The mesonero threw him an inquisitive glance, then continued to wipe the bar.

"Can't find him. The cops found his friend, though. Not good." Alex pushed the crime scene photo across the bar. "I won that. Dice. Bet m'brother looks the same." He took a long pull from his glass as if to drown his sorrow.

"Looks like the guy who cleans at Kotovsk's." The bartender pushed the picture back. "The cops toss dice for the strangest things."

Alex continued his act until his glass was empty, then stumbled to the door. Outside, he leaned against the wall, caught himself reaching for cigarettes again, and buried his hands in his pockets. Bengt appeared a minute later. "Get anything?"

"Maybe. You made those poor suerte players pretty nervous."

The mischievous grin that flitted across Bengt's face surprised Alex. "Kept them from cheating." The Skanian laughed. "Not that I know the rules. Anyway, what did he say?"

"The mesonero thinks our guy could be one of Kotovsk's people. That's a boxing gym down the road; bookmaking, probably drugs, you know the kind of joint I mean."

Bengt nodded disbelievingly. "He was a boxer?"

Alex laughed. "In his dreams. But he might have worked there as a janitor." He briefly considered their options. His usual subtleties would get them nowhere here; to these guys, cops were the enemy, and nothing he said would change that. "This time we'll do it your way. Show them the picture, ask directly, play hardball."

"Would what this Kotovsk is doing theoretically be enough to close him down?" Bengt asked.

"You bet."

"Excellent. Then let me do this."

Alex threw him a doubtful look, but he seemed perfectly sure of himself. Well, he'd survived two years of security in the mines. "Bueno. Here we are. Be my guest."

Four concrete steps led up the side of the building to a wooden door that was covered in graffiti—and locked. When Bengt knocked, the spy hole opened. "What do you want?" a voice asked from the other side.

"We would like to talk to Señor Kotovsk."

"Not in." The spy hole closed.

Bengt looked at Alex with raised brows and a pained expression. Alex grinned. So the Skanian had a sense of humor.

Again Bengt knocked, and again the spy hole opened. "Scram! I told you he's not here." The hole closed.

Bengt shook his head sadly, took a step back, and without ado kicked the door down. The bouncer must still have been standing right behind it. Now he was sitting on his ass holding his bleeding nose.

"My apologies," Bengt said politely.

Alex chuckled, then turned to the bouncer. "Come on, friend. Kotovsk. We don't have all night."

The bouncer came to his feet like a cat, noticed that Bengt stood a good two heads taller than him, and stepped aside. With murder in his eyes, he pointed at a door in the back wall on the other side of the ring.

The gym was brightly lit—a raised training ring in the middle, benches and hooks around the walls. Two men sparring were too busy with each other to notice what was going on at the door; only an older man with a towel around his neck, the coach probably, glanced over briefly.

Bengt had already crossed to the appointed door, and Alex hurried to keep up. It opened into a kind of office, claustrophobically small and full of smoke.

A man sat behind the desk, cigarette between clamped lips. When they entered, he squinted at them against the smoke in his eyes. "What the hell? Who are you?"

"ICE." Bengt pointed his thumb at Alex. "Policía. We'd like to ask you a few questions."

The man drilled meaty fists into his desktop and started to get up. "Eb tvoyu mat."

"I doubt that," Bengt said matter-of-factly. "Had you tried, my mother would have ripped your balls off."

This time, Alex almost burst out laughing. Who would have thought the evening would turn out to be so entertaining?

The guy sank back into his chair. "What do you want?"

"Are you Kotovsk?"

He nodded.

Bengt fished the photo out of his pocket and shoved it across the desk. "This man used to work for you. We need his name and address."

"Na khuya?"

"Because I can close this joint down so fast it'll make your head spin."

Kotovsk threw a cursory glance at the picture. "Never seen him."

Bengt sighed theatrically, leaned on the desk, and abruptly shoved it forward, trapping Kotovsk against the wall, chair and all. He shoved a little more, until Alex almost expected to hear the sound of cracking ribs. "Look again," the comisario recommended gently.

"His name is Jesús Oviedo," Kotovski gasped. "He didn't work here full time. Just helped out once or twice. I don't have an address. I swear! I don't even think he had one." His face had turned red; he was desperately straining against the desk without effect.

"When was the last time you saw him?"

"Couple of weeks ago, at least."

"Where were you Sunday night?"

"Here. Please. I'm always here. Ask anyone."

Bengt looked questioningly at Alex. They wouldn't get anything else from this guy. Hell, they weren't even sure about the time of death yet. Alex nodded, and Bengt let go.

The bouncer waited for them by the door with his ballooned nose, but didn't try anything.

Outside, Alex barely made it down the steps before he lost his composure and burst out laughing. "His face, when you talked about your mother . . ."

"And the bouncer's nose . . ." Bengt joined in his mirth.

They doubled up laughing, gasping for air, until Alex had to wipe tears from his eyes. "Madonna, I haven't done that since . . ." He shook his head, unable to come up with a memory.

"Rumbled a boxing joint?"

"Laughed like that." He hadn't wanted to say that. That was . . . How the hell did this guy get under his skin so easily? "There's a working-girl beat nearby, maybe one of the hookers saw something," he said, serious again. He didn't look at Bengt, just started walking.

After a few steps, the Skanian caught up with him. "What's wrong?"

"Nothing fits here. A drifter gets killed, mala pata. But someone methodically restrained him, cut him up, and then went to the trouble of bringing him somewhere else without hiding him. I'll eat my hat and boots if that was the Securitas."

Bengt didn't comment on the change of topic, but he checked at Alex's last sentence. "The Securitas? Why would they want to kill a drifter?"

"How would I know? Maybe he knew something, saw something. Some kind of torture is the only explanation I can come up with for that weird head injury."

"Whoa, hold it, I meant . . . You make it sound as if the Securitas torture people on a daily basis."

"Your point being?"

"They're law enforcement."

"And pigs fly." Alex stopped walking when Bengt suddenly did. "I think you're laboring under a misapprehension, mi amigo. The Securitas is no law-and-order, help-the-citizens troop. They're the patrón's personal army. Anything threatens his superiority, the Securitas is there to clear up the problem. They do his dirty work. They couldn't care less what happens to us djeti. And if a Securitas occasionally pursues his own agenda . . ." He shoved both hands in his pockets and pulled his shoulders up. "As long as it doesn't hurt the familias, it doesn't bother them. The Securitas has more dead bodies buried across this island than you can possibly imagine."

Bengt had disbelief written all over his face. "No way. We investigate all murders, remember? And the miners on the mainland have far worse statistics than you here."

Alex snorted. "They obviously don't hide their victims well enough. No, think, Bengt! Do you seriously believe the Securitas would inform you of a murder they themselves committed? No one ever hears from these victims again. Often we don't even know if they're actually dead or not." He frowned. "And that's the point. The Securitas doesn't litter the beaches with their victims. And if they didn't dissect him, who did?"

Bengt stood before him as if he'd been struck by lightning. Denial, disbelief, resignation flickered one after the other across his face. He opened his mouth, shook his head, finally said, "No wonder you think us all stupid."

"No. Not stupid, just . . ."

"Naive then. Same difference in this case."

Alex shrugged. It was true; the Skanian met the world with an openness and curiosity that didn't seem to know any fear of consequences. Like a child. Although Alex couldn't remember ever having been like that, even as a child. Yes, it might be naive, but it was also enviable.

"You're far away," he finally said, trying to be conciliatory. "I'm sure I don't know any more about your world than you about ours. We're much too isolated from each other to change that." He took his hands out of his pockets. "Come on, we still have time to question some of the girls, then we'll call it a day." And when Bengt didn't budge, "Oh, come on, big guy, I don't want to spend the night here."

Finally the Skanian started to move, but for the rest of the night, he was distant and morose, and didn't participate in any of the chats Alex started with the ladies of the night. Of course, none of them had heard or seen anything, much less known the victim.

They made it back to the hotel in the wee hours. Alex was dead on his feet, and Bengt maintained his stony silence, which made for short good-byes. Alex didn't complain; he'd talked too much today anyway.

CHAPTER 6

When Bengt woke up the next morning, he briefly looked at his watch and burrowed back into his pillows. No one could possibly be awake after only four hours of sleep. A fold pressed into his cheek, forcing him to shake up his pillow before he could be comfortable. Then his arm started to fall asleep. *Really?* He groaned and sat up.

The sun blazed through the window and had long since started its daily battle with the A/C. Bengt reached for the blister pack on his nightstand, swallowed the pill dry, and peeled himself out of bed. His face itched—sunburn.

In the shower, he just stood there, letting the tepid, metallic-tasting water rain down on his head and shoulders. There was no pressure to speak of. He stared unseeingly at the tiles. *The Securitas is no law-and-order, help-the-citizens troop. They're the patrón's personal army.* Why did nobody know this back home? Because nobody wanted to know. Suddenly the strange rules of the game Alex played to investigate made sense. Investigations in enemy country. *Do you seriously believe the Securitas would inform you of a murder they themselves committed?* Bengt groaned and wiped the water out of his face with both hands. What a fucked-up country.

Yesterday he had believed for a moment that something like a friendship was possible between him and the Santuarian. Until Alex had slammed the door in his face again. Shit, he wasn't good at living only in his own head, was used to having friends around and family, missed Svenja's insights. He pulled himself together and turned the water off. This assignment wouldn't last forever. Until then, he'd just have to manage.

In the lobby, he bought a paper to read over breakfast. The first headline almost made him choke on his tea.

BJÖRBO—A GAME BEGINS THE CULTURAL EXCHANGE

While the politicians drag their feet, the people are already celebrating the longed-for fall of the borders.

Tierraroja - This coming Saturday, the Castañeda arena will see the first björbo match on Santuarian soil. The Skanians have composed two all-star teams especially for this event. The best björbo players of Jardvegur will be demonstrating their national sport. The fiesta starts in the morning on the Plaza Concilio and is expected to last far into the night.

Advanced ticket sales . . .

Dazed, Bengt let the paper sink. The best björbo players. Kjell would be here. He shook his head. It didn't make any difference. It was over. Kjell didn't mean a thing anymore. Except that he was someone who knew what snow smelled like, who knew Bengt's family, who had sat at their table every first Familyday of the month, with whom he could talk, with whom he . . . Oh, please no! Hadn't he debated that topic to death with himself already? Given in to temptation and forgotten their differences again and again? They'd broken up and made up so many times that it made Bengt dizzy. How could he still not be sure?

The problem was that Kjell was too easy to love. For everyone. The golden boy, the star, the media personality. Bengt had always had to share him with the whole world, had stepped into the background, especially during björbo season, when Kjell had nothing in his head but goals and points, or how he'd come across during his last interview, what people said about him, if he earned enough money. At first it had been exciting—travel, attention, the fast life. But over the past year, Bengt had found it more and more annoying. It was simply unthinkable for Kjell to spend a few quiet weeks with him. Even if they managed to lose everyone else, Kjell himself set a feverish pace. No, he was sure. It was over.

The waiter came to his table. "Perdone usted, señor. There's someone on the phone for you. I told him you were in the middle of breakfast, but he insisted on waiting."

Bengt got up and followed him to the reception desk. Probably Alex. Another day of foot work. They had nothing, not one clue. He wondered why the Santuarian hadn't come over. Maybe he'd stumbled onto a lead and was following up? Bengt took the receiver off the desk. "Found something?"

Soft laughter sounded through the line, sending a shiver up his arms. *Please, no.*

"I'm sorry, I don't have the foggiest idea what you just said. Was it important?" Skanes. Upbeat, caressing. Kjell.

Bengt closed his eyes for a moment. "Where are you?"

"In Tierraroja, in a fantastic hotel. Palacio or something like that, close to some Plaza or other. If you want details, I'm sitting in a hot tub letting the water bubble the traveling dust off my skin."

Blond, athletic. Bengt immediately had the picture in his head and made a fist. "No, actually I didn't want any details. What's up?"

Kjell's voice dropped a notch. "As if you needed to ask."

Bengt groaned.

"How are you?" Kjell asked in a more normal voice, but still with that caressing undertone.

"Brilliant. The case is hopelessly stuck, I don't know the rules, I have sunburn, my A/C only works three hours a day, my computer can't get a connection, and no one is talking to me."

"I'm talking to you?" A question, an offer.

You gorgeous bastard, don't make this harder than it already is. "No Kjell, we've already—"

"My A/C is working, no problem. There's a conference room here with everything you need, and a phone in my room." Pleading.

If he gave in now, the whole drama would start over. Who needed that? "Let's not—"

"There's a king-sized bed." Challenging.

He knew he should pass. And that had nothing to do with a dark-haired teniente who was just driving him bonkers anyway. "Fine."

The game was Saturday, the day after tomorrow. Sunday at the latest, Kjell would be gone again. Three, four days tops. "What's your room number?"

"153."

"Let reception know. Could be a while until I make it, though." He handed the receiver back to the receptionist. "Is there a bus connection to Tierraroja?"

"Sí señor, right in front of the entrance. The next bus is at nine thirty."

That gave him half an hour. "Could I make another phone call?"

The receptionist politely motioned toward the pay phones on the wall. The reception phone, he apologized, had to stay available for incoming calls.

Bengt called the Comandatura Three, informed Kazatin of his move, and gave him the hotel name and room number. On his way to the stairs, the receptionist stopped him again. "Perdone usted, señor, there's mail for you." A large brown envelope from the lab in Hentavik, the autopsy report. Bengt went over it on the stairs. Surgical cuts with a precision instrument, probably a scalpel, disinfectant on the skin. Small, round, third- and fourth-degree burns—electric marks. Cause of death: heart failure, probably due to electric shock. Electric shock?

He packed quickly, checked out, and asked to have his mail and messages forwarded. The bus stop had no shade, so people waited under the canopy at the entrance. Bengt joined them absentmindedly, preoccupied with the report. Why electric shock? Torture? Questionable therapy? An execution? But why take the trouble to open the skull for an execution?

The bus was only half full, so Bengt was able to claim a bench for himself. There wouldn't have been much room for anyone else anyway. He had to sit sideways to fit his legs. Despite the open windows, the heat was oppressive.

The trip across the unpaved road was supposed to take two hours; that would be a wonderful commute. *Brilliant decision, Bengt.* Was he kidding himself in thinking it would be over again on Sunday? It had been a brain-dead move any way he looked at it. If he knew that, why was he sitting here? It would make trying to stay in contact with Alex a pain in the ass. Not that Bengt particularly wanted to think about Alex just now.

POLICIA

When the bus reached the city, Bengt looked around, surprised: wide, palm-fringed boulevards filled with people, cars, suits, uniforms; groomed hedges covered in flowers, white multi-story buildings with open-scrolled brickwork, large plazas, fountains, flower beds. Santuario could look like this? He realized that, without thinking, he had imagined the whole island looked like the provincial Cuevas or the backwater Peones. He strolled across the plaza toward the hotel entrance and recalled the "simple living quarters" as his eyes took in the elaborate façade. Had the author of that dossier ever set foot on Santuario?

The receptionist gave him a key and had someone take his luggage up. Señor Kjell, he said, was awaiting him upstairs. *You bet your ass he is.*

The door was torn open as soon as the page knocked. "Bengt, am I happy to see you."

Shit, the kid looked good enough to eat. Bengt waited until the page had set down the luggage, received his tip, and closed the door behind him. The wide windows looked down on the pool below and, beyond that, a large garden, or rather, a park. "I really don't know if this was a good—"

Hands touched his back, stole around his waist, crept up his chest. Lips softly brushed across his neck.

Bengt breathed in sharply. That infinitely familiar scent. He caught Kjell's wrists and twisted out of his embrace. "Do you really want to start this all over again?"

Kjell pouted. "*You* said it was over. I never wanted that. You made that decision alone. You never gave me a second chance."

You had two hundred chances. "And what would change if you had one?" *Nothing.*

Pleading eyes the color of the woods in summer. "Everything. And we didn't just fight. It was wonderful too, wasn't it?" Kjell freed his wrists and got busy with the closures on Bengt's shirt.

"Nobody said it wasn't." Bengt closed his eyes and savored the soft touches. That was exactly his dilemma. Kjell kissed the corners of his mouth, started to nibble on his lips, the phone rang, Bengt's lips returned the kiss of their own accord, he grabbed Kjell's hips, drew him closer.

The phone rang. Bengt lifted his head.

"Let it ring," Kjell murmured against his chin.

"It could be the office, or the comandatura." He let go of Kjell and went to the desk.

It was Alex. "What in the world are you doing in Tierraroja?"

"Liked the hotel better. We have the autopsy report." He quickly summarized the pertinent points. Kjell nestled against his back and played with the phone cord.

"Electric shock? Seriously?" Alex asked.

"That was pretty much my reaction." Bengt tried to concentrate on their conversation while Kjell was stripping the shirt off his back.

"Vale. No use speculating. We have news. Tierraroja has a third body."

Suddenly Bengt was perfectly focused. He pushed Kjell aside and sat on the edge of the desk. "When? Where?"

"Huelva called this morning. Workers found a body on the city dump. Madonna!" He paused. Apparently, some situations managed to unnerve even the indifferent teniente. "Same injuries, he wasn't killed at the dump site." Another pause. "Huelva says he was maybe fifteen, sixteen."

"Fuck." Bengt shoved Kjell, who had nuzzled against his shoulder again, almost roughly away.

"Mendez is sending both of us to One to help with their investigation. Since you're already there, would you drop by the comandatura and make sure the pictures of all three victims are given to the press? I don't really think someone will come forward, but you never know, and as yet, nobody has stepped on my toes because of the investigation."

Bengt let the allusion to the Securitas go. "Sure. Shall we meet there?"

"Vale." Alex gave him the directions. "I'll hurry. You okay?" Was that concern in his voice? Couldn't be.

"Sure. Why?" Kjell was sitting on the bed pouting.

"I'm sorry for yesterday."

Bengt was dumbstruck. An apology? For what, exactly? "Don't worry about it," he finally managed. "Erm . . . see you soon, then."

Shaking his head, he hung up. Immediately, Kjell was with him again. "Finally. That took forever."

"Listen." Bengt raised his arms, denying Kjell access. "I have to go. Like, right now."

Kjell blocked his way to the door. "Then why did you even come?"

Because he needed someone to talk to? Someone to encourage him and help him not to feel so fucking lost? All unbelievably poor reasons to choose Kjell, of all people. "I don't know."

"I'm not going to just let you disappear again."

Well, he'd thoroughly messed that up. "You don't have a choice. It's really urgent, Kjell. Look, can we argue about this later?"

"You always have to go." Kjell balled up Bengt's shirt and threw it at his head.

Bengt caught it reflexively. "Come on, Kjell. You're the one who can't sit in the same spot for five minutes." He'd grown louder, felt the familiar pressure in his stomach of anger he had to swallow. He should have stayed in Cuevas.

Again Kjell came to him. "Just half an hour, what difference can it make?"

It wouldn't be half an hour. Bengt grabbed him by the shoulders. "Grow up. There are more things in life than your fun."

"You're hurting me."

Bengt let him go.

"You can hardly call the way you treat people fun." Kjell had crossed his arms in front of his chest like an angry child. "Go. Go join the locals. You must feel quite at home here. That's why you want to go. You like it here. Finally, people who don't think loss of self-control a big deal. From what I heard, a miner more or less makes no difference to this lot."

Bengt felt the blood leave his face. Something seemed to warn Kjell because he took a step backward. Bengt put his shirt on and left the room without another word.

Kjell had been angry, disappointed. Who could blame him? He had thoughtlessly lashed out with the first thing he could think of, but the blow had hit home, had struck a spot that, after all these years, was still tender. And telling himself that Kjell hadn't meant it made the resulting guilt-fueled fury no easier to deal with. He badly wanted to break something.

In front of the hotel, Bengt stopped to get his bearings, breathed the hot air in deeply, [and] relished the climate's assault on his body because it forced his mind off Kjell. With Alex's directions in his head, he made his way through the tangle of streets to the low, white building that was the Comandatura One. Alex must have called Huelva again, because the cabo was already waiting for him. Even though the thought of having the pictures published obviously made him uncomfortable, he immediately went to work, so Bengt had nothing to do but twiddle his thumbs and wait for Alex. The cabo brought him the ubiquitous coffee and offered him a seat at an empty desk. Bengt thought it was less out of politeness than to get the stranger out of the way, and stared at the drink that smelled so much better than it tasted.

Alex arrived barely an hour later. Bengt didn't dare imagine how he must have driven. He was covered in dust and had deep shadows under his eyes. Someone else who hadn't slept enough. Alex briefly saluted the room at large, exchanged a few papers with Huelva, then turned to Bengt. "Want to go directly to the morgue? Get it over with?"

Bengt agreed and followed him into the street. He stole a glance at the Santuarian from the side. He hadn't shaved; Bengt assumed that someone had kicked him out of bed rather precipitously. A single drop of sweat ran across his face along the chin cord. Bengt would have liked to say something, connect in some way, but by now he was so unsure how Alex would react to even a trivial remark that he kept silent.

As if he'd read his thoughts, Alex suddenly looked at him. "You look like I feel. Sunburn?"

Bengt nodded. "Not that bad."

They fell silent again, but Bengt felt better.

The entrance to the morgue lay in a side street. Alex greeted the desk officer with a wave of his hand, and they followed directions down a flight of stairs.

The boy lay on a metal table. Slender, delicate, with dark hair; a pretty lad. He had a tattoo under his belly button: a chain with the word 'Vigo' inside it. The pathologist who'd come over from the hospital promised them a preliminary report the following day, but already assumed from scarring that the boy had had anal intercourse at a very young age or brutally, or both.

Alex made a face. "Chapero?"

The doctor nodded. "Probably."

Bengt looked at them inquiringly.

"A rent boy. Kiddie stroll. The low end of the pecking order." Alex turned back to the doctor. "Can you say how old the tattoo is?"

"Not exactly, but no older than about a month, I'd say."

Bengt nodded. "Then we should try to find Vigo."

Alex rubbed over his stubble. "And trawl through clinics and hospitals."

They returned to the office, where Alex called Three to give Kazatin the latest news and their plans for the day. Bengt informed ICE. If this continued, the pathologist might as well stay here.

On their way to the hospital, Alex suddenly stopped and dragged Bengt into a store. "You need a hat," he mumbled. He briefly talked to the vendor, who measured Bengt's head, doubtfully screwed up his face, and disappeared into the back. Bengt stood stunned in the middle of the store, and watched Alex rummage idly through the contents of a shelf. He'd never make sense of the man.

The vendor came back with a light brown hat. Oilskin or something similar, wide brim, chin cord. Bengt tried it; it fit as if made for him. Alex also pressed a jar of aloe gel into his hand. "Helps against sunburn. You're paying. I'll wait outside."

Bengt breathed deeply, felt a smile tug at the corners of his mouth. Suddenly, he knew that he'd be able to live with the Santuarian's terse manner.

Neither in the hospital nor in the two general practices they visited did they get any new information. Back on the street, Bengt caught the smell of grilled peppers, and his stomach began to growl. "I have to eat something. My breakfast was a cup of coffee and half a sandwich, and it's nearly two thirty. Don't you ever get hungry?"

Alex looked surprised, seemed to have to think about that. "Well, yeah, 'course I do. Actually, they didn't give me time for breakfast at all this morning." He smiled ruefully. "Sometimes I just forget to eat."

Bengt rolled his eyes. Alex crossed the road to a couple of tables under umbrellas and sat down. A waiter brought a jug of water and two glasses. There was no menu, since, as Alex explained, they only served one dish here: cubiertas, small, thin pancakes rolled up with meat or vegetables in a sauce, which were eaten with one's fingers. Bengt chose vegetables, leaned back in his chair and poured himself a glass of water as they waited for their food. "Where are we going next?"

Alex gulped down his first glass in one go, then drank a second more slowly before he answered. "We should check the street clinics and the illegal ones, and tonight the kiddie stroll." He made a fist on the table. "We have to find something."

"What about Cuevas?"

Alex shook his head. "Cuevas doesn't have a clinic."

Bengt raised his eyebrows. "No doctor?"

"No one with the kind of equipment we're looking for. Drink, your body needs it. You're not drinking enough."

The waiter brought their rolls. The smell made Bengt salivate. He looked at Alex, who was already chewing and watching him quizzically.

"Don't worry. You won't die," Alex said around the food in his mouth. "But be careful, they're a bit spicy."

Bengt tried a little piece at first to let his tongue get used to the new flavor. The aromatic sauce was spicy indeed, but not painfully so. "This is amazing."

Alex laughed at his surprise. "What did you expect? That I'd poison you?"

Bengt shook his head and concentrated on his cubierta. It wasn't easy to eat the little rolls. If he bit into one end, sauce came out the other. He was licking his fingers clean so he could pick up his glass when he became aware that Alex was still watching him, contemplative now.

"Is there a trick to it?" he asked, wondering whether he had committed a faux pas.

Alex blinked. "What? No, not really. You'll get used to it." Short, cool, with the same expression on his face he'd had yesterday when

Bengt had asked about his pet name. Shuttered. This time Bengt didn't apologize. Whichever invisible line had been crossed just now, it hadn't been him doing the crossing. Alex would get over it, and maybe one day Bengt would figure out where this line ran exactly.

With a gesture Bengt had noticed before, Alex's hand wandered to his breast pocket, like some of the miners when their provisions hadn't come in yet, or they'd underestimated their cigarette use. "Did you just stop?"

Looking caught, Alex put his hand on the table, but raised it again immediately to wave the waiter over. "Check please." He didn't look at Bengt.

"Fine." Bengt sighed. "What is it?"

"Nothing."

"Oh, come on, Alex. If you raise that wall any higher you're going to run out of bricks."

Alex chewed on his cheek. "I'm sure you know what you're talking about," he said finally, keeping his eyes on the waiter who brought their check.

Bengt watched him concentrate on counting out the money, waited for him to look up, but he wouldn't make eye contact. Bengt gave it up. "So be it. Let's look at your street clinics then."

Alex left the zorro in a guarded lot outside the slums, and they walked through increasingly neglected streets in which the heat raised the stench of trash.

Finally, the Santuarian stopped in front of an apartment building where the door was ajar. Inside, merciful half-light hid most of the hallway. Something crunched under Bengt's foot. It was too dark to make out what, and Bengt didn't even want to know. Climbing the stairs close to the wall—the wooden steps didn't look very trustworthy—he tried to ignore the mustiness as well as the off-key, moronic singing from one of the upper floors. Alex stopped in front of a door, where a small girl sat playing with buttons.

When they entered the apartment, the singing stopped. An older man on a sofa looked up, but his expression turned vacant when Alex squatted in front of him to ask him some questions. Bengt crossed the room and entered the kitchen where the stench was worst. A mix of sweat, body odor, raw alcohol, and decay. Bengt barely kept his lunch down. A young woman looked at him sharply. She was cleaning a wound on the forearm of a woman who was sitting on the table; the flesh looked cooked. The woman whimpered softly, her eyes rolled back and showed only the white; she seemed barely able to hang on to consciousness.

Bengt took in every detail with a morbid fascination that gave him just enough distance not to puke right there on the floor.

"What do you want? Can't you wait outside?"

He pulled himself together and held out the photos to the doctor, or whatever she was.

"Never seen them," she said before he could ask.

"Does the kind of injury seem familiar? Have you ever seen—?"

"No! And now piss off. I have work to do."

Even if she knew something, Bengt was sure he wouldn't get an answer out of that one.

When he returned to the main room, Alex rose out of his crouch and shook his head.

Back on the street, they both breathed deeply, then continued their search. With rising disbelief and outrage, Bengt registered blankets under outside stairs and in archways, filthy dressings, cheap booze serving as analgesic and antiseptic alike, soup kitchens with "herbal corners," abortions in back rooms. Hour after hour, they asked and talked their way through the *barrios* of Tierraroja. The shadows under Alex's eyes became canyons, and Bengt knew that shock must be written all over his own face. He stank of sweat and the tenacious miasma of countless unwashed bodies.

Alex stumbled from one of the makeshift divisions on the ground floor of an abandoned building onto the street outside, stretched, and breathed in long gulps of the somewhat cooling evening air, then simply dropped onto the stone steps behind him. "So, how do you like Santuario?"

"No comment." Bengt sank down next to him and closed his eyes for a moment.

A bitter laugh escaped Alex. "How diplomatic." He leaned his elbows on the step behind him and let his head fall back. "Now I'd really like a smoke."

"Why did you stop?"

"It's not easy to get good tobacco, so you smoke anything you can get your hands on. A disgusting habit. And one that controls you," he added.

"Why did you start?"

Alex sighed. "That's much harder to answer. I was a kid." He fell silent. The dust had left a line on his skin where his collar fell open now. Bengt could see the regular beat of his heart against his throat.

"Don't you have any family?"

"No."

Just the one word, but softly this time, exhausted. No family. One of the worst scenarios Bengt could imagine. No parents, no siblings, no children, no partner, no one.

"You?"

"I have a baby sister, and a younger brother who has a family of his own. My mother's still alive, as is my mother's sister. Once a month, we all meet for dinner."

Alex rose. "Well, come on then, let's finish this so they'll have you back soon."

Huelva had mentioned an illegal clinic to them, but when they got to the address he'd given, there was only a rusty half-open gate into an inner court. No other doors, no hint that anyone had been here in the last few days or even weeks. The plaster was falling off the walls, and on one side somebody had sprayed the word "svoboda" in large red letters.

"Does that mean anything?" Bengt asked.

Alex shrugged. "No idea. I mean, it's the Rus word for freedom; I'm sure whoever wrote that had a purpose, but whether that's relevant for us . . ." He slowly did a three-sixty, scrutinizing every corner in the dusk.

"Could Huelva have had the wrong address?"

Again a shrug. "Possible." But not probable, his tone said. "Let's go back and check outside again. I have a feeling this is—" Something cracked under Alex's boot. He bent down and picked up the fragments of a disposable syringe. "Looks like he had the right address."

"Maybe they changed locations?"

Alex shook his head. "No reason for that. No one would close down a clinic, however illegal. We need them too much. And this must have been a fairly professional outfit from what Huelva said. It can't have been out here in the court, either. There's got to be an entrance somewhere."

But even though they walked around the whole block, they found no entrance to the building from ground level. High up under a roof on the street side was a loading hatch with a pulley above it. Both looked neglected and didn't seem to have been used for years. The whole building looked like an abandoned warehouse to Bengt.

Alex chewed on his cheek. "Someone warned them." He stepped back into the street, throwing a last glance at the court. "We've scared someone, or at least made them nervous. Someone who knew we'd come here."

"That information would have to have come from one of the comandaturas."

"I wouldn't be surprised."

Bengt sighed. "Shouldn't surprise me anymore either, I guess. Now what?"

"Not a lot we can do here for the moment. I'll tell Huelva to keep his eyes and ears open. When the clinic reopens, we'll try again without telling anyone. But I hope to all the saints that by then we'll have some more leads. Come on, next stop, gay kiddie stroll."

When Alex started toward a bus stop, Bengt followed hesitantly.

The boys were hanging out at one end of a parking lot behind a dance club. Bengt estimated the youngest to be about twelve, the eldest sixteen; his insides tied into a tight knot. He stayed back, let Alex talk to the kids, trusting that the Santuarian's laid-back style would get them talking.

A few minutes later, Alex rejoined him. "I might have found someone who's willing to talk to us, but not here. Come on." He led Bengt down a narrow walkway between the parking lot and a building to a small side court filled with trash cans, crates, and boxes. Through a narrow milk-glass window high up on one wall, diffused light fell into the court. The smell of food hung in the air, but Bengt didn't feel like eating anything ever again. Alex hunkered down on a wooden crate and motioned for him to do the same. The boxes didn't look very sturdy, and Bengt preferred to lean against the wall.

"How much money have you got?" Alex asked.

"About two hundred, why?"

"Give me fifty and add it to your expense account."

Bengt just managed to swallow his comment about bribes, dug a bill out of his wallet, and handed it over. The Santuarian laughed and winked at him as if he knew that Bengt had just bitten his tongue.

The boy glided like a shadow into the court. Maybe thirteen, skinny. Bengt could almost smell his fear. Alex waved him over. "Thank you for coming, Jurij. That over there's Bengt. He's with me. Don't worry, he's not going to move a muscle. You knew the boy in the picture?"

Jurij nodded. "He used to work here. But in the last few months he hardly ever showed up anymore."

"Do you know his name or where he was from?"

"Ramón. I don't know where he came from."

Alex looked at the money in his hand. "Any idea why he stopped coming here?"

The boy followed his glance. His eyes grew wide when he saw the bill. From that moment on, he never took his eyes off it. "I think he found a protector, someone with money. He had better clothes and often real cigarettes. He gave me one once as if it were nothing."

"Do you know anything about a tattoo?"

The boy shook his head. "He never said about a tattoo."

"Did he ever mention the name Vigo?"

Jurij nervously shifted his weight from one foot to the other. "Maybe, but if he did I never thought anything of it. Really, Teniente." Suddenly his face brightened. "Maybe that's the name of the guy who gave him the clothes and cigarettes."

Alex sighed. "It's possible. Anything else?"

The boy shook his head, nervously kept his eyes on the money, visibly worried the teniente would change his mind.

Alex gave him the bill, and in the blink of an eye, they were alone again.

Bengt stretched his arms. "Supposing Vigo is the unknown 'protector,' would he have killed the kid?"

"I'd think it highly unlikely. I'm pretty sure the killer is the same for all three victims. And whoever has these men"—Alex made a face at the word—"on his conscience did his best to choose people no one would miss. So, why leave a trace like this with the boy? I think the killer either didn't notice the tattoo or didn't think it important."

He stood and flexed his back. "Let's go back. I still have quite a ways to drive and really need a few hours of sleep."

Bengt pushed himself off the wall and led the way back to the street. "We continue here tomorrow?"

Alex briefly considered their options. "We should, and out of uniform this time. I'll pick you up at the hotel. Around nine thirty?"

Bengt nodded. The thought of repeating this torture tomorrow made him nauseous. To take his mind off the prospect, he changed the subject. "Say, do you feel like watching the match on Saturday? I can get us tickets."

Alex looked at him, surprised, then smiled. "Why not? Yeah, I'd like that."

They left a message for Huelva that they'd be back in the morning, and Alex dropped Bengt off at the hotel before heading home. Bengt stood in the driveway for a moment, looking after the zorro, prolonging the moment when he'd have to go up. Finally, he braced himself, crossed the lobby, and went up the stairs.

Kjell had obviously made an effort. He'd ordered a cold dinner. The table on the balcony was laid for two. A bottle in a cooler had been set on a side table. But even though Bengt was hungry, he couldn't possibly eat. Even the thought of alcohol turned his stomach. He couldn't get over how widespread and normal downright squalor seemed to be—no doctor, not even shelter. And that "kiddie stroll," as Alex had called it, right out in the open, with not even a thought of rounding the boys up and providing at least the younger ones with a home.

Kjell came out of the bathroom, barefoot, in dark blue satin shorts. When he saw Bengt standing in the balcony door, he came over and caressed Bengt's face. "I'm sorry," he whispered. "You look so tired."

Kjell rarely noticed how Bengt felt, and Bengt swallowed hard. All he wanted was to forget this day, to feel the warm body in front of him against his and let go, stop thinking. He pulled Kjell roughly against him and Kjell immediately put his arms around Bengt's neck and kissed him. "Right now?" he asked, breathless.

"I need to take a shower first; I've rarely felt so filthy," Bengt returned hoarsely.

Kjell winked at him. "There's room for two in there."

CHAPTER 7

The Plaza Concilio was busy with set-up activities for the Fiesta the next day. An expectant bustle hummed in the air that Alex found infectious. No one had kicked him out of bed this morning with bad news, and he'd had ample time to shower and shave. He was almost whistling as he ran up the stairs to the hotel.

At the entrance to the restaurant, a man in a suit stopped him. "May I help you?" he asked.

"I'm expected in the restaurant."

"Allow me." He waved Alex ahead of him. Bengt sat close to the patio. Alex felt a moment of surprise to see another Skanian with him, then realized that the hotel was more or less in Skanian hands. Of course, the björbo players, every one of them built like a ton of bricks and ducking under doorways. Bengt waved at him, and the guard at Alex's side nodded and went to resume his post.

"Good morning," Bengt greeted him in Skanes. "Join us for a minute. Have you had breakfast?"

Alex nodded, his brain scrambling for vocabulary. "But I will have another coffee."

Bengt signaled the waitress and indicated the man sharing his table. "Alex, this is Kjell, one of our best strikers, and my friend."

Kjell smiled, and Alex mirrored the smile. "So, this is how you get the tickets."

Bengt opened his eyes wide in mock surprise. "Connections are important."

The waitress came, and Bengt asked for a third cup, which she brought at once. "How do you drink it?"

"Black, thank you." Alex leaned back, cup in hand. Good coffee. Expensive hotel. "Bengt must explain me the rules," he said to Kjell.

"Well, that shouldn't be a problem. I'm sure he knows them by now," Kjell returned sunnily and winked at Bengt.

Alex drank his coffee. "How long will you stay?" he asked Kjell.

"Our flight goes back Sunday at noon. Although I'd like to stay longer." He threw Bengt a look Alex found disconcerting.

"I do not want to rush you," Alex turned to Bengt. "But if you have finished, we should start."

Bengt folded his napkin and stood up. "Ready." He gave Kjell a room key. "Would you leave that with reception in case you're not upstairs when I come back?" Kjell nodded. Bengt kissed him on the lips. "See you later."

For a heartbeat, Alex saw the scene without making the connections in his brain. Then it clicked, and all the puzzle pieces fell into place—the winking familiarity, the saucy look, the kiss . . . "Quebracho," he murmured under his breath.

Bengt looked at him questioningly. "Something wrong? You don't look good."

Alex looked from one to the other. No, indeed. He felt sick. Then shock gave way to anger. "Maricón," he spat across the table.

Bengt still seemed clueless. "Alex? What in the—"

Alex jumped to his feet. "You . . ." he couldn't think of a fitting word in Skanes, and that made him even more furious. "I thought . . . I trusted you, I believed . . ." He was too loud, became remotely aware of other people staring at them and realized he'd automatically fallen back into his mother tongue. "I should've known better. No, I did know better. I just should have followed my own advice."

Kjell looked at him blankly at first, then suspiciously. Finally, he turned to Bengt with raised eyebrows. "Is he jealous?" he asked.

Alex raised his arm, prepared to lunge, noticed the cup in his hand and flung it down on the table, where it shattered. He stormed out to the patio and down into the park.

Gay! Bengt was gay. Shit, damn, and mierda! And he'd been stupid enough not to notice. For the first time in his life he'd let down his guard with a stranger. He'd trusted him. Had thought . . . felt . . . It was his own fault, really. He knew he should have kept his distance. You didn't give others a chance to leave you or hurt you. They always took it. The buddy-buddy act, the offer of friendship; all lies, just to . . . *Jealous, my ass!* He wasn't jealous, how could he be? That would imply . . . And he didn't. He'd only . . . He'd . . . *Don't go there.*

He groaned and looked around. A fence closed the area off to the outside, barring his way. He must have crossed the whole park.

Suddenly exhausted, he randomly followed the path to the left and finally sank onto a bench, buried his face in his hands and pressed his fingers to his eyelids to counter the pressure behind them. He'd always known that closeness was dangerous. Only enemies couldn't betray you.

A cop with a gay partner. Madrios. And with his explosion just now, he'd made sure that at least the whole hotel had noticed. Why had he lost it like that? That wasn't like him. He'd almost attacked Kjell. He rested his forearms on his knees and stared at the ground. His hands trembled. He wasn't one of those guys who just lost control. That had never happened before. Not more than once, anyway.

He couldn't sleep, tossed and turned in the heat, until he finally gave up and snuck down the stairs in his pajama pants for a smoke outside. He tried to be as quiet as possible. He'd catch hell if his mother caught him smoking. He was fourteen; old enough.

At the foot of the stairs, he heard voices from the kitchen. He froze. Luìz must be back from Tierraroja. Turning to sneak back up, he heard a yelp of pain and a loud slap. "Damn it, woman! Pay attention!" Luìz yelled. His mother's answer was inaudible. Alex paused on the last step, listening to Luìz knocking her around again. "What did you just say to me?"

Then a crash and his mother screaming. Without thinking, he barreled down the corridor and into the kitchen. A broken teacup in a puddle on the floor. His mother trying to pull herself up on the sink, one arm raised, palm out, to protect her face. On her cheek, tears mixed with blood. Luìz hitting and kicking her. The look on her face changed from fear and outrage to empty resignation when, finally crushed, she gave up fighting and curled into a ball against the cabinet.

With a hoarse scream, Alex flung himself at Luìz, and together they crashed against the counter. Luìz didn't seem to know what had hit him—time enough for Alex to hammer his fist into Luìz's face and split his lip. Then the advantage he'd gained from surprise was used up. He saw the blind rage in Luìz's eyes, had enough adrenaline in his own blood not to feel the first couple of blows, but then the pain hit him. When he stopped defending himself, Luìz stood him up against the wall and systematically beat him until he slid to the floor. He felt the first kick to his ribs. The second smashed his head against the wall and flicked the lights off.

Alex shook his head as if that would get rid of the memory, and shoved both hands through his hair. He'd made a fool of himself, then and now. Sooner or later, he'd have to meet Bengt again. He looked at the fence that was just visible through the greenery and made a face. It would be sooner rather than later, since he'd have to go back through the restaurant if he wanted to leave. A cigarette would be welcome just about now.

He took a deep breath and blew the air out. All he'd had to do was stay calm. That wasn't usually a problem. Just accept that the joke was on him and keep going. Wide-eyed Alex, thinking Bengt might want his friendship. Yeah right. You couldn't be cheated out of something that didn't exist. Sitting here and thinking about might-have-beens only postponed the inevitable. He got up heavily, took another deep breath, and walked back to the restaurant.

Bengt was standing on the patio, leaning against the doorframe; Kjell was nowhere to be seen. Thank God for small favors. When Bengt saw Alex, he started toward him, a worried crease between his brows.

Don't bother; I won't trust the buddy act twice. "I apologize," Alex said before Bengt had a chance to open his mouth. "I have . . . I don't know what happened in there." He swallowed. *Madonna*, this was hard. "We have to work together for a while yet, so I suggest . . . It won't happen again," he concluded lamely. He could have kicked himself.

Bengt looked at him mutely, eyebrows raised. Then he nodded. "Apology accepted," he finally said.

Alex nodded. "We should split up. With Skanians all over the place, you won't attract any attention. That'll make it easier to strike up a conversation and ask around. We'll meet at," he checked his watch, "five at the fountain in the plaza."

Bengt hesitated. "At five," he agreed in the end.

Alex turned on his heels and fled through the lobby. *Don't think about him. Concentrate on the job.* But where to start?

At the northern end of the plaza, a stage had been erected, where two marimba players were testing their instruments. A couple of people were taking the opportunity to try out their dance steps in front of the stage. It wasn't noon yet. Alex doubted the fiesta would wait until tomorrow. By sunset, the plaza would be cooking.

On a whim, he returned to the general hospital, this time to talk to patients rather than the staff, but with no better results. Then, back in the lobby, he noticed an old woman with makeshift bandages around her arm, looking lost. "Are you all right, abuelita?" he asked gently.

She raised huge, confused eyes to his. "They say they can't help me," she complained.

"You don't have any money?"

"I told them I will pay as soon as I can. That was always good enough in Soria." She held up her arm. "I burned myself."

The word Soria caught Alex's attention. That was the barrio in which they'd searched for the disappeared clinic last night. He gently took the old woman by the shoulders and steered her back to the front desk.

The nurse looked up, regret clearly written on her face. "I can't admit her," she said.

"I'll pay for her," Alex answered softly.

The nurse breathed a sigh of relief. "In that case . . ."

She filled out a form, gave Alex a receipt, and a male nurse took charge of the old lady, leading her off toward the emergency treatment room.

Alex waited on one of the benches that lined the wall. So there was indeed a clinic in Soria. Bengt would— It didn't make any difference what Bengt would or wouldn't do. He didn't want to think about Bengt. He checked his watch. Why was this taking so long? He jumped to his feet and started to pace.

Finally, the old woman came back with a proper bandage around her arm, which she held up triumphantly. "They helped me after all."

"So I see." Alex took her other hand and placed it in the crook of his arm. "Have you eaten, abuelita? Or would you care to join me?"

She raised a scolding finger. "Are you flirting with me, young man?"

Alex laid his open hand on his heart. "I'd never. Or only the tiniest little bit."

She let him lead her down the street to a small taqueria, where they lunched on tapas.

Alex nodded toward her arm. "Why didn't you go to Soria?"

"They had to close for a bit," she said. "And they're so nice there, but the coronel told them they had to." She leaned toward him confidingly. "My niece told me that. She does laundry for them."

Alex nodded. "And did the coronel also tell them why he wanted them to close?"

"Because otherwise they would arrest the people working there," she said indignantly. "Can you imagine that? They are good people and good doctors. Sometimes the coronel even brings in his own people, even though they could go to the hospital, and he even pays for them." She nodded emphatically.

Alex smiled at her. "He must be very nice, the coronel."

But about that she didn't seem so sure. "He is a little scary," she admitted. "But he takes good care of everyone."

Alex carefully asked her a few more questions, but she didn't seem to know any more than that. He paid and walked her to the bus. On his way back, he strolled through cafés and tapas bars, stopped occasionally at a cubierta stand, always starting a conversation, always trawling for information. Twice he talked to men who knew about the closure of the Soria clinic, but neither of them knew any specifics.

He arrived back at the plaza shortly before five. A band had established itself on stage, and people were dancing merengue everywhere. Food vendors and small stalls had appeared like magic all around the plaza, and a boy selling björbo rules dashed around between the groups of people. Bengt was sitting on the stone rim of the fountain, lost in thought, trailing one hand through the water.

Alex slowly walked over. "And? Found anything?"

The Skanian started out of his reverie. "Hola. Yes, I think you were right. Until yesterday morning there was apparently a clinic, but no one seems to know why it closed. And something else: every time I ask about 'svoboda,' they all turn mute as fish."

Alex watched the crowd. "An old lady told me 'the coronel' temporarily closed the clinic so they wouldn't all get arrested."

"Which coronel?"

"That, unfortunately, she couldn't tell me, but only the Securitas has that rank."

One of the girls who'd been applauding the dancers looked over and smiled.

Bengt meditatively regarded the ground between his feet. "Meaning the Securitas warns an illegal clinic about an impending visit from the policía?"

The girl swayed with the rhythm of the music, swishing her skirt back and forth with both hands. She sported a small medical plaster over her right earlobe, which she'd tried to disguise with makeup.

"Funny, isn't it? Why is the Securitas interested in an illegal clinic? That they're raining on our parade is a sign we stepped on their toes. Or on Andúja's."

"Andúja?"

"Yeah, the patrón. This is his land. And his Securitas. They only let us investigate as long as we don't get in their way."

"So you usually regulate traffic?"

"Something like that. That's why it's so weird that this thing landed on my desk. And as far as Mendez is concerned . . . but that's a different kettle of fish."

Bengt stretched. "So now what?"

Alex hadn't taken his eyes off the girl with the adhesive. The telltale orange of antiseptic was hard to cover up. The kind of antiseptic only a clinic would use; everyone else made do with alcohol. "Dancing," he threw over his shoulder as he walked toward her.

She smiled victoriously when he approached her. Alessa's age, no more than eighteen. "I hope you're not here all by yourself, hija," he said.

She lowered her eyes. "My brother is here. Somewhere." A dimple appeared in her cheek.

Alex laughed. "Somewhere? How convenient. Would you like to dance, señorita?"

"Anna. I thought you'd never ask."

Alex surrendered his body to the rhythm, flirted, let her talk. A mambo followed the salsa. He put a finger under her chin and turned her head to one side as if he'd only just noticed the adhesive. "Ouch," he said softly. "That must've hurt."

He glanced back at Bengt, who was watching them from the fountain, hands in his pockets, brows drawn together.

Anna waved her hand dismissively. "Little brothers. He ripped out my earring, and it got infected. But it doesn't hurt anymore."

Alex winced in sympathy. "Did you go to a hospital?"

She laughed. "Yeah, Soria. Inés helped me. She's not really a doctor, but very good with stuff like that. If you ever need help, go to her. She won't hurt you so much."

"She sounds nice."

"She is. And she'd have every reason to be bitter. Something's wrong with her legs. She walks with crutches."

That was all she had to tell, but Alex was satisfied. When the mambo ended, he said good-bye. If her brother was really here, he didn't want to be caught with more than two dances. She pouted a little, but didn't try to hold him back. Clever girl.

Alex sauntered back to Bengt. "Now we have—"

"Really? Girls? Is that all you can think about? We've been at this case almost a week now, we're stuck solid, and you just don't give a shit."

Alex stared at him. Did Bengt still not know how he worked? He would've thought . . . but he'd been so very wrong about Bengt before. Fuck him. Deep down, he knew he deserved payback for this morning, but was too pissed to acknowledge the thought. If this was how Bengt wanted to play it, fine. "Relax, life is short. You have to find your fun where you can."

Bengt opened his mouth for a comeback, but was obviously distracted by something happening behind Alex's back. Alex turned. To the left of the stage, a brawl had erupted. Before the audience could react, Securitas cut in, but seemed to fuel the fight rather than end it.

Bengt made a step toward the melee. Not a good idea. Automatically, Alex grabbed his arm, but let go again quickly as if he'd burned himself. "I wouldn't do that," he said instead.

Bengt turned back toward him, then pointed at a closed van with antennas on the roof. "See that?" he shouted. "The collective media is here today and tomorrow. Something like that," he pointed at the fight, "is a field day for anyone who is against the annexation."

"Exactly," Alex shot back. "And that's why you don't have the slightest chance of stopping it." He sighed when Bengt looked at him with a mix of fury and incomprehension. "Come on, sit back down."

"Fuck you."

"A viente! There won't be an annexation, you blockhead. That would be the worst that could happen to the familias. Now sit the fuck back down before I get a crick in my neck and the boys in camo start noticing us." Demonstratively ignoring Bengt's challenging stance and balled fists, he sank down on the fountain rim.

"You're this close to talking yourself into an early grave," the Skanian hissed at him, holding thumb and index finger paper-close in front of Alex's face, but he did sit back down.

Alex realized he was on the brink of overdrawing his patience account for the day and took a deep breath. "The patrones' power is based on two things: the energy monopoly, because they control the trade in solar cells, and military might."

"Is this going to be a seminar in internal politics?"

Alex counted to three in his head. "You can't power one technical gadget, let alone a vehicle, without access to their solar panels or the batteries they charge."

"Oh, sorry, energy management."

"Just shut the fuck up for five minutes, will you? This total control only works as long as nothing gets into the country and no one gets out of it, entiende? If there's an annexation, sooner or later they'll be finished. There'll be more fights like this one, you can bet your ass on that."

Bengt's eyes went wide as he followed Alex's reasoning. "And they organized the game to have a podium, media and all, so that even the last Skanian understands what a gigantic mistake it would be to eliminate the borders?"

Alex nodded. "That, and entertainment for the masses. Keeps people quiet. Two of the soup kitchens we visited yesterday are run by Andúja as well." He shook his head. "They're not stupid."

"And yet there's a lack of everything for too many people."

"Not enough hospitals, almost no secondary education . . ." Alex fell silent. Useless to talk about it.

Bengt looked at him searchingly. "But you didn't gain this depth of insight from eight years of public school."

"Me? I went to the Academy," Alex said haltingly.

"You managed to get yourself accepted. That doesn't mean you've earned the badge on your collar. If you work hard and don't do anything stupid, you might one day. But with any kind of offense, you will have

forfeited that badge and any chance at graduation. So take good care of it."

Twenty-eight boys stood lined up in front of the speaker. Lonely, terrified, fourteen years old. Four years of academy lay ahead of them. Half of them wouldn't even make it through the bullying of the first. The older students saw to that.

They caught Alex three weeks before the end of the year, when he had started to believe the worst was over. Four of them had rushed him and torn the badge off his jacket. He ran after them blindly all the way to the storage cellar. When he caught up with them, they were standing smirking around a cage made of dense mesh, about as long and deep as Alex's forearm. The cage was bolted to the wooden floor and filled so densely with rats that the animals had started to tear each other to pieces. A small hatch gave access to the top. Alex's badge lay on the bottom.

He wasn't the only one to attend the finals with a thickly bandaged hand.

At the end of the second year, they demanded he do the same thing to the first years. At first, nothing happened when he refused. But when Luìz found out later that he'd been assigned to the policía for the last two years rather than the Securitas, he started his third year with broken ribs.

Bengt was watching him expectantly, but Alex had no words to explain the Academy to an outsider. Not that he wanted to, least of all to Bengt.

But to hold back information about the case because Bengt had ticked him off was childish. "The girl I danced with just now?" Alex started. "She had an adhesive bandage on her ear. And iodine."

Bengt looked confused for a second, then closed his eyes and opened his hands in defeat. "Alex, I'm an idiot. The clinic in Soria?"

Alex nodded. "She gave me a name, Inés. A woman who walks on crutches, who helps people with minor injuries but is not a doctor."

"So we have Vigo and Inés. Not much. But at least a place to start looking."

Alex got up. "Not tonight. I find the audience entirely too explosive. One wrong word . . ." With his head he indicated the south end of the plaza, where a fight quickly dominoed into a free-for-all, the mottled Securitas uniforms like dead leaves in the center. "I recommend spending the evening in your room."

Bengt also got to his feet. "Tomorrow, then?"

"I have to catch up on some stuff first. Don't know how long I'll be."

"The game starts at eight. If I don't talk to you before then, I'll wait in the lobby."

Alex hesitated. Hadn't he been clear enough? How much more brutally did he have to say he wanted nothing to do with Kjell and . . . all that? But he'd kicked up enough dust for one day. Besides, the stadium might offer opportunities to talk and listen and watch people. He nodded once, touched his hat in a farewell gesture, and walked over to the zorro.

During the drive back, he puzzled over all the different knots the case was presenting him with. Inés? Well, they wouldn't be able to deal with her until the clinic reopened. Vigo? A garden-variety name. More pavement pounding. The coronel? That was rather more interesting. How many coronels were there in the Tierra Andúja? Five max. He couldn't imagine a rank that high existing more than once per rajon. And Andúja had no staff officers, he knew that much. Luìz as protector of Soria was ridiculous, so four. Maybe Mendez had more current information on that. He growled. Mendez and his assignments. He'd have to corner the old fox on that sooner or later. Better sooner.

He parked the zorro behind the comandatura, glanced at the roster to see when Mendez would be back, and bade Gijón a good night. Would be good to have someone else lock up for once, and get a good night's sleep.

The moon hadn't risen yet. The water to his right lay invisible in the darkness. Despite that, he stopped in his usual spot to look north. Old habits died hard, and Jarðvegur had been the Promised Land for so long that it wasn't easy to . . . And why should he? Bengt was not the be-all and end-all. *Maricón!*

He walked on, forced his thoughts back to the murders and managed, after a fashion, to stay focused on the case until he got home. There he tried to make tea. After miscounting the spoonfuls three times, he slammed the lid on the can and threw the spoon in the sink. *Chingalo!*

He stormed back out to the beach, tearing his boots and his clothes off as he went, and threw himself into the cold salty water. He loved this bay because it dropped away steeply under him, so he didn't have to wade out for miles. The slow, rhythmic movement of swimming calmed him. *Shit,* the two had kissed in public. What did Bengt's colleagues have to say to that? He couldn't imagine that they would simply accept it. And yet Bengt's stunned confusion had been real. No use breaking his head over it, though. The sooner he resigned himself to the facts, the better. And why should he care? The Skanian was a stranger who'd disappear again as soon as the case was closed. So why did he care? Because he'd thought he could trust Bengt? Because there'd been something . . . *Oh, grow up, Alex!* There'd been nothing. *Nada.*

He swam until he was tired enough to sleep, and the next morning walked purposefully into Mendez's office. Before the capitán could open his lips, Alex closed the door, took a seat opposite him, set his elbows on the desk, and rested his chin on his fists.

Mendez looked at him blankly for a moment, then closed the file he'd been reading and returned Alex's gaze.

Bastard. This wasn't working out as Alex had planned it. So he asked, "How long have we known each other?"

Understanding crept into Mendez's eyes. Holy shit, the guy was fast. "Over two years."

"In that time, how often have you ordered me to investigate a murder?"

"Never."

"And how often have you thought it necessary to coordinate the investigations of two rajons?"

"Never."

"Why now?"

Eyes lowered to the desk, Mendez mulled that over. Finally he raised his head. "How often have you seriously imagined that you might change something?"

"Never."

"And why now?"

Slowly, Alex leaned back in his chair. It was true that with this case, for the first time, he had the feeling he was doing something meaningful, but that was not something he'd consciously thought about. For the first time in the two years they'd been working together, he wondered what kind of man Mendez was behind the uniform, what had dug those deep lines into his face, why he'd ended up here, why he backed Alex against Vilalba now and then. "I don't know."

"Because it's suddenly possible. The time is ripe and 'freedom' has become more than just a word. Because for once, we had a body before the Securitas got to it. Because ICE is here, giving us an advantage we never had before. And we should use that advantage." The capitán leaned forward. "But don't forget that nobody is bulletproof." With that, he rose and went to talk to Gijón.

Alex had guessed that Mendez had had trouble before. Now he was sure. And he admired his courage.

He hadn't agreed on a time with Bengt and didn't feel like driving into Tierraroja for no good reason. He walked toward the village, going over the conversation with his capitán again and again in his mind. "Freedom," was it? The market held the weekly crowd of sellers and buyers; he bought a papaya, had it peeled and deseeded, and ate it while walking.

Andrés was sitting on his porch as Alex had hoped.

"Cómo es usted?"

"Oh, if my old bones play along, it's not too bad. Do you want a coffee?"

"Please, don't bother."

Andrés snorted and disappeared inside. A few minutes later, he came back with a mug. "Here, sit and don't talk nonsense," he said with a wink.

Balancing on the porch railing, one foot on the lower beam, Alex sipped his coffee. "May I ask you something, Andrés?"

"Sure."

"Does 'svoboda' mean anything to you?"

The old man was silent for so long that Alex thought he'd fallen asleep. "That word hasn't meant anything in Santuario for decades," he finally said.

"Maybe it's starting to mean something again."

"With words like that, Sasha, one has to be careful. Very careful. I remember your mother well."

Impatient at Andrés's topic change, Alex set the mug down on the post. "Would it have meant something to her?"

"Your mother had many friends. Quite a lot of friends, Sasha. Never forget that."

"I won't." Andrés didn't seem to be having his best day. But even he would notice if Alex tried to lead their talk back to "svoboda." He gave up. He wasn't even sure Mendez had meant anything by his little "freedom" speech. It was Bengt's idea that svoboda had any significance. And Bengt's ideas . . .

That night, the Plaza Concilio was a teeming anthill. The media people had set up a gigantic screen across from the hotel for those who hadn't managed to get tickets or couldn't afford them. Alex saw people coming to blows all over the square, the Securitas never far from those eruptions.

Bengt came toward him just as Alex was about to run up the steps to the hotel. Alex nodded a greeting, then turned and shoved his way through the crowd.

Even though it was almost an hour before the game would begin, droves of people were already blocking the stadium entrances. Alex moved left toward a side entrance, flashed his badge, and motioned for Bengt to follow him. Inside the stadium, it was the calm before the storm. The first visitors were already looking for their seats.

Alex waited for Bengt to catch up. "Where are we sitting?"

Bengt fished the tickets out of his pocket and read, "Block A, row S3, 14 and 15."

Alex furrowed his brows. "S3? Show me. Damn." He looked at Bengt in disbelief. "That's the VIP lounge."

Bengt nodded. "Should be right."

Alex turned without a word and led the way. So much for opportunities to talk and listen. Andúja would be there. Alex congratulated himself for the decision not to wear his uniform, but still felt like an offering on a silver platter.

The lounge had glass walls that separated it from the stands. Two Securitas guarded the entrance, checked their tickets, then waved them inside. Five rows of seats in the front partition, a buffet table right behind them, and a bar. They were the only ones there. A cozy tête-à-tête, how romantic.

A waiter appeared silently out of nowhere. "Would the gentlemen like something to drink?"

"Water," they said in unison.

"Coming right up." The waiter waved in the direction of the buffet. "Would you like to eat something? Please, feel free, Señores."

Alex struggled to maintain his usual façade, but managed to stroll along the damask-covered table and calmly thank the waiter who brought their glasses. Bengt's presence was a hard-to-ignore pressure between his shoulder blades.

"When exactly were you planning on talking to me again?" the Skanian asked quietly.

"I am talking to you."

"What you call talking."

They'd reached the end of the table. Through the glass, Alex watched the seats slowly filling up.

"Fine," Bengt started again. "Then at least listen to me for a moment."

Alex focused on the dishes in front of him. He was trapped in the corner. He took a plate from the side and started loading it with bits of food.

Bengt sighed. "I haven't quite grasped why the fact that I'm gay makes any sort of difference. Or do you seriously believe that you'll have to walk with your ass against the wall from now on?"

Alex concentrated on the delicate operation of balancing olives on a fork to add to his plate.

"Just because you happen not to be doesn't mean you nail every woman who has a pulse either, does it?" Bengt continued.

"That's different," Alex murmured.

"How?"

"That's not even the point." He pushed Bengt back with his plate. "And anyway, you're crowding me."

Bengt stepped aside. "What is the point then?"

Damn, why did he act so naive? He couldn't possibly not know what he was talking about. Or could he? Alex turned slowly, searched for hints in Bengt's face and only saw open confusion. "This is all perfectly acceptable to you, isn't it?"

"What, damn it? What exactly are we talking—" He stopped short, surprised realization in his eyes. "I broke a taboo. Is that what you're trying to tell me? That homosexuality is taboo?"

Alex swallowed, tried to grasp the implications of that question. "Where you're from, it isn't?" he finally managed.

"Of course not. I've never . . . Sorry, it's obviously not a matter of course." He wiped his hand across his face. "But the rent boys?"

Alex put his plate down. "I didn't say it wasn't done," he said slowly. "But while being caught with a hooker has at least some negative prestige . . ." He faltered. "To . . . those kids . . . That's just sick."

Bengt leaned against the glass. "I agree, but it's their age and exploitation that make it so disgusting, not their sex. Does it have to be a prostitute? Aren't there any normal relationships between men?"

"Normal rel—?" Alex desperately hunted for words that would explain what he wanted to say without breaking any more china. "It doesn't get much more normal than Vigo and Ramón. Anyone I've ever met who'd consider . . . where it was obvious . . . is seriously twisted." He stared fixedly at the wild conglomeration of appetizers on his plate, thoughts stumbling through his head in a similar pandemonium. He finally managed to grasp and hold on to one of them. "Are you trying to tell me you worked in the mines for two years and never clued in?"

Bengt shook his head. "It didn't even occur to me in my wildest dreams to think about it. Of course, there were dirty jokes, but they were more about women. To question something that's as natural as breathing . . ." He raised both hands in a gesture of capitulation.

Alex took his plate and glass and found his seat. There was a small folding table in one of the armrests that was just large enough for both of them. He had the feeling that if he tried to think more than one thought at a time, his head would explode. Yet, the tangle in his brain had neither beginning nor end.

The stadium filled up, and one by one, the VIPs with tickets for the lounge seats arrived as well. Voices and the tinkle of glasses and cutlery filled the room.

Bengt sat down next to him, but the opportunity for a private conversation was over.

Alex chewed thoughtfully on a piece of bread, watching the activity behind him reflected in the large glass pane. Suddenly, he sat up straighter. "Andúja," he murmured to Bengt. "The whole family."

The patrón was immediately surrounded by people wanting to talk to him, so Alex could turn around without drawing attention.

"The one in the blue suit jacket is Vadim Linares, his secretary," Alex explained. "The gray-haired one is Diego Andúja, the patrón. His wife, Elena, and his two sons. The older one, Santos, got married last year. The younger, Vigo, just finished school." As he said the name, it went through him like an electric current.

"Vigo," Bengt whispered.

Alex could feel the familiar flutter of fear in his stomach. "Don't jump to conclusions. There's got to be hundreds of men in the city with that name."

"Maybe, but we can at least ask some questions."

"No, we can't." Alex knew they'd have to eventually, and felt sick. The seats filled up, but Bengt seemed to want to discuss the problem at length. "Listen," Alex whispered quickly. "I promise you, I'll check around. Just leave him alone for now."

Bengt opened his mouth, when suddenly there was a commotion on the pitch below. Forty or fifty spectators had climbed across the barrier and stormed onto the green. As if they'd shot up out of the ground, a line of Securitas enclosed them. Rifle butts crashed on heads, batons smashed into unprotected faces, and boots dug into twitching bodies, even though there was no serious resistance. Alex's stomach churned. He was about to turn away from the carnage in disgust when he suddenly recognized a face. He jabbed Bengt with his elbow. "See the redhead in the blue shirt?"

Bengt nodded.

"Securitas," Alex said. "The guy on the other side with the visored cap as well. And the one on the left there." Now that he'd started to notice, he could see four, no, five men among the agitators who he knew were Securitas wearing plain clothes, and at least as many others who looked like they might be. "They are thorough. Where there are no riots, they'll provoke them."

"I'm sure that'll look spectacular on the TV screens," Bengt commented bitterly.

After the field had been cleared, the players came on the pitch, fifteen on each team. Kjell waved in the direction of the lounge, and Alex leaned back and watched with surprise as Bengt's face turned to stone.

The lower halves of the H-shaped goals were covered by a net, the crossbar hung at two meters fifty, the morning paper had explained.

"If the ball goes in the net, three points. That's a goal," Bengt said quietly when the game started. "If it goes over the crossbar but between the goalposts, that's a small goal, one point."

Alex nodded. There were several referees on the pitch as well; the ball sailed past one of the posts, and the ref behind it waved his arms. Each team played with two attackers (one of them Kjell), who constantly changed positions to escape their markers.

After thirty-five minutes, they switched sides. Throughout the game, Bengt kept up his low-voiced commentary. "The players are not allowed to pick the ball up from the ground, and they can't throw, but when they catch the ball, they can run four steps with it in their hands. After that, it has to touch the ground, but they can't bounce it twice in a row, it has to touch the tip of the foot in between."

That rule created a complicated running rhythm that looked fantastic with these players, who were masters at their game. The stadium went wild with enthusiasm. Even Alex let himself be carried away by the match.

The Andúja clan disappeared immediately after play ended. The others lingered at the buffet for a bit, talked about the game, and shared a glass or two.

Alex took the dishes back. "Do you want anything else to drink?" he asked Bengt.

"Just water."

Alex was standing at the bar waiting his turn when someone leaned against the wall next to him. Black combat boots, Securitas uniform, scarred face with ice green eyes, dark crew cut turning gray at the temples. Luìz.

As long as he lived, Alex would always flinch inside when the coronel suddenly appeared out of nowhere like that; would always, for a fraction of a second, try to figure out what he'd done this time, but he had long since learned to let none of that reach the surface. "Coronel."

Luìz's lips twisted. No one could call that a smile. "Cómo estás, hijo? Haven't seen you in a while. I was worried about you."

"What do you want?"

The grin disappeared. "You're working too much, Alex. Take a break."

The warning Alex had been anticipating for a week now. It was almost a relief to actually hear it. "Mind your own business."

Luìz pushed away from the wall so his face was only a hand's breadth from Alex's. "You forget yourself, hijo. You owe me a certain respect, as your father and as an officer," he hissed under his breath.

Alex was only too conscious of the crowd behind him and the curious looks of the barman. Not another scene. Abruptly, he stepped left, slid through the door and past the guard outside, and let himself be carried along by the crowd leaving the stadium.

CHAPTER 8

Bewildered, Bengt stared at the door through which Alex had just disappeared. Now what? The older man in uniform who had talked to Alex looked over, nodded a greeting as if he knew Bengt, then stopped to exchange a few words with the guards at the door and left. Shaking his head, Bengt went to get his water from the bar, rolled the cool glass across his forehead, and sank back into his seat. Kjell would look for him here, would want to discuss the game.

A culture in which it socially ruined a man to be gay? Which so marginalized homosexuality that perversion was the only outlet? No wonder Alex had reacted with such force. Bengt tried to imagine what his life would be like under such conditions and failed. What kind of culture was this that laid down such brutal rules, but whose dances were as soft and sensual as its language?

Yesterday, Alex had moved into the rhythm of the music perfectly naturally, seemingly unthinking. And even when he wasn't dancing, he moved as if an echo of that rhythm were pulsing through his veins without pause.

Bengt closed his eyes and gave himself up to the images in his head. They had created a perfectly matched unit—the girl following the music, fitting herself against Alex, Alex framing her with his arms and shoulders, his long legs anticipating every beat. Goose bumps raced up Bengt's arms. Maybe part of his much-too-forceful reaction at the fountain yesterday had simply been envy, the knowledge that he wouldn't be able to take any of that beauty back with him, except in his memories. Of course, he was kidding himself if he didn't also admit how effortlessly Alex managed to provoke him.

Yet their argument hadn't started the dynamic of losing control and feeling guilty that Bengt was so used to. Alex had countered and that had been that. It had even cleared the air. The memory made the corners of his mouth twitch. It took a considerable amount of brass to yell back at someone who was more than a head taller than you and rather pissed. But there'd been no accusations for breaking any rules as there would have been back home, the kind of accusations that Kjell managed to wield against him so effectively.

"Are you asleep?"

Bengt flinched. Talk of the devil. "Almost," he grumbled. "Took you long enough."

Kjell laughed. His hair was still damp from the shower. "We had to give an incredible number of interviews and autographs. The game was a real hit. They love it." He was excited and so magnetic that Bengt had a hard time remembering why he'd broken up with him. No wonder the media loved him.

"Shall we go and join the crowd for a while?"

Ah, yes, the mingling with the fans. Bengt sighed. "Let's check what's going on outside first. If the plaza's boiling like it was yesterday, we'd do better to restrict ourselves to the hotel bar."

Kjell was already making for the door. "Did you see my goal in the eighteenth minute? Wasn't that a dream?"

"Fantastic." Bengt couldn't remember, but didn't have the heart to tell Kjell that he'd missed almost half the match because his thoughts had been somewhere else and he'd been busy explaining the rules to someone who occupied his mind more than he would have liked. No need to disappoint Kjell like that; he'd be talking most of the time anyway and only expect agreement from Bengt now and then.

At the exit, they met with exactly the kind of uproar Bengt hated most. Kjell barely had a foot through the door when the masses pounced.

Bengt hung back to escape the worst crush, as well as to keep an eye on the crowd. People elbowed him in the back. Everyone kept throwing flowers at the players, and their heady scent mixed with the smells of different foods. Fans who couldn't close in fast enough started fighting with others trying to force their way through.

Suddenly, Kjell shot forward through a gap in the barrier to settle a fight that had started next to him, and in the blink of an eye, had two Securitas aiming their guns at him. The scent of gun oil hit Bengt's nostrils; the sound of the slide made his hair stand on end. Ruthlessly, he elbowed his way through the mob, badge at eye level, stepping on feet, knocking people aside left and right, and drew his friend back behind the barrier. "Have you lost your mind?" he hissed, trying to catch his breath.

"The guy hit one of my fans," Kjell said.

Bengt shook him. "Shit, kid, the two uniforms almost shot you."

"Don't be ridiculous." Kjell freed himself angrily. "And now? Do you plan on spending the night here?"

Bengt looked around. "Stay with me. We'll go back inside and use the side entrance."

Kjell followed him, grumbling to himself.

The door Alex and Bengt had used a couple of hours ago stood ajar. The guard jumped when Bengt opened it from the inside, but relaxed when he recognized him, and touched his hat in a salute. It was quieter here, but Bengt still chose a roundabout route through side streets to escape the commotion, eliciting some snide remarks from Kjell. In the end, they had to turn back to the main road, where they were quickly swept along by the crowd. By the time they reached the hotel entrance, Kjell was surrounded again. Some Securitas were guarding the doors, keeping the fans back with curses, batons, and kicks.

The clash was preprogrammed, but Bengt wasn't close enough to prevent it. A man asking Kjell for an autograph was pushed against one of the guards, who immediately started to bludgeon him. Outraged, Kjell lunged at the guard to defend his fan. The guard didn't even try to use his fists against the huge Skanian, but went straight for the stun gun in his belt.

Kjell screamed when the tip touched him, more surprised than hurt since he was immediately jostled aside. At last, a gap opened in the crowd, and Bengt grabbed Kjell's elbow and dragged him into the lobby with brute force. Kjell furiously ripped his arm out of Bengt's grip, and loudly and creatively vented his anger about dust-born Santuarians in general and the brutish Securitas in particular. He was clearly shocked about having been physically attacked outside the game. Bengt had never seen his friend like that. He let him rant until he noticed the camera team.

"Kjell!"

"Did you see what that bitch-ass fart knocker did to me?"

"Yes, but can we talk about that upstairs?"

"People want to see a game and then celebrate, what's the big jerking deal? We won! Did you even notice? Do you think I'm going to let some megalomaniac monkey in a uniform ground me?"

"You don't seem to be in a celebratory mood anyway. Just get the hell upstairs."

"Don't order me around."

"Fine, whatever. I was looking forward to going over the game with you, but if you prefer to have your skull bashed in, I'll find someone else."

"We won."

"You were clearly the better team."

"Maybe they'll air highlights."

"Let's go upstairs and check."

Kjell still wasn't convinced, but let Bengt drag him in the direction of the stairs. When Bengt looked back, he saw Alex sitting on one of the sofas, following the whole drama with interest. What the hell was he doing here? However justified his disappearance into thin air might have been, did he have to reappear at the most inopportune moment?

Upstairs in their room, Bengt slammed the door shut behind them with relief. He had a few sharp comments on the tip of his tongue, but a lecture would make Kjell even more resentful. Instead, Bengt fetched him a glass of water.

"Calm down." He hesitated. "I'll have to go back downstairs for a sec to talk to Alex."

Kjell's head shot up, a storm in his green eyes, indignation in every rigid muscle of his body. "You are not going to leave now?"

"Gives you time to get a grip on yourself. Tantrums are not especially attractive."

"Look who's talking." Still, the remark seemed to have hit home. Kjell didn't raise any further objections, and Bengt quickly left the room before the kid changed his mind. His patience was stretched dangerously thin, and by the time he got back to the lobby, he would have loved to have rammed Alex's mocking grin down his throat. "Before you start," he hissed, "I'm not in the mood. So keep a lid on it."

Alex raised a warning finger to his lips and nodded toward the reception desk. The camera team was making a beeline for them. Bengt felt Alex's hand at his elbow and let himself be steered toward the park. A glance back showed him the media people trying to convince security to let them onto the patio.

Alex let go of his arm. "Walk with me."

"Fine, but don't tick me off."

The Santuarian didn't answer. Bengt fought for control and stole a glance at him. The white shirt made a stunning contrast with his dark skin. He wore the collar open and had rolled up the sleeves over his elbows as he always did, but he looked younger out of uniform, less . . . hard wasn't the right word. Seasoned, maybe.

Knee-high lamps lined the path to light the way without obscuring the stars.

Alex looked at him from the side. "Trouble?"

"Let's just say it's time the kid got home." The bushes and trees looked weirdly contorted through the light from below. Bengt rubbed the bridge of his nose with his thumb and middle finger. "We'd actually broken up even before I came here." Why was he telling Alex that? "It was a mistake not to leave it at that. Had I known yesterday what you told me today, I could have saved us all a lot of headaches."

Alex buried his hands in his pockets and pulled his shoulders up. "I'll survive," he said calmly. He'd obviously done his own thinking, and Bengt gave him credit for having his prejudices under enough control to walk here alone with him.

Bengt decided it was safe to ask the question that had been puzzling him. "Why did you disappear like that?"

"I've had enough drama this week." Alex stopped and looked at Bengt. "We might have a problem. Luìz, the guy I was talking to in the lounge, suggested that it would be healthier to conduct our investigations less, say, intensely."

"A threat? To be taken seriously?"

Alex looked at him, disbelief written all over his face. "From a coronel of Securitas? Are you kidding?"

Bengt's ears pricked up at that. "Coronel?"

"Forget it. I couldn't imagine Luìz as a protector of widows and orphans if I tried." He laughed and shook his head. "Madonna, that's a good one."

"You know the coronel well?"

The wry amusement left Alex's eyes. "You could say that."

That was all he said. One thing was for sure, the yelling matches were a lot less stressful than these clamming-up tactics. It always felt like a personal attack when Alex suddenly retreated like that. It smelled of mistrust and secrecy, and always happened when he least expected it.

"So, we'll be careful."

"We better sleep with our eyes open. Let's go back. It might be better for you to stay inside tonight." He nodded in the general direction of the hotel entrance. "The goons have been told to crash the party, and I don't trust every idiot out there to think of the possible consequences if they extend the head-bashing to you guys. Me, I think I'll use the general fiesta to have a few drinks. Maybe someone feels like chatting with me."

Bengt walked next to him for a few steps in silence. "That's what you meant when you said we couldn't just interrogate Vigo Andúja. That that would result in reprisals?"

"As sure as night follows day."

On the patio, Alex paused. "I'll call you tomorrow, but I might not make it here until noon. Have to type my report for Mendez."

Bengt rubbed his neck. "You had to mention the r-word?"

"I'm afraid it's bound to be mentioned by someone sooner or later."

"I guess investigation reports are a universal truth. Take care, don't let anyone catch you."

Alex raised his hand in parting. "I won't," he called as he crossed through the restaurant and disappeared into the lobby.

Bengt stayed for a few minutes, savoring the coolness of the night and bracing himself for the fight that still lay ahead.

Upstairs in their room, he found Kjell sprawled naked on the bed, fast asleep. The small night light threw his body into stark relief.

Bengt carefully took a pillow from the bed and the extra blanket out of the closet and spread them on the floor. Then he slipped into the bath and shut the door quietly behind him. These evening showers were like a treat at the end of the day to get rid of that mix of dust and sweat that settled into every pore. His thoughts went to Alex, who was probably sitting in some cantina right now, drinking with the guys or bending his narrow ass over some pool table in concentration. In Jarðvegur, anyone who was even remotely interested in men would hit on him hard. Unfortunately, the male part of that demographic wouldn't survive the response.

When he came out of the bath, Kjell was sitting up, leaning against the headboard, arms around his knees. "You're mad at me," he stated.

Bengt stopped short, and Kjell pointed an accusing finger at the blanket and pillow on the floor, then at the towel around Bengt's hips. "You wouldn't even have woken me up."

"No, I wouldn't have. My taste for drama has been satisfied for the next few years." That had sounded harsher than he'd intended. He sat on the bed next to Kjell. "It was a mistake to come here. You shouldn't have talked me into it."

"Oh?" Kjell looked up, surprised. "Now it's all my fault?"

Bengt shook his head. "I shouldn't have let you talk me into it."

"But why?"

Because you'll never grow up? Because I don't have the patience anymore? Because I can't see where this is leading us? The morass of poverty, apathy, and exploitation he'd been wading through the last few days put everything he dealt with at home to shame and made nonessentials irrelevant. The differences between him and Kjell had never seemed more insurmountable. He smiled. "Because I feel like I'm a hundred years old when I'm with you."

"You're only six years older than me." Kjell looked at him searchingly. "This place is changing you. You're really serious this time, aren't you?"

Bengt nodded silently.

"I guess I'll have to accept that," Kjell said slowly. "This must've been the shortest stretch we've had yet." Again that searching look. Then he shook his head as if to get rid of the heaviness of his thoughts and grinned. "But that doesn't mean you have to sleep on the floor."

Bengt stood up. "A night on the carpet won't kill me."

Kjell laughed. "You can't resist me."

"It's difficult," Bengt admitted, wrapping himself in the blanket and lying down on the floor. "Now turn the light off and go to sleep."

For a few minutes, there was only their breathing in the dark, then, "Bengt?"

"Hmmm?"

"Is there someone else?"

"Bullshit."

Pause.

"Good night."

"Night," Bengt said toward the wall.

The phone jolted Bengt awake. He shot upright, trying to remember where he was, then reached for the phone on the desk and settled against the wall with the receiver to his ear. It was a quarter after six. "Buenas días?"

"What do you think I just saw in the news?" Skanes. Loud, upset. Sunne.

Bengt swallowed. "I can guess."

"Oh, you can guess. Well, isn't that something? I think I spoke of this case as a delicate matter. I gather having your friend lose it in the hotel lobby is your idea of appropriate procedure."

"No, of course not," Bengt tried to get a word in. "Unfortunately, I was—"

"Shit, Bengt, I'd hoped this investigation would diffuse the potential violence, not fan it."

"Yes, me too. Only—"

"And where's my report, by the way?"

Bengt closed his eyes and banged his head against the wall. "Almost done. I'll envoy it."

"And our golden boy?"

Sleeping the sleep of the wicked. "Packing."

"The sooner you get him on that plane, the better." Her voice became more conciliatory. "Everything okay with you?"

Apart from having just been skinned alive? "All's well."

"Good. I expect the report before noon, then. I have no idea what I'm supposed to say to the press." She disconnected.

Bengt took a deep breath. The annexation would fail miserably. He had to somehow make it perfectly clear in his report how the political power was divided up. Which made him painfully aware that he still knew too little about that. Maybe, if Sunne was elected, she could . . . If, could, and maybe. Chances for the annexation had never looked worse. *There won't be an annexation, you blockhead.* The patrón and his Securitas had done their job only too well.

Bengt pushed himself up to cradle the receiver. His joints cracked and his neck felt stiff. He was getting too old to spend the night on the floor.

Time for that report. He looked around the room for his netpad. It was a constant puzzle to him how Kjell managed to achieve this level of chaos within three days and with a limited amount of luggage. Bengt finally found the netpad under a stack of magazines and three half-empty blister packs of pills. For a while, his typing was the only sound in the room.

Finally, he leaned back and, satisfied, stretched his arms. That was done. After a quick shower, he went to the reception desk to get the key for the conference room and envoyed the report to the office.

Kjell jerked awake when he came back. "You startled me. Where were you? What time is it?"

"Almost nine. How about getting up?"

Kjell stretched lazily under the blanket. "Yeah, yeah, don't push me."

After he'd finally made it out of bed, he spent over half an hour in the bathroom.

Bengt had just started to pack his suitcase for him out of sheer boredom when the phone rang again. This time, he had it on the first ring. "Alex?"

"Well, aren't you awake already?" He sounded tired, but Bengt was sure he heard a smile in his voice.

"Shoot."

"You were right," Alex said. "Vigo Andúja is indeed Ramón's Vigo. Just after three this morning, I was playing cards with a piss drunk waiter who witnessed Vigo bursting into tears at a party and lamenting how someone had murdered his beloved Ramón. Vigo must've gotten quite a hiding from his father and brother, but only after the cat was already out of the bag. Too many witnesses. It didn't sound to me like the grief was an act, though, so I think we should take Vigo off our suspect list for good. We should concentrate on that coronel. See who twitches first."

"And Vigo?"

Silence on the other end, then, "What about him? He's an asshole, and a whiny, stupid one at that, but that's no crime."

"Is there no law against sex with a minor?"

"Only with children. At fifteen you can marry, with parental consent. Granted, those rent boys fall through a legal gap, but where there are no parents, there's not going to be a judge. There's nothing you can charge Vigo with. Had he laid a finger on Jurij, that would have been different, but he obviously wasn't quite that stupid."

Bengt slapped his palm against the wall. "You can't be serious."

Kjell came out of the bath and started to collect his things.

"Afraid so."

Bengt played with the phone cord, trying to come up with a way to teach Vigo Andúja a lesson. "But theoretically, Vigo is still a suspect in a murder. We could at least interrogate him. Strictly speaking, we even have to."

"You can, of course, do that, but then our investigation here is over and done with. That much you should know by now. You don't seriously believe it was Vigo, do you?"

Bengt sighed. "Well, I'm sure the autopsy reports will confirm it was the same perpetrator in all three cases, and we don't have a motive for the other two. Still, we shouldn't exclude the possibility that he was somehow involved—or that he at least knows something about Ramón that may give us a hint."

"Vale. I'll type my report and pick you up around one."

"I'll be waiting in the lobby." He hung up. This case was like a morass, where every step was a fight and a potential disaster. And yet, he had a feeling that it must break soon, one way or the other.

Kjell sat next to his packed bags on the bed, watching him. "Are you going to have breakfast with me?"

"Sure. We should get a move on, though, or you'll miss your plane."

Kjell got up. "I'll take everything downstairs to check out. Are you keeping the room?"

"Yeah, less fuss that way. Oh, come on, don't give me that face. You said yourself it's no fun to be with me, the way I treat people."

"You could try to change," Kjell suggested.

Bengt almost laughed out loud. "At thirty-two, that's not bloody likely. Maybe you're right. Maybe I really fit in better here. At least the Santuarians don't seem put out by the occasional loud argument. They just yell back, and that's that." He grew serious again. "No, really, Kjell, I wish you all the best. Let's have breakfast." That would at least keep his mind off king-sized beds. He was relieved and grateful that Kjell had backed off so easily, but that also exposed how superficial their relationship had always been. Yes, they had fun and the sex was great, but for some reason Bengt was reluctant to explore, that just wasn't enough anymore.

After seeing Kjell off at the entrance, Bengt still had two hours to kill before his meeting with Alex. He'd go stir-crazy here in the hotel. He went out onto the plaza, which was buried in trash and wilted flowers. Enough to make him wish for a fresh breeze, and not only because of the heat. At the other end, a few workers were taking down the stage. Other than that, no clean-up effort was visible.

The coronel the old woman had mentioned to Alex stuck in Bengt's head. There had to be more they could find out about him. Remembering Alex's instructions, he picked his way through the tangle of streets to the Comandatura One. None of the desks were occupied, but when he entered, someone came from one of the back offices.

"Señor? May I help you?"

Bengt had trouble remembering the rank insignia, but recalled that Mendez wore the same.

"Buenos días, Capitán. I'm looking for your cabo, Huelva."

"It's his day off today. Won't you tell me what I can do for you? You are the comisario. From ICE. Right?" He beamed at Bengt. "Come. Sit. Have a coffee with me. I have very much regretted that I have not yet had the pleasure of making your acquaintance, señor."

Bengt was getting dizzy from the flashy smile and the baroque politeness. He wondered whether the capitán—his name tag said Ronda—had ever considered a career as a toothpaste model. When Ronda disappeared to get the coffee, Bengt considered his options. Keeping Alex's warning in mind, he would try to be less direct.

Unfortunately, he was a lousy liar, so he'd best play what he was: a stranger who didn't know his way around.

"It's fresh, I just made it. How would you like it, señor, and don't you say hot." The arch admonishment came complete with wagging finger.

"Sugar and milk, please. I need your help, Capitán," Bengt added before Ronda could unleash the next volley of words.

"Por supuesto, I am wholly at your disposal, just ask me if—"

"I have to contact someone. Unfortunately, I've only been told that he is a coronel. With the Securitas?"

When Ronda promptly paled, Bengt smiled understandingly. "Sadly, I'm not acquainted with anyone in the Securitas, and you'll understand that I don't just want to ask a stranger. That's when I remembered your helpful cabo. But to have you here personally is a piece of good luck I would never have dreamed of." The capitán's flowery style was contagious.

The poor man looked anything but lucky now, though. "Well, I mean, I will of course do what I can, but . . ."

"Of that I am convinced. Please believe that I won't let that go unmentioned in my report. If you'd be so kind as to give me the names of those with that rank, I'd be most grateful."

"Oh, of course. Here, I'll write them down for you." It was almost embarrassing how relieved the man was to get out of the affair with such little effort.

"And where I might find them, too, please. If you happen to know their areas of operation, that would also be of interest. It is, after all, entirely possible that one of them won't be in his office, and I will have to search for him."

Ronda sweated all over the piece of paper he was writing on. He stayed perfectly courteous, but didn't offer Bengt more coffee. Instead, he said his elaborate farewells before Bengt had even risen from his chair.

"Thank you very much indeed. If I ever have another problem, I'll know who to turn to." Bengt was convinced the good capitán would spend his lunch hour in the next church lighting a candle to the Madonna, praying he'd never set eyes on Bengt again.

Back on the street, he wiped the sweat off his brow. It still took too much concentration to remember all those Santuarian addresses and polite phrases. But he wasn't aware of having made any mistakes and was quite satisfied with himself.

The hotel's A/C received him like an old friend. Relieved, he sank into one of the armchairs in the lobby and, to get the bitter taste of the coffee out of his mouth, ordered a tea, which was, as always, served lukewarm.

With his cup, the waiter brought him an envelope. "The receptionist asked me to give this to you, señor."

"Gracias."

Mail from Hentavik. Bengt ripped it open and went over the autopsy report. Almost identical to the first one. This time they'd also found gauze fibers in the wound, which made the whole clinic scenario even more likely. He let the report sink to the table, took a sip of his tea, and then busied himself with the list Ronda had composed for him. The first name caused a classic double take. Luìz Rukow. Rukow? How common was that name? Alex had said he didn't have any family. But Bengt didn't believe in coincidences.

He continued going through the list. Five names, but Luìz Rukow was the only one in Rajon One. Why should someone from another rajon be interested in the clinic in Soria? On the other hand, why Luìz Rukow? He tried to recall the man who'd saluted him in the stadium's lounge. Alex had called him Luìz, but thought it impossible that he could be "the coronel." Still, Bengt would have liked to have talked to the man. The large clock in the lobby sounded one, and he automatically looked toward the door. Alex would be here any moment. He folded the list and dropped it in his jacket pocket, not sure whether the Santuarian, who admittedly knew this Luìz well, was completely objective in this instance.

CHAPTER 9

Alex had parked the zorro in a side street because road access to the hotel was still closed off. Aside from a few workers sweeping up trash, the plaza was quiet now. The media people had already taken down the screen, and the stage had disappeared as well. Alex was walking slowly across the plaza in its Sunday slumber when, with the familiar, heart-shocking jolt, he saw Luìz.

The coronel was sitting on the rim of the fountain, but when he saw Alex, he got up and ground out his cigarette under his boot. He must have heard that Alex had been fishing for leads last night. Too late to slip past him. Stomach churning, Alex forced himself to walk up to him.

"You must have missed me badly," Luìz said in lieu of a greeting. "Or I must not have made myself very clear last night."

"On the contrary," Alex said. "I followed your advice and took the whole evening off. Did me good."

Luìz's eyes narrowed. "Next time, take the evening off in Cuevas, you smartass. The nightlife here is extremely unhealthy. And you shouldn't be working on a Sunday either. Go to church or something." He shoved the ball of his hand against Alex's shoulder, forcing him to step back to keep his balance. "But keep your nose out of my business. Am I clear this time?"

"Perfectly. Do you also have an idea what I'm supposed to tell ICE about why their investigation is suddenly dead in the water?"

"Think of something, hijo. Be creative. But don't cross me again. And something else." He pointed his thumb at the hotel building. "If that lumbering hulk in there gets too enterprising for my taste, you'll have a problem."

Without another word, Luìz turned on his heel and strode from the plaza. Alex exhaled slowly. His stomach was still fluttering, and he cursed himself for that.

In the lobby, Alex found Bengt sitting at one of the low tables, reading some papers he'd spread out in front of him. With a sigh, Alex dropped into the other chair.

"Did you see a ghost?" Bengt asked.

"Not yet. Can't be long now though. Luìz ambushed me outside. He's pretty mad about my little act last night."

Bengt frowned. "Did he say anything concrete?"

"He never does. Not really. Just that I should stay out of his business. I think he'd like it if you complained to ICE about the Securitas, so there'd be a nice fat scandal. Adiós, political rapprochement—and adiós, Alex."

"You be careful."

"Right. What are you reading?"

Bengt shoved the papers over. "The second autopsy report just came in. Same MO. Almost certainly the same killer."

Alex scanned the text before handing it back. "Everything all right with Kjell?"

Bengt looked up quickly, and Alex bit his tongue. Shouldn't have asked that. Why did he find it so hard to keep his distance around the big guy?

"Depends on how you look at it," Bengt answered. "We called it quits last night, and he took it better than expected." He made a face. "Better than last time anyway." He shoved the papers back into the envelope. "Shall we?"

"Not like we have much of a choice. Let's go by One first. I want to see if Huelva has any news for us."

"Already did. Huelva's not working today. I met Capitán Ronda instead. Man, I bet that guy won't even shut up when he's dead."

"And?"

"I didn't want to ask about the clinic too directly. With you guys, one never knows . . ."

"Hmmm."

Bengt toyed with the envelope. "I'll just run this upstairs. Be right back."

Alex watched him go, a crease between his brows. Bengt obviously hadn't left right away after not finding Huelva in, but had stayed to talk to the capitán. About what? Or who?

It was quiet in the lobby. Now that the teams were gone, the hotel must be half empty. Alex leaned back and tried not to think about Luìz. Good things came in threes. Bad ones, too? Luìz wasn't exactly famous for either his patience or his chattiness. Alex had the feeling that the courtesies were over. He just couldn't get caught a third time.

When Bengt came back, Alex got up. "Did you get your report sent off?"

Bengt groaned. "Don't remind me. Sunne called way early this morning to read me the riot act about Kjell's stunt last night. It was on the news. And don't say," Bengt stabbed his index finger at Alex, "that you told me so. I don't want to hear it."

"I'm not saying anything. Sunne is your CO?"

Bengt nodded. "And a good friend. But that newscast made her really furious."

Alex opened the door; the noon heat closed like a second skin around his body. "I hate air conditioning. It only makes you conscious of the heat when you leave. Normally, I never think about it."

"How nice for you," Bengt growled.

He sounded so resentful that Alex had to laugh. "Sorry. So, you have women working at ICE? As investigators?"

"Of course. Why wouldn't we?"

"I just thought . . . Just surprised."

Bengt rolled his eyes. "Let's start before you think any more."

Around five, Alex suddenly stopped walking in the middle of the road. "I'm hungry."

Bengt laughed. "Really? I thought that would never happen. By all means, let's eat."

They chose a small restaurant with tables on a patio. Bengt leaned back and stretched his legs. "I guess our only hope is that that stupid clinic will reopen soon."

They reached for the menu at the same time, their hands touching. Alex flinched and looked up at Bengt, but the Skanian just opened the menu as if he hadn't noticed. "Do you think they have those little rolls here?" he asked.

"Possibly."

Bengt closed the menu again and shoved it across the table. "You look first; I have to disappear for a second."

Five minutes later, Bengt was suddenly behind him. He gripped Alex's shoulder and leaned in close. Alex froze.

"Don't look over right away," the Skanian whispered into his ear. "But when I sit back down, check to see if you know the guy who's sitting by the door."

Alex tried to ignore his goose bumps that had nothing to do with what Bengt had said. He waited until Bengt sat back down, then risked a glance. "Nope, never seen him. Why?"

"Because he keeps looking over. Am I starting to get paranoid too, now, or what?"

Alex sent a silent prayer to the Madonna. "I hope you're just paranoid. Did you see him come in, or was he already there when we arrived?"

Bengt looked guilty. "I don't know. Didn't pay attention."

"Well, neither did I." *And God knows I have more reason.* Alex forced himself not to stare at the guy.

When they left, he stopped Bengt at the corner to look back, but no one left the restaurant behind them. The street was empty. From a nearby church, they heard the bells ring the end of evening mass. Alex grinned. "I need to go to church," he said.

"Excuse me?"

"Advice someone gave me today."

As they rounded the corner, the area in front of the church was filling with members of the congregation saying good-bye or staying around for a chat. Unfortunately, their conversations didn't include any interesting information.

"Let's call it a day," Alex finally said. "We're just wasting our time. At least he can't say I didn't do as I was told." Not that that would make a difference.

"Who?"

"Nobody important. Tomorrow at ten?"

"And that clinic better be open by then."

Alex didn't know what had woken him up. A sound or his sixth sense. Straining to see in the dark, he was fishing for his shorts on the floor when someone forced a sack over his head and chest and wound a rope around his arms. He couldn't breathe. Heart pounding in his throat, he kicked out at the attacker, but his legs were still tangled in his blanket. The sack smelled of breath mints. Something hit him hard on the head.

Concrete under his cheek . . . blinding light in his eyes. The sack was gone. Blazing pain at the back of his head.

"He's coming around." Leonid. Alex tried to sit up. Not a chance. His wrists and ankles were tied together behind his back, forcing his body into an unnatural arch.

"What're you waiting for then? Get going." Luìz.

Someone—Leonid?—grabbed his arm and dragged him to his knees. It felt as if his shoulders were being ripped apart at the joints. The rough floor tore his skin open. He stretched his head back to alleviate the pain in his shoulders, could just see the outline of a figure behind the light. "I warned you." Luìz. So it was Leonid who stood next to him.

Alex closed his eyes against the light. "I know. And I did go to church."

The blow struck his unprotected face. He couldn't see what Leonid had hit him with, but it made his eyes water under closed lids.

"You should have gone inside instead of snooping around town."

Alex didn't answer.

"Did you forget what happens to children who don't obey their parents?"

When he came to after the fight in the kitchen, he was hanging from his wrists and looking directly up into the crown of the old oak tree. Luìz stood in front of him, obviously waiting for him to wake up completely, his face white with rage. Alex felt the fear in his throat more than the blows and kicks he'd just received. He'd often been beaten, for a lot of things. But never before had he attacked Luìz. God alone knew the punishment for that. His shoulders started to protest against his own weight.

Slowly, demonstrating every inch to him, Luìz dragged the belt out of the loops on his pants and snapped it tight, making the leather crack between his hands. Then he grabbed the end with the holes and circled around Alex.

Alex closed his eyes, felt tears running down his cheeks and wished he was already dead.

"One!" The buckle tore through the flesh between Alex's shoulder blades. He screamed, screamed with every blow and then without pause.

A tremor ran up his arms. He wasn't fourteen anymore, but the terror from long ago still lingered in a dark corner.

"We should help your memory along."

A kick in the belly. The reflex to double up tore at his arms. He toppled over sideways. Again Leonid pulled him to his knees, struck his face. Water ran over his lips. A wet towel. Rolled and folded to make a blackjack. A kick struck his thigh, the flexed muscle. Alex felt the sound in his throat before he heard it. Then two quick blows to the face. *Madonna,* please speed up time. Let it be over already. He heard a rib crack when a boot met his chest. The impact threw him off balance again. He gasped for air—stabbing pain, groaned when Leonid pulled him up, closed his eyes expecting the next blow. The tension in his arms and thighs was unbearable.

"Are you finally going to do as you're told?"

Alex nodded.

"What?"

"I will."

Only now did the next blow strike him. Then Leonid kicked him in the upper arm with the tip of his boot. He screamed out the pain that raced through his muscle. Crashed, head first, to the concrete.

"Don't forget it again."

Leonid grabbed his arm, digging his thumb into the tender spot. By now, Alex's knees were raw meat on the concrete. He blinked into the interrogation light that suddenly dimmed when the damp towel covered his face. A hand in his hair forced his head back. Leonid behind him now. Alex could hardly breathe under the towel.

"What have your investigations turned up?"

"Not much," Alex gasped, fighting for air.

Suddenly there was water everywhere. In his nose, his mouth. He fought for air, lost his balance, held only by Leonid's hand in his hair. The water ran down his neck. No air in his lungs. Don't panic, breathe shallow.

"What do you want with Vigo Andúja?"

The voice sounded far away, dreamlike. What did they want with Andúja? "Andúja? Nothing."

Water again, like a seamless skin, a vacuum under the towel. Don't panic! He couldn't breathe, the pain in his muscles made him gasp, but there was no air. He lost all direction, didn't know which way was up or down, was breathing wet cloth in his desperate effort to get air into his lungs.

"What did you want in Soria?"

The clinic? What had they wanted with that? He couldn't think.

"Hold on for a minute, he's blacking out." Then, very close. "Alex? What's in Soria?"

"Clinic." Alex could hardly talk through the towel in his mouth.

"What's in the clinic?"

Breathing had never been so hard. "Instruments."

"Shit, I know that. Let him breathe; he's not making any sense."

The towel disappeared. Air! As much as possible as fast as possible. Breathe! Never mind the screaming ribs.

"He's still fighting," Leonid said.

"Horseshit, the kid's done. He's never been able to take much. Let him go."

Alex almost lost his balance again when Leonid did, but Leonid caught his shoulder against one knee. Even that touch was unbearable.

Then suddenly the light was gone. It took a while for his eyes to adjust enough that he noticed there was still a normal ceiling light on in the room. Luìz stepped in front of him looking down. First, he was only a silhouette, but after a while, Alex could make out every wrinkle in the hard face. When had he gotten old? Only the eyes were the same. Like that light green glass they made water bottles out of.

"You'll now give me a report of your investigation results. That's an order. You know the punishment for disobeying a direct order?"

Alex dragged his tongue across his lips. "I'm not Securitas," he croaked.

"But you are my son."

"Chingate!"

Without a word, Luìz raised his right hand. Holding a gun.

Alex waited for the blow with the barrel, then swallowed hard when Luìz pulled the slide back with his left. He felt Leonid nervously shift his weight. "Coronel . . . ?"

Luìz ignored him. "I should probably offer you a last cigarette."

I quit, Alex wanted to say, but couldn't form the words. A chuckle escaped him instead. He didn't doubt for one second that Luìz would shoot. He'd ignored too many orders, defied him once too often.

"Coronel? He's of no use to us dead."

The muzzle came closer, rested against his forehead, the metal cold against his skin. He saw the veined hand, the finger around the trigger, the short nail.

"Coronel? He's your son."

No, he isn't.

"Shut up, Leonid."

Was Leonid drunk? Good thing Bengt was at the hotel. Even the Securitas couldn't just drag him out of there in public. He had the power of ICE at his back; he was safe. Alex tried to swallow. *Come on, what the fuck are you waiting for?* He was fighting to control the fear and suddenly knew what Luìz was waiting for. For the fear to creep up into his eyes, where he could see it. And there was nothing Alex could do to stop it. *Madonna, I beg you, don't let me plead, don't let me start bawling.* He couldn't take his eyes off the finger around the trigger, saw the nail go pale. He'd always been sure that death wouldn't faze him. He had nothing to lose, had no idea why he suddenly wanted so badly to live. Fear of the inevitable turned to naked terror.

Then the click of the trigger.

Leonid jumped beside him. The blow against his forehead drove his head back, overstretched his throat.

Nothing had changed. Alex stared at the ceiling, straining to understand what had just happened. Felt blood run down his face. Leonid's knee was still digging into his shoulder. Alex's muscles were still screaming in pain. He raised his head. Luìz wiped the blood off the muzzle, fished around in his pocket, then, very deliberately, shoved the magazine back into the gun. It had been empty? The click. The trigger had only clicked. Luìz hadn't shot at all. He'd merely rammed the barrel into Alex's forehead to complete the illusion. Alex closed his eyes, searched for the anger that had to be somewhere, but came up empty.

Again Luìz pulled the slide back. "Get the towel. We're starting over."

No! Alex opened his eyes wide.

Luìz squatted in front of him. The lamplight reflecting in his eyes made them shine like silver. "Unless you're finally ready to tell me what I want to know."

"Three bodies," Alex started haltingly. "Two bums, one rent boy. Same killer, precision cuts with surgical instruments, death by electric shock."

"What about Vigo?"

"The boy had his name tattooed on his belly, was Vigo's lover. But Vigo's not a suspect, just a source."

"That's it?"

"If you start again, I'll just invent something."

Luìz shook his head. "Why do you always have to challenge me, hijo? You know you'll lose in the end." He stood up.

Leonid took a step toward him. Alex lost his balance and toppled over to the side again. Was it possible to go insane with pain? This time they let him be.

"So they don't know any more than we do. If it's the truth," he heard Leonid say.

"Look at him. He's said everything he knows." Disappointment rang in Luìz's voice. "He's always been a wimp."

"Bull," Leonid mumbled softly.

"Did you say something?"

"Nada, Coronel."

"Keep it that way. Now, take him back." Luìz hunkered down again in front of Alex. "I hope for your sake we don't need to repeat this lesson. I've got my eyes on you. Don't ever forget that."

Leonid pulled the sack back over Alex's head, carried him outside, and laid him almost gently on a metal surface. Cargo bed of a truck? Alex swallowed a curse, felt fabric on his skin. Then the endless drive, knocks and bumps that made him swear like a cheated hooker.

Suddenly quiet. Leonid carrying him again, then letting him slide to the floor. Wooden boards. He didn't bother to remove the sack, just cut Alex's bonds.

"The coronel can't tolerate defiance. Why provoke him?" If it hadn't been so absurd, Alex would have thought that Leonid was apologizing.

The door slammed shut. Silence.

For a moment, Alex didn't dare to move. Then, carefully, inch by painful inch, he freed his hands and feet from the ropes, raised his protesting arms, and pulled the sack off his head. He was at home, and alone. He tentatively stretched his limbs, gritted his teeth against the pain of the blood flow returning. He fought the rising pressure behind his eyes until pain and exhaustion got the better of him, then rolled himself into a tight ball on the floor and let the tears flow until there were no more.

A rafter cracked. Alex raised his head. The sun was high in the sky. With an effort he regained his feet, his body held together by nothing but pain. He couldn't have said where one left off and another started. The way to the bathroom had never been this long. He had to stop more than once, couldn't breathe deeply. In the shower, he sat on the tiles, opened the tap and flinched when the water hit his skin. Carefully, he cleaned the scrapes and cuts.

Foregoing the rough towel, he checked himself over in the mirror. Not as bad as he'd feared. His face was red and swollen from the blows with the towel, but that would pass. A split on his left temple from hitting the floor, a gouge on his forehead where Luìz had rammed the gun between his eyes. His brow, on the other hand, had almost healed. He tried a grin, but only managed a grimace.

Someone hammered on the front door. Alex jerked around so sharply he almost lost his balance.

"Alex!"

Relief made his knees weak. Bengt. He wrapped a towel around his waist before starting the long trek to the door. "It's open!" he yelled.

"Are you aware I almost pissed myself with worr— Shit, Alex, what the fuck . . .?"

Bengt stopped short when Alex stepped into the living room.

Alex slowly sank into a chair. "I'm afraid I missed our appointment. What time is it?"

"No idea, after one . . . Who gives a shit what time it is? What the hell happened to you?"

"Luìz reminded me that it's bad for me not to follow his orders. Leonid lent him a helping hand."

"I'm going to kill them."

"Can I watch?"

"You need a doctor."

"Good idea. You got one?"

Frustrated, Bengt banged his fist into the wall. "Do you at least have some meds in the house?"

"There should be some aloe."

"Aloe? For that?"

"That's all there is."

"Man, you're really well equipped for emergencies. Where?"

"In the kitchen."

"Could you be a tad more imprecise?"

Alex closed his eyes in amused relief. The banter felt good; normality trickled back into the day. "There's an odds-and-ends drawer in the table."

Triumphantly, Bengt came back a minute later with the little jar and pulled the other chair over. Alex held out his hand. "I can do that myself."

"Hands off, you can't see a thing." Bengt carefully turned Alex's head to one side. "Do you find that your face is missing something without any cuts?"

"Don't make me laugh. My head's exploding." Alex didn't feel fit enough to fight, and gave himself up to the Skanian's surprisingly gentle hands and his own thoughts. After a while, he asked, "What are you doing here, anyway?"

Bengt checked his handiwork, then started to apply the gel to Alex's torn arms. "When you didn't show up, I tried calling your office, but of course your phone wasn't working again. At some point, I just couldn't bear it anymore and went over to Huelva to check for news, and he helped me get a seat on the mail plane. From Cuevas, I took the bus. When Mendez hadn't heard from you either, I came here. Gijón drove me. I sent him back on foot to let Mendez know I found you.

Alex savored the feeling of his muscles slowly relaxing. A thought flitted through his head and spread warmly in his belly. "So, there's a cavalry after all," he murmured.

Bengt looked at him inquiringly, but then turned to Alex's bloody knees.

Alex watched him through half-closed lids, noticed his scrutiny, and tried to keep his breathing shallow to control the pain in his chest.

"Mendez mentioned something about Svoboda possibly being a movement," Bengt said.

"Mhmm."

Bengt screwed the top back on the jar, put it on the table, and looked around. He picked up the sack and ropes and sniffed them. "Did you fall in a peppermint patch?"

"Leonid brought those. It was a party with a dress code."

"I'll keep that in mind. Oh, I almost forgot the best. Huelva says the clinic is open again."

Alex groaned. "Now you mention that." He thought for a moment. "Can you drive the zorro?"

"No idea, how difficult is it?"

"Easy as pie. Help me up. I've got to get dressed."

Bengt crossed his arms in front of his chest. "To go where exactly?"

"To the clinic, bonehead. We'll never get a better opportunity. The way I look, everyone will believe that I belong there. With a bit of luck, I can look around, or at least hear something about your Svoboda."

"We can hope," Bengt said drily. "Aren't you afraid they'll catch you again?"

Alex flinched. "Luìz won't expect me back so quickly. Besides," he growled through his teeth, "it would almost be worth it, just to see his face when he realizes that he himself gave me that perfect excuse."

During the drive to Tierraroja, Alex kept his eyes closed and his teeth firmly clenched. Still, considering Bengt had only a ten-minute introduction and the steering wheel was between his knees, he was handling the driving just fine.

When they reached Soria, Alex sat up. "Best let me out here. Wait for me in the little café across the road."

"You want to go in there by yourself?"

"Bengt, you stand over two meters in your stockinged feet and weigh, what? 150 kilos?"

"175."

"Everyone would know immediately who you are. Me, I'm just a patient. What could possibly happen to me?"

"It's three now. If you're not back by four, I'm going to take that place apart brick by fucking brick."

Alex smiled. "Good to know, but say five. After the closure, the wait is probably fairly long." He climbed out of the zorro, feeling like an old man, and limped slowly, one arm pressed to his ribs, along the few streets to the address where they'd found nothing but the shards of needles before. When he walked around the corner, he knew why. Someone had fixed a removable stair to the pulley under the eaves. A long row of patients waited on the steps, some standing, some sitting. The loading hatch stood open.

"Hola," he said quietly and installed himself at the end of the queue.

A woman who sat three steps above him watched his labored movements and elbowed her teenage son. "Move, Misha. Can't you see the man there needs help more urgently than you with your thumb?"

Alex smiled gratefully before picking his way up to where she sat.

Her prompt caused others to turn around to him. One after the other silently let him pass. When he finally made it up to a young woman with a screaming baby in her arms, he leaned against the wall fighting for air. His turn came right after hers.

The room he entered was a former warehouse. Halfway up the walls hung ropes to which sheets had been tacked. These curtains divided the floor into several small examination areas and effectively blocked any view of the back part of the room. A boy led Alex into one of the makeshift cubicles, furnished with a cot. Against one wall was a shelf with bottles and boxes on it. A few minutes later, a young woman entered walking on two crutches.

"Buenos días, my name is Inés. You hurt your head?" Small-boned, arched eyebrows, a hard crease around the mouth.

"I'm afraid I broke my ribs," Alex said.

She pointed to the cot. "Please sit there and take your shirt off. Juan, let the doctor know he's needed here." She drew her brows together when she saw his arms and chest. "Did you fall under a bus?"

"Just under the Securitas. They didn't like the way I looked."

She avoided his eyes. "They're not all like that."

Alex raised his brows. "Oh? Who isn't?"

She flashed him a warning glance and put a finger to her lips. True, the coronel sometimes brought his men here, and the curtains weren't exactly soundproof.

"They do whatever they want with us," he murmured under his breath.

Inés sat down beside him to inspect his face, set the crutches to one side and accidentally touched one of his knees. He flinched, which made her struggle to her feet again and command, "Pants off and lie down."

Alex stretched out on the cot in his shorts.

"Did you clean the wounds?" she asked.

He nodded.

"Disinfect them?"

"No."

She took a brown glass bottle from the shelf, and a gauze package. "Did you apply anything?"

"Aloe."

She nodded. "I'm sure that felt good. I'll have to take it back off to disinfect the wounds; it will sting a little."

Anna had been right. She was very gentle. Her speech betrayed a good education. Alex doubted she was a *djeti*, but then what was she doing here?

A man came in, tall, gray-haired, gaunt. His lab coat was stained, and he appeared harassed. "What do we have here?" he asked Inés.

"Multiple contusions, possible rib fracture." She turned to Alex. "This is Dr. Martinez," she explained.

The doctor pressed several points on Alex's chest, which made Alex close his eyes and hold his breath.

"Keep breathing normally."

Alex shot him an exasperated look, but tried. He was asked a few more questions, told to sleep on his injured side, breathe as normally as possible, and cough now and then to clear his lungs even if it hurt.

"I'll tape the rib to save you some pain, but you can rip the tape off if you find it too restricting. It will eventually heal on its own. If you can get ice, that may also help with the pain."

Inés had taped a gauze pad to the gash in his head and reapplied some salve to the abrasions on his skin. "Did I find them all?"

"I think so, except if that thing on the back of my head is not just a bump."

She carefully moved his head to one side. "A considerable bump," she said. "Headache?"

"You could say that. The Securitas is anything but delicate. Time someone finally showed them some manners." This time, he kept his voice down.

Martinez looked at him. "You've had trouble before?"

"Oh, they used to harass my parents. If it wasn't for the Securitas, they'd both still be alive." He continued to rant for a while, hoping to elicit a response without risking his neck.

The doctor tore the last strip of tape off his roll, turned, and left without a word.

Alex looked after him, surprised. "Is he always that talkative?"

Inés handed him a glass of water and a pill. "He's a good doctor. Here. Take that." She gave him four more pills in an envelope. "That will have to be enough against the pain. I'm afraid I don't have more to give you."

"I'll manage." Alex reached for his pants and fished out a bill he'd crumpled into his pocket for this. "That won't be enough," he said, embarrassed. "But I don't have more than that."

She smiled. "It's enough. Thank you."

He didn't have to feign the embarrassment. He hated pretending he couldn't pay for his treatment and silently vowed to make an anonymous donation.

She left him to dress, and he saw her enter one of the other divisions when he peeked through the curtain. After closing his buttons, he filched a piece of gauze from the open package she'd left, then checked around. The whole floor seemed to consist of these little divisions, but they were too high to see over. He had made his way to the back of the room, searching for some kind of surgical ward or equipment, when Dr. Martinez stepped out from behind one of the curtains right in front of him, eyes narrowed. "Looking for something?"

"You," Alex said promptly and held out his hand. "I wanted to thank you."

"De nada. Keep away from the Securitas."

"I wish someone would tell them to keep away from me."

Martinez kept standing in front of Alex, blocking his way, so that he had no choice but to limp back to the exit. Most of the divisions were still occupied. Alex counted four people in lab coats, not exactly an overwhelming amount of personnel.

"Pssst."

He turned.

"Señor."

The boy, Juan, half hidden behind one of the curtains, was furtively waving him closer.

Alex stepped inside the division, and Juan took his hand, folded Alex's fingers around a piece of paper and vanished before Alex could ask any questions. Alex shoved the paper in his pocket and, on leaving, thanked those again who had let him pass earlier. The climb downstairs was easier on his lungs, but harder on his knees and thighs. He swore softly, knowing that he was comparatively mobile now, but that tomorrow morning he'd find it hard just to get out of bed.

Bengt was sitting at one of the rear tables, glasses and a carafe in front of him. He got up when he saw Alex. "That was faster than I thought."

"Wine? You?" Alex pulled out one of the chairs. "I'm fine. Don't fuss."

The Skanian doubtfully watched his slow movements as he folded himself into a sitting position, but sat back down. "Had to flush the shock out of my system. What about you?"

Alex nodded, filling the second glass. "Why not. Salud. Since you're driving," he added sarcastically.

Bengt almost choked. "It's only the one glass." Then he saw Alex's grin and chuckled. "Fuck you."

Alex pulled the paper from his pocket.

TUESDAY, 12 NOON
NUESTRA MADONNA
SVOBODA

"Did you find anything?" Bengt asked.

"I'm pretty sure Inés comes from one of the familias. Unfortunately, I couldn't look around much. Martinez, the doctor, got suspicious when he found me trying to take a peek at the back." He handed Bengt the piece of gauze he'd pocketed. "We should have this tested for similarities with the fibers found on the second body. Apart from that, I think I might have raised some dust with wild talk. A boy slipped me this." Alex gave him the note.

"That's tomorrow. What's 'Nuestra Madonna'?"

"The little church a couple of blocks east of here."

Bengt frowned. "You're not going there alone."

"You want to go?"

His answer was an accusing stare. "I could at least be close by. Like just now."

Alex shook his head. "Not that it doesn't give me the warm fuzzies to know you have my back," he admitted, "but if they were that stupid, we'd have heard of them before, or they wouldn't exist anymore. I'll take the bus." The wine made his eyelids heavy and had him thinking longingly of his bed. He shouldn't have downed it so fast. When he noticed Bengt's scrutiny, he sat up straighter.

The Skanian raised his hand to signal the waiter. "Check, please." With it, the waiter brought him a take-out bag.

"I thought you might want to go home," Bengt said, embarrassed. "So I had them pack something to go. I can't cook worth shit," he added when Alex didn't answer.

Madonna! "Listen, Bengt. That was a joke about you driving. I'm fine. How would you get back? You can't keep the zorro."

Bengt left money on the table and grabbed the bag. "Wouldn't be the first night I spent on some floor," he said, walking out the door.

"Just a minute! Bengt? Mierda!" Alex heaved himself to his feet. That was decidedly going too far.

By the time he'd limped out to the zorro, Bengt had jammed himself behind the wheel.

"I don't need a nanny," Alex fumed.

Bengt started the engine. "Are you going to stand there all evening?"

Alex banged his fist on the hood, flinched with the pain, and capitulated. "Don't get any ideas," he growled when he climbed in the passenger seat.

Bengt ignored him, but a satisfied smile played around his lips.

Alex leaned back in his kitchen chair, stretched his legs, and watched Bengt get out plates and glasses, divvy up the contents of the bag and open the bottle that had come with it. The Skanian had insisted that Alex not budge. And Alex was admittedly quite happy not to have to move anymore.

It felt weird to see Bengt bustle around so intimately in his kitchen. On the one hand, it made Alex feel less vulnerable than he would have expected after last night's events; on the other hand, it was unsettling, to say the least.

Bengt's powerful hands made short business of the cork and warmed the glasses. When Bengt poured, the wine reflected the lamplight. Alex looked up, straight into Bengt's eyes, which were watching him in turn. Trying to ignore the shiver that flashed through his body, he looked away and sat up. "So, what did you get us? Cubiertas? I should have known. You seem quite taken with them."

Bengt seemed surprised for a moment, then laughed. "They're just amazing."

Alex forced his thoughts back to the clinic. "Too bad that Martinez popped up right as I was making for the back. There could easily be something like an OR, or at least some gear back there."

"Hmmm, we still have no idea why, though. And what's their motive? I think while you're trying your luck at the church tomorrow, I'll let my computer do some work. As far as I can see, we have no other lead to follow for the moment, and I should make use of the fact that I have net access now. Let's see what I can find out about heads and electroshock. It might at least give us some ideas."

Alex nodded. The wine and the analgesic were starting to wash the pain out of his muscles. He felt light-headed, but filled his glass again anyway. If tonight wasn't a good time to get drunk . . .

Bengt fought to keep the sauce inside his cubiertas. Alex felt a smile tug at the corners of his mouth when Bengt started licking his fingers like a child. Another shiver raced across his skin.

He started out of his reverie when Bengt got up.

"You belong in bed."

Alex yawned. "Probably. Although I have no clue if I can stand. Are my legs still there?"

"They look like legs." Bengt helped him up, intent on not touching him anywhere it hurt, but so close . . . His skin smelled of soap and suntan lotion. Warning bells went off somewhere in Alex's fogged brain, but he was too tired to pay them any heed.

He barely managed to get to the bedroom and carefully sat on the bed, only to realize that the cracked ribs prevented him from bending over far enough to take his boots off. He swore and kicked the heels down with the toes of the other foot. "I have no idea how I'm supposed to get those back on tomorrow," he muttered. "Look in the top of the closet. There should be a couple of blankets. If you spread out the sofa and chair cushions, you should be reasonably comfortable."

Bengt got his blankets and started to leave the room. At the door, he turned back. "And you?" Worry in his eyes. Those damned eyes . . .

Alex blinked. "Err, never better. Don't worry about me." When Bengt left, he stared at the closed door and rubbed his arms to get rid of the third shiver of the evening.

CHAPTER 10

For a moment, Bengt stayed behind the closed door, then shook his head and set up camp in the living room. He had the impression that last night had left Alex with more than contusions and a few broken ribs. He'd been completely different today, as if he didn't have any energy left to defend his protective wall. Or he'd realized that wall wouldn't protect him anymore. Or maybe he'd simply felt lonely behind it.

Bengt rubbed the bridge of his nose, sat down on his makeshift mattress, and looked around. No pictures, no books, nothing that gave any hint about who lived here, not even a cupboard. What did Alex do in his spare time? Movies? Theater? He seemed to have hardly any friends. Was it possible to live that much within oneself?

Bengt turned the lamp down and lay back, hands behind his head. Alex had accepted his help today, even asked for it, trusted Bengt with his cover. He'd let himself be touched. Just before dinner Bengt had, for the length of a fluttering heartbeat, felt something like attraction from him, a certain look . . . But it had been gone too quickly.

Alex had probably just been tired and hurt and grateful for a helping hand. The rage Bengt had felt when he'd found Alex rose again, this time intensified by worry. He couldn't call a murder investigation off, but he wished there was some way he could keep Alex safe. Bengt tried to find a comfortable position and balled up a pillow under his cheek. Staring into the darkness, Alex's scent in his nose, he reviewed the day and finally dozed off.

He didn't sleep long, couldn't shake the thought that someone in Soria might have recognized Alex. He jumped at every cracking of a beam, searched for the root cause of every noise until he'd found it.

He got up early and pulled together whatever he could find in the kitchen for breakfast. Opening the different tea tins, he breathed in the scent of the herbs that was so much a part of Alex, but couldn't decide on one. Finally he knocked on the bedroom door. "Alex?"

"Hmm?"

"If you want to take the bus, you'll have to get up."

"Coming." His voice sounded sleepy. The creaking of the bed, a groan, and a string of curses.

Bengt carefully withdrew out of the line of fire.

A bit later, the curses came from the bathroom. When Alex finally showed up in the kitchen, Bengt left him alone for a bit.

The Santuarian threw a glance at the bread, fruit, and cheese on the table, grumbled something that, with a charitable interpretation, could have passed as "good morning." He poured himself a glass of water and dissolved one of the pills he'd been given at the clinic. Then he put the kettle on and swallowed the analgesic with eyes firmly shut while the water in the kettle started to simmer.

"Do you really think it's a good idea to go to this meeting?" Bengt asked. He didn't expect Alex to change his mind, but couldn't help trying.

Alex turned his back on him as he washed out his glass in the sink. "You got a better idea?"

Bengt looked pointedly at Alex's naked feet. "You can't even put your socks on."

"Chingalo . . ." The kettle whistled. Alex made tea, and Bengt watched his spare, graceful movements until an appetizingly fresh scent filled the kitchen.

"Smells good. What is it?"

"Hibiscus."

Bengt fell silent. Any further comment concerning the meeting could only start a fight. He wouldn't be able to keep the Santuarian away.

"What did Ronda tell you?" Alex asked out of the blue as he sat down and reached for the fruit.

"Sorry?"

The swelling in Alex's face had abated somewhat, and he'd removed the dressing from his forehead. With a small crease between his brows, he stared at the slice of pineapple in his hand, the juice running down his fingers. "We have three dead bodies, an illegal clinic, and an angel of mercy that could be connected, possibly, to an underground movement, and, in the stands, a whiny gay asshole and a merciful coronel." He looked at Bengt, eyes a little more awake now, but still with deep shadows underneath. "You asked Ronda about the coronel."

Shit, why now of all times? It had been a stupid idea not to talk about it right way. "He didn't know any more than you probably do. He only gave me the names and rajones." Bengt pulled the note from his wallet. "Read it, but it doesn't help us any." He hesitated. "Unless you know something about Luìz Rukow that I don't."

Alex flinched. "I know a lot of things about Luìz Rukow that you don't, but none that would tie him to Soria."

"What would a coronel from one of the other rajones have to do with it?"

"How the hell would I know?"

"And how do I know that Luìz doesn't have anything to do with it?"

"Or that I don't?"

"Bullshit."

"That's it, isn't it? That's why you didn't tell me. You don't trust me."

"Come off it. I don't think you're perfectly objective where Luìz is concerned, that's all."

"Luìz is as much in the dark as we are. He tried last night to beat out of me who the killers are."

"Or he knows and wanted to find out who we think did it."

"Horseshit."

"Not necessarily."

"Chingate!"

"Shit, Alex, this isn't getting us anywhere." Bengt pinched the bridge of his nose. He'd done a brilliant job of antagonizing Alex. Now what? Leave it? Then it wouldn't be long before they weren't talking at all. He'd better try to set things straight right now. Even if that involved a question he might not want to hear the answer to. He took a deep breath. "To be perfectly clear, I trust your integrity. I merely happen not to share your opinion. But what I'd like to know now is: Do you trust me?"

Alex stared at him without moving a muscle, as if he'd been carved from stone, but Bengt could guess how feverishly he was considering everything that stood between them. He almost held his breath.

Finally, Alex nodded. "I told you yesterday that it's good to know you have my back, and I meant it."

For a second, Bengt closed his eyes in relief. He had the feeling the decision had been pretty tight. "Why does Luìz threaten you?" he asked gently.

Alex ate the rest of the pineapple, then got up laboriously to wash his hands. "I think our search for Vigo flushed him out of the woodwork. Something he said. The patrón, of course, wants us to leave his son alone, so he sends his lackey. Apart from that, Luìz is in an unfamiliar situation. Someone is running around killing people left and right, and for once Luìz has no idea who or why. The whole thing is outside of his control. It drives him nuts." The thought seemed to amuse him. "No, I think we should focus on the clinic personnel. I'd like to check out Inés a bit more closely, and maybe I'll find out something about the doctor, Martinez, at this meeting today." He wiped his face with his wet hand. "I'll walk past the office and let Mendez know where I'm going. He has a bad habit of getting annoyed if he finds out about activities like that after the fact. Are you going to be at your hotel? I can call you as soon as I know something."

Bengt looked demonstratively at Alex's feet. "Are you gonna go like that?"

"Gives me the right look," Alex replied calmly. He'd either gotten a hand on his anger or the pills deadened more than just the pain.

Bengt drummed his fingers against his pant leg. "Fine. I'll look forward to hearing what you find out."

Alex was already at the door. "Nothing's gonna happen to me," he said over his shoulder as he left. But that didn't make Bengt feel any better at all. Frustrated, he banged his fist on the table, making the teapot jump.

Back at the hotel, the third autopsy report was waiting for him. Bengt bagged the gauze sample and addressed it to the lab, then read the report on the stairs. It confirmed the assumptions of the doctor at the Tierraroja morgue. This time, they'd found traces of drugs, but nothing that would have been relevant at the time of the murder. The pattern was the same as with the other two, except the cause of death had been cerebral hemorrhaging triggered by electric shock. The boy's heart had simply held out longer than his brain.

Bengt threw the papers on his bed and made time for a quick shower and fresh clothes before installing himself in the conference room with his netpad. He appreciated being the only one who used the room.

The system came up, searching for a connection. Bengt stared at the screen without paying attention. He couldn't get the image out of his head of Alex standing there yesterday, face unrecognizable, his body covered in abrasions and bruises, and worst of all, that shell-shocked emptiness in his eyes. Bengt would have liked to have done more than the superficial care of the little cuts and scrapes, but he'd been far too aware of how close they were sitting and the fact that Alex wasn't wearing anything but a towel.

The system beeped as it found a connection. Bengt opened his account, called up his favorite search engine, and ran the words "head, skull, electricity."

He couldn't remember when he'd started to trust the Santuarian, when his utter confusion had changed to intuitive comprehension. During the last few days, there'd often been situations he'd enjoyed. More than he would've thought possible. Last night . . . Bengt had been glad his hands were busy with the bottle when he'd noticed how Alex was watching him. He might otherwise have been betrayed into a gesture or touch that would have driven Alex back behind his wall. He realized he was well on the way to falling in love with a man who was different in every respect, and he had no idea how to stop himself.

"Señor Comisario?"

Bengt looked up. Two men were standing in the doorway, one of whom rang a faint bell. "Yes?"

"My name is Linares. Would you be able to spare me a moment?"

The one in the blue suit jacket is Vadim Linares. Andúja's secretary. Bengt closed the window with his search results, got up, and shook Linares's hand. "Good to meet you. Please take a seat."

The second man remained standing against the doorframe, arms folded across his chest. Bodyguard. Bengt ignored him. He was curious to find out what Linares wanted.

The secretary sat down, crossed his legs, and studied the tips of his fingers. "I hope you are enjoying your visit to Santuario?" he finally said, looking up.

"I can't complain, thank you," Bengt said carefully. Had Andúja sent the man? And if so, did he consider Bengt something of a Skanian ambassador?

Linares's lips formed a strictly allotted smile. "A very diplomatic answer."

"Which in this case happens to be the truth. At first, the climate proved a little difficult, but now I'm fine." It was none of the man's business that he needed medication to cope with the heat.

"Our cultures are very different," Linares continued. He smelled of sweat, wool, and old furniture. Razor nose, keen, light-blue eyes, cynical parentheses around his mouth.

Bengt shrugged. "All in all, the similarities are surely more surprising than the differences."

"Naturalmente." Linares made a conciliatory gesture. "And yet, there are certain things that are hard for a stranger to know."

Bengt began to guess the direction this was going. He drummed his fingers on the tabletop. "And a young teniente from a backwater village might not be the best advisor in such matters?"

Linares leaned back in his chair. "I see we understand each other." His lips did the allotment thing again, but the smile never reached his eyes.

The hairs on the back of Bengt's neck rose; he struggled to hide his antipathy. "You, on the other hand, know your way around very well, I assume."

"At least, I am much better informed about the current political tide."

It was Bengt's turn to lean back. "Why don't you educate me?"

Linares drew his brows together. He'd obviously not expected such a direct attack. "Well, the relationship between our cultures could be, shall we say, smoother?" he began hesitantly. "If an innocent member of a highly regarded family should now become the subject of a police investigation, that would not be, if I may say so, exactly helpful. The patrón has so far regarded the issue of annexation quite positively."

And pigs fly.

"But he can only take the accusations against his son as a personal affront," Linares continued.

Bengt raised his brows. "I'm not aware of having accused Vigo Andúja of any crime," he said gently.

"Surely this is all a misunderstanding," Linares said peaceably, while his eyes sent a clear warning. "I'm convinced that now that you know how your investigations must look to the patrón, you will do your utmost to make the problem go away."

With that, Bengt was warned as well. Keep out or risk political complications. Mutual mistrust had always stood between their two cultures. Support for the annexation was still tentative in Jarðvegur. Bad press like Andúja was threatening could easily sink any chance of it for years to come. And politically annihilate its supporters. But then, the familias were planning to provoke a scandal no matter what he did. Not that Vigo was particularly interesting to the case, anyway. He stood up and held out his hand. "Don't worry."

For a moment, Linares stared at him from narrowed eyes, seemed unsure whether he'd accomplished what he wanted. But he shook the offered hand and let Bengt accompany him to the door.

The bodyguard stepped aside for Linares, but blocked Bengt with his body, standing so close that Bengt could smell the mint on his breath. When Bengt's brain made the connection to the sack Alex had been tied up in, the little hairs on his arms stood on end. He looked more closely at the tall, massive Santuarian. So that was Leonid. Bengt stuffed both hands in his pockets to keep them from closing around the Securitas's throat. He'd get his opportunity. Or make it.

Leonid matched him stare for stare, not a muscle moving in his face. But a spark in his eyes hinted that he knew what Bengt was thinking and that he looked forward to the challenge. Then he turned and followed his charge into the lobby.

Bengt closed the door and wiped his hand on his pants. Alex must be at the church by now. Barefoot and with broken ribs. Shit. Bengt caught himself pacing the length of the room. He sat back down, brought up his results, then tried new searches, now and then replacing the search terms "electronics, electric shock, brain, cortex." He scrolled through articles, stopped suddenly when his eyes caught the word "Esprus."

> ... not known how these ships are navigated, since there seems to be no input device for the computers. When questioned, the engineer answered with an Esprus word that was translated as *direct connection*. Dr. Hemavan could find no explanation for the term. The possibility of a cortical connection was discussed briefly during the conference, but could not be confirmed. The asylum seekers were given the island of Laholm, which they renamed Santuario, in the South Sea ...

Bengt stared at the ancient article in utter fascination. Direct connections between a computer and a human cortex? Was that even possible? Or was it just the fiction it sounded like? And even if it were possible, would anyone be desperate enough to try it today? And why? Every computer used today had touch screens, keyboards, or mics.

He wondered what had happened to the old ship's computers. And what happened to the ship itself after it had been stranded in Jarðvegur?

He feverishly started a new search, changed parameters again, waded through newspaper and data archives and finally sent envoys to a few friends and colleagues who might be able to help him.

He leaned back and stretched his shoulders. Alex must now be ... He had no clue what Alex was doing at the moment. It was tempting to just go and check up on him, but that might endanger him even more. Bengt decided to have lunch to kill the time before the answers to his envoys came in. He left a message with reception to please let him know immediately if someone should call for him, and then settled uneasily at a table. He wasn't really hungry, so he just ordered a salad. He had to force himself not to jump up every ten minutes to go and look for envoys. Again, he checked his watch. Alex had had an hour. He should call any minute now.

Bengt forced himself to eat slowly, but his gaze kept wandering to the door. Finally, he threw down his cutlery and returned to his netpad. He'd received four envoys: one "No idea," one "So, where the hell are you again?" one "What ships?" Bengt cursed the Skanian information policy concerning Santuario and opened the last envoy.

BENGT,
FROM WHAT I COULD DIG UP ON SUCH SHORT NOTICE, THE SMALLER SHUTTLES WERE SENT TO SEVERAL RESEARCH FACILITIES. THE MOTHERSHIP WAS SCUTTLED TO BUILD THE COLONY ON SANTUARIO. BUT NO ONE BOTHERED TO LIST ANY EXACT DATA. WHEN NO WEAPONS SYSTEMS WERE FOUND ON BOARD, THE GOVERNMENT APPARENTLY LOST INTEREST (NO COMMENT).
SUNNE
(YOU'RE MAKING ME CURIOUS; SEND ME A SHORT INTERMEDIATE REPORT)

Shit, so did these computers still exist or not? Bengt wished there was a way he could reach Alex, talk all the possibilities over with him. But above all, he needed to give Alex the information he'd found so he could ask the right questions.

But then, maybe all this was widely known here. He rubbed the bridge of his nose. Huelva would know that. Bengt powered the netpad down and brought it up to his room. Back in the lobby, it dawned on him that he might miss Alex if he left now. He turned, checked for change to make a phone call from the lobby, then stopped dead in his tracks when he saw a man come out of the conference room. The coronel who'd been talking to Alex on Saturday.

For the second time that day, Bengt curled his hands into fists and shoved them in his pockets. Control. Not another Skanian temper tantrum in the lobby.

The coronel had obviously been looking for him. He raised his hand to his cap in greeting and came over. "Señor Bengt?"

"Coronel."

Luìz regarded him for a moment. "Can we talk somewhere in private?"

"In the conference room. Please." *There I can also take you apart in private.*

Luìz led him back the way he'd just come. He sat on the table when Bengt closed the door. "I'm here to help you," he began. "But just so there are no misunderstandings . . ." He let his gaze wander demonstratively over Bengt's aggressive stance, then tapped his fingers against the handle of his pistol. "You'd do well to stay a few feet away from me."

Bengt had to muster every ounce of will he possessed to relax his muscles. He breathed deeply and leaned against the doorframe. "You want to help me? You have a strange sense of humor."

Luìz shook his head. "It's not that strange, but I don't expect you to understand that."

"But you expect me to believe you."

"That would indeed be best for all involved."

Bengt barked a laugh. "Which I would also have to believe. Why do you suddenly want to help me? Or are you our anonymous donor after all?"

"I have no idea what you're talking about."

"Oh, come on. You're the coronel who has his people treated in Soria and pays for it. And who throws in the occasional tip-off before a swoop."

Luìz stared at him for a moment, then sighed deeply. "I really can't understand your exaggerated interest in Soria," he complained. "What makes the clinic so important to you?"

"You first."

"That's not why I'm here. And time is of the essence."

"I don't believe a word you're saying. Give me a single reason why I shouldn't take you apart piece by piece."

"Nine millimeter?"

"Oh, please! It's one thing to torpedo the political detente, but even we can be provoked too far. You start eliminating ICE personnel, and I guarantee you this whole island will be dumped into the ocean, patrón and all," Bengt bluffed.

For a few seconds, Luìz studied the tips of his boots before looking at Bengt again. "We don't have time for games. Your young friend managed to get himself into a situation he won't be able to get back out of. If I were you, I'd go check on him."

Bengt felt the blood drain from his face. "Alex? Where is he? What . . .? Why would you suddenly be so interested in his well-being?"

Luìz banged the heel of his hand against the edge of the table. "Enough!" With two long strides, he covered the distance between them, shoving his face up into Bengt's. "My motives are none of your fucking business, amigo. Fact is, you can't take the risk not to believe me."

He was right. Which finally snapped Bengt's patience. His right hand closed around Luìz's throat, and he shoved the coronel back to where he'd been sitting before and forced him backward onto the table, their faces only inches apart. Luìz's pulse beat against Bengt's fingers, then Bengt felt the barrel of Luìz's pistol in his ribs. The coronel's face was distorted with pain, but his eyes burned with fury.

"Stalemate," he whispered with effort. "You'll no sooner . . . kill me . . . than I'll . . . kill you."

"Pray," Bengt hissed. "Pray to your god that Alex is all right, or you won't live to see your mistake. Where is he?"

CHAPTER 11

The church was cool and empty. Alex dropped a coin in the box and lit a candle. He needed any help he could get. Then he sat in one of the pews and waited.

Only a few minutes later, the door opened; two men entered the church and came toward him. "Perdone usted, would you have the time?" the younger one asked.

Alex checked his watch. "Five after twelve."

The two looked at each other, seemed to have expected a different answer. The older one nodded his thanks, and they left again.

Alex was sure he'd blown his contact, but not how or why. And he couldn't ask, either. What if they weren't the ones he was waiting for? He stayed another fifteen minutes, but no one else came. Shit. He got up angrily and went back outside.

The sun was blinding after the dimness inside, and he stopped in the door for a moment to let his eyes adjust, when he was shoved hard from the left. Instinctively, he crossed his arms in front of his body to protect his ribs and stumbled against the second man, who pinned him against the wall with a hand around his throat. When Alex tried to pry the fingers open, an arm was pressed against his chest. He screamed and kicked out blindly, connecting with a shin. The pressure against his chest eased a little.

"Who are you?" the attacker hissed in his ear.

Alex thought feverishly. They were the two guys who'd asked after the time. No uniforms. They just had to be the men he was here to meet. "Chingate," he forced out, "you're worse than the Securitas."

The pressure eased some more. Suerte.

"I'm Alex. Someone from Soria sent me. I have a note."

"Show me!" the one who'd shoved him said.

Gingerly, Alex fished the note from his pocket and handed it over. The man was still suspicious. "Who've you been talking to?"

"Inés and Dr. Martinez, but it was the boy, Juan, who gave me the note."

"Seems real enough to me, Jesús. And he does look like the description we have."

"Madrios," Jesús swore and let him go. "One day we'll be seriously fucked if nobody ever knows the password."

Alex kept his breathing as shallow as he could.

The older one held out his hand. "I'm Xavier. Sorry about the ribs. Someone's been sloppy; it's not the first time."

Jesús lightly touched his shoulder in apology. "No offence. I was 'specially careful."

Alex tried a smile. "Nothing else broken. I think. If you treat the Securitas like that, I'm your man."

"Not here." Xavier looked around. "Come."

They led him to a flat not far away. The main room had been converted into an office with an old desk taking up the back half. A woman in her fifties offered him a seat in front of the desk, and the two men took their leave.

For a while, she studied him in silence, then asked his name and what he did. She wanted details about his trouble with the Securitas and had him explain why he was here and what he expected to happen now. Alex stayed with the truth as far as possible. They would check his answers; otherwise this interview made no sense, and he might want to be back for more information later on. He left out the murder investigation and told the woman the Securitas had beat him up because he'd fought back against their harassment.

"Bueno, Alex, you can go get yourself something to eat next door, if you want. Tell them Ena sent you. Then go home. We'll contact you."

"That's it? Can't I do anything?"

"Not for the moment. We'll let you know."

Mierda. So, the only thing he knew now was that there was indeed an underground organization that seemed to recruit its members through the clinic. If the mysterious coronel ever found out, he'd surely be a little less protective of said clinic.

The house next door was a soup kitchen, the rows of tables packed. Alex got himself a bowl and squeezed between two men at the loudest table. The whole group wore shoes. Leather gloves and a few helmets on the table indicated they worked construction. But for the moment, all they were interested in was a Santuarian björbo team.

"They wouldn't stand a chance against a Skanian team."

"Not necessarily. Body checks are against the rules, and I didn't see too many during the game."

"Oh, and maybe you didn't see their longer reach either."

"Well, I wouldn't wanna try to catch a ball they fired off."

"We don't have to play against the Skanians."

"But we need someone who's familiar with the game and the rules."

"Can't you read, or what?"

"What does reading have to do with it? This is about tactics and experience. If we dive in blind, we'll just end up with a pile of cracked heads."

"Inés'll sew us back up."

"Inés is slowly losing her nerve."

Alex ate his soup, trying to melt into the background.

"If you had to work with Martinez, you'd lose your nerve, too."

"Martinez may be a cold bastard, but he's a damned good doctor."

"And he gives me goose bumps."

"He doesn't give a shit about us. Why does someone like that become a doctor anyway?"

"Am I his mother? Thing is, he helps."

"Does he? There's something off about that guy. Me, I've no clue what his 'big' secret work is and what good it's supposed to do us."

"I guess he wouldn't even tell his mother that, but he did patch you up, didn't he?"

"Yeah, well, but you don't seriously think he'd do that after every match."

The discussion turned back to björbo; Alex carried his bowl to the counter where the dirty dishes were piling up. He didn't see any staff other than the woman doling out the soup. "Do you work here all by yourself?"

"Unless you want to help me," she replied curtly.

"Why not? I ate. I can wash dishes for a bit."

She looked at him in surprise, but made room and gave him a dish rag. "I wish everybody thought like that. For most folks here," she nodded to the packed tables, "the glorious fight for freedom and justice doesn't include soup and dishes."

"Well, it's maybe not the most heroic occupation," he admitted ruefully over the running water.

That made her laugh. "I'm Nadya. Are you new?"

He nodded. "Alex. Dr. Martinez seemed to think it a good idea to send me here." Her face darkened. "You don't like him," he added.

"Do you like him?"

"Can't say, I don't really know him well enough. He's a bit brusque, but there could be many reasons for that."

She silently filled another bowl and handed it to a newcomer. "They say he used to work as a private doctor for one of the familias. Had a life as cushy as you can imagine. It's rumored they pulled his license because he lost a patient."

"Reason enough to be bitter."

"Maybe, but that doesn't make him any more likeable. Look at Inés; I'm sure it can't be easy for her, but I've never heard anyone talk badly about her."

"True, she was really nice. And gentle. A friend told me to go to her because she 'doesn't hurt you so much.'" He smiled, but didn't get an answer. "I felt sorry for her with those crutches. Pretty girl, doesn't talk like a *djeti*."

Nadya pulled her shoulders up. "There are rumors. But whether they're true . . .?"

Alex's fingers were getting pruny in the dishwater and his thigh hurt from standing for so long. He'd remember that kick Leonid had given him for a while. "That's the thing with rumors. But I thought she must have some medical training; she was using all those terms."

Nadya thought about that for a moment, but then shook her head. "She'll have picked those up over the years. Far as I know, she's an engineer or something like that. She's connected somewhere with the Andúja clan. Maybe she really severed all ties because she fell in love with a *djeti* or because she owes her crutches to the carelessness of her bodyguard. I don't know which is the truth. And I don't think it's any of my business, either," she added with a meaningful look at him.

Whoa, Alex, shift back a few gears. Bengt's direct style was beginning to rub off on him. He wouldn't get anything else from her, but it couldn't hurt to keep his options open. "I didn't mean to pry, just to chat a bit. Since I don't know anyone here yet."

"Now you do. Thanks for the help. If you feel a longing for dishwater again, do drop by."

He made as if to throw the rag at her, and she laughed. These Svoboda people were starting to interest him—not only because of the case. He would have liked to stay, but Bengt was probably on the brink of tearing up the clinic as it was.

Juan was hanging around outside, smoking. He grinned at Alex's disapproving face. "Hola señor. Quetal?"

"Not too bad, no thanks to you."

The boy shrugged. "I'm just passing on messages. Inés wants to see you. In the yard behind the clinic."

What the hell? Had the note been hers then? Or had someone told her already that he'd shown up here today? That he'd been asking questions about her?

"Why in the back?"

Another shrug. "She didn't say. Just to wait here and give you the message."

Alex hesitated. Something about this didn't feel right. But he'd come here for information, and this might be the break they needed. He slowly walked the few streets over. There were no patients sitting on the steps, the whole street lay deserted. The gate stood ajar; it squeaked when Alex opened it further, the handle leaving crumbs of rust in his hand.

A man was leaning against the wall, chewing on a blade of grass, watching, waiting. Alex recognized Kolya, the Securitas from Rajon Four with whom he'd had the altercation at the Hotel Aldea. Alarm bells went off in his head. There'd been two of them. But he knew, when he heard a sound behind him, that the realization had come too late. A blow to the head caught him mid-turn.

". . . too obvious. There'd be hell to pay. Are you forgetting it's supposed to look like an accident?"

"I really don't know why we can't just disappear him."

For a dizzy moment, Alex didn't know who the voices belonged to. Just to open his eyes was a Herculean task, and when he finally managed, the sun made the pain explode in his head, so he closed them again. His wrists were tied behind his back.

"He wants to avoid further investigations, but if you want to argue with him, be my guest."

"Don't think this makes you the boss, Castillo. Gimme a hand here." Kolya's voice. Carefully, Alex opened his eyes a slit. He was lying on the ground by a wall. Kolya and his wolfish sidekick were busy breaking open the lock on a door. There was a click, and Castillo stepped back. "See? That's how you do it."

Kolya came over to Alex, gun in hand. "On your feet."

Alex pushed himself up the wall, trying to ignore his protesting ribs and hammering skull. For a moment, the world danced dizzyingly in front of his eyes. Castillo watched his efforts with the detached interest one might have for a bug struggling on its back. Kolya's eyes glowed with an unholy joy. "Too bad we can't touch him," he murmured.

"But you'll have the pleasure of putting him on ice."

Kolya looked at his pal blankly, then grinned. "Good one," he chuckled, then to Alex, "In there. Go on."

Alex stepped into a warehouse with a concrete floor. The only light came from a row of narrow windows just under the ceiling. Floor and walls were covered with crates and boxes, overhead cranes ran along the ceiling.

Kolya cut his restraints and made himself comfortable on a large crate. "Strip!" he ordered.

"Madrios." Castillo threw his arms up. "We don't have time for your games."

"I don't know what you want," Kolya replied, innocently fluttering his eyelids. "It'll go much faster that way."

"Point. So yeah, strip!"

"Chingate," Alex hissed.

"Do you think anyone would notice if I just pushed a bit on those ribs again?" Kolya asked in a chatty tone.

"Naw." They both looked expectantly at Alex. "You can have it easy or hard. Your choice," Kolya said.

Alex stared into the barrel of the gun. Déjà vu. He couldn't think straight, couldn't see a way out. Hesitantly, he took off his pants and shirt. Castillo walked over to a metal door and slid the bolt open.

"Hold on," Kolya called. "He forgot a piece."

Castillo rolled his eyes. "You're starting to get on my nerves." He heaved the door open and turned back to Alex. "What's your problem? You waiting for a written invitation?"

Kolya suddenly came up from his makeshift couch. Alex's time was up. He stepped past Castillo into the room beyond. Cold air all around him, even the floor was painfully cold under his feet. Floor-to-ceiling shelves were packed with boxes, cartons of food, crates. Alex didn't turn when he heard the door slam shut behind him, leaving him in the dark. He tried to think, but found it hard to concentrate. Goose bumps ran up his arms, and he rubbed both hands across the skin. He had to get out of here. This time there'd be no cavalry, Bengt had no clue where he was. The door didn't budge when Alex leaned against it, the metal cold enough under his hands to make his skin stick. He found a switch and turned the lights on. The shelves ran from wall to wall, no windows. He could see his breath in the air.

He pulled a cardboard box from one of the shelves, emptied it out, and flattened it to stand on. Better. For a while he was busy making something of a nest for himself with boxes and paper. The movement helped, but the cold crept into his bones. His fingers and toes started to hurt. He shivered uncontrollably. Again, he tried the door. The hinges were on the outside, and the door closed so tightly that he couldn't even get a nail in the crack. He could have kicked himself. How could he have been so stupid to walk into such a simple trap? If he ever laid his hands on Juan again . . . but the boy had probably really just passed on a message for a few coins. He should have . . . what? Called in Bengt, so all his sources would immediately clam up? He slammed his fist against the frame. What good was his knowledge now? If you could even call it knowledge. He gritted his teeth to keep them from chattering. He was shivering violently. He had to move. He started to jump up and down, but the pain exploding in his head and chest forced him to stop. He chose squats instead, ignoring the protest of his beat-up muscles.

Kolya and Castillo were Securitas. So, was Luìz behind this? But wouldn't Luìz send Leonid, or at least guys under his own command?

Why two strangers? Or had Andúja himself given the order? But again, why them? Stuff like this was what he had Luìz for. Or the mysterious coronel who protected the clinic?

How long had he been in here? The pain in his thigh forced him to stop again. Why was he bothering to stay warm anyway? He was kidding himself. No one would come, and there was nothing he could do. He sank onto his cardboard nest, wrapped his arms around his knees, and rested his head on them. They'd just let him freeze to death in here, no effort. They were probably playing cards outside.

Powerless. Like a child.

"When is he going to leave, Mama?"

"I don't know, Sasha. Sleep. Happy dreams."

So cold. *"Is he really my father?"*

"Only your heart can decide that, Sasha."

Languid indifference crept into his body, though deep down he could still feel the twitching wings of fear.

"I am your father, and that's what you will call me." Luìz's fingers dug mercilessly into his shoulders.

"Sí, señor."

"Say it."

"Sí, señor."

"Father! Say it, you defiant little shit!" Luìz yelled, his face a grimace of rage, as if it was melting. Alex's arm was going numb. With a dry sound, his collarbone snapped. The new pain made his knees buckle, and the last "Sí, señor" was no more than a whimper. Disgusted, Luìz let him go.

He flinched when his shoulder touched one of the shelf posts, but was too tired to raise his head. An easy way to die. But he'd much rather lie outside in the sun. A smile flitted across his face. He'd have liked to have been able to tell Bengt good-bye, joke with him about some nonsense. Amazing, how used to a stranger one could get in just a few days. The face with the high cheekbones now almost as familiar as his own. The little wrinkles in the corners of the eyes from squinting against the sun. The way every drop of sweat outlined the muscles in his neck. A shiver ran across Alex's skin that had nothing to do with the cold. He shied away from the direction his thoughts were threatening to take. He wouldn't have to deal with this strange, threatening, and yet alluring friendship anymore. But then, who was he to call a friendship strange? What did he have to compare it to? He idly wondered why he wasn't freezing anymore, if he'd miss the music. Thoughts like quick little fish under the sunny surface of the bay.

Hands. Soft fabric against his skin. The scent of soap and suntan lotion. The familiar deep voice. "I can't let you out of my sight for two minutes." Bengt. Warm. Huge. Sun on Alex's eyelids, humid air. Arms like a fortress around his body. To just surrender and be safe. A shoulder under his head, pulse against his lips. Bengt's sudden deep breath.

Then twinges like maggots in his hands and feet. Burning. Solid, steady pain. Unyielding muscle. No escaping those hands, massaging the blood back into his limbs. Finally, mere pins and needles. A flush of warmth.

Tender hands in his hair. "Sleep, Sasha. Happy dreams."

Alex yawned languidly, unwilling to open his eyes and leave his comfortable nest. Stretched his arms, felt the body underneath him move—and was suddenly wide awake. He was lying between Bengt's outstretched legs, wrapped in a blanket, the Skanian's arms around his shoulders, his head on Bengt's chest. When he jolted upright, Bengt gave him a worried look. "Easy, or you'll just keel over again."

Cursing, Alex jumped to his feet, stumbled, caught himself against a tree, and looked around. The sun rode low in the sky; it was late afternoon. He was standing on the narrow strip of grass that circled the warehouse. Adrenaline chased the last of the languor from his muscles. He ignored Bengt's, "Alex?"

The zorro was parked a couple of meters away, and the door into the building stood wide open. Alex hesitantly walked toward it. Kolya lay right behind the entrance with a broken neck, Castillo at the door to the refrigeration unit in a pool of blood. Alex stared at the bodies, incapable of associating them with the image he had of Bengt. Alex's clothes still lay where he'd dropped them, and he got dressed quickly.

Although he had his back to the door, he knew when Bengt entered, didn't look at him. Couldn't. He was too aware of the clothes against his skin, but they were still not enough protection. Don't think. Do something. Anything to kill that demanding silence. "Where are we?"

"About twenty-five kilometers north of Tierraroja."

When Alex finally turned around, Bengt's eyes asked a silent question. He looked away again. He needed fresh air, but would have to pass the Skanian to get it. No, way too close. Just do something already! Snap out of it. He opened the door to the cold room, grabbed Castillo's body in a fireman's grip and dragged him inside. His ribs screamed and his vision swam. Short of breath, he leaned against one of the shelves. The more he regained the function of his body, the more it remembered the beating he'd suffered.

Bengt brought Kolya and dropped him beside his comrade. With a worried frown, he laid his hand on Alex's shoulder. "Give yourself some time to recover."

Alex pushed him aside with a quick move of his arm. "I'm fine. I owe you a life. Don't touch me."

Bengt recoiled as if he'd been slapped. "You don't owe me anything," he said quietly.

"I don't?" Alex barked a laugh. "And here I thought you'd already chosen your payment." But he knew that wasn't true. He shoved past the Skanian, crossed the warehouse to the door and, as deeply as he could, breathed in the outside air. He needed to get away from here, get some distance, needed to clear his thoughts, but mostly to regain some control.

"Shit, Alex, are we really back at that?" Bengt, right behind him.

Alex automatically started to walk away and jerked around when Bengt grabbed his elbow.

The Skanian didn't give him a chance to say anything. "We can't work like this. You'll just have to believe me when I say I won't bother you. You can't go berserk or hide behind your wall every time I bump into you. I'm not exactly famous for my patience. We should clear this up once and for all." Bengt was getting louder with every sentence, his neck reddening, a vein pulsing in his throat. Impossible to pull out of his iron grip.

Clear what up? He did believe Bengt, that wasn't the point. No. There was nothing to clear up. Especially not now, when he didn't know which way to turn. Alex closed his eyes, trying to breathe more calmly to lessen the stabbing in his chest. "Let go!" he hissed between clamped teeth. "Just let me the fuck go."

Bengt didn't budge. "Talk to me, damn it."

"Let go!"

"And where are you planning to go, Alex?"

"Away!"

"You can't get away. You're lugging your own prison around with you and patching up any holes from inside. Brilliant tactics, really! How does it feel?"

"Safe!"

"Safe? You provoke a man like Luìz Rukow at every turn and run into the lion's den without backup, and you talk to me of safe? You don't even know how to spell fear."

"I've been afraid all my fucking life."

"Yeah, of yourself."

Alex recoiled, finally pulling out of Bengt's grasp. "Asqueroso!" He turned and stumbled toward the zorro.

"Alex! Please, Alex, that wasn't . . . I know it's not . . . I'm sorry!"

Alex gave Bengt the finger over his shoulder. "Tu madre!"

He scrambled into the zorro, started the motor and, ignoring the pain in his thigh, stepped so hard on the pedal that the zorro jumped forward in a cloud of dust.

CHAPTER 12

Fuck! *Well done, Bengt! Attacking someone is really the best way to start a peaceful, reasonable dialogue.* A forceful kick slammed the warehouse door against the wall, but it brought him no relief. He picked up the blanket and his gaze fell on the pool of blood. Whoever was using the warehouse would have a heart attack, but there wasn't anything he could do about that.

Kolya's gun was still stuck in the waistband of Bengt's pants. Sheer dumb luck that his shot had gone wide—luck and maybe the surprise factor. They hadn't expected to be disturbed. Castillo had gone for his gun in nothing but reflex. Bengt had realized too late that the man hadn't actually been armed. He balled up the blanket between his hands. Fuck. The two must have felt perfectly safe. Stupid assholes. He turned abruptly and left the building, feeding his fury so he wouldn't have to deal with his guilt. Fuck Alex for leaving him with two bodies. Fuck himself for losing his temper with Alex, and fuck those two goons and whoever had started all of this in the first place.

Apart from Castillo's gun, Bengt also found a two-way radio in the Securitas's zorro. He moved the bodies from the cold room to the back of the zorro and covered them with the blanket. Then he sat at the wheel for minutes without starting the motor, staring blindly through the dusty windshield. Two dead. Fuck!

The horizon was changing to a pale orange when he reached the Comandatura Three and killed the engine. Mendez and the second teniente, Vilalba, came toward him. Bengt reached behind him and pulled off the blanket. Mendez merely raised an eyebrow, but Vilalba turned as pale as the two in the back of the zorro.

"Where do you want me to take them? The slaughterhouse?" Bengt asked.

Mendez nodded to Vilalba. "The teniente will take care of that." He frowned in mock indecision. "I wonder whether we should rent one of their meat lockers."

The corners of Bengt's mouth twitched, but he wasn't really in the mood for jokes, even caustic ones. He left the zorro to Vilalba, taking with him just the radio and Castillo's gun.

The capitán looked at him searchingly. "You're the second man to park a zorro here today with thunderclouds on his face." He pointed his chin at the other vehicle just visible behind the barracks.

"Alex is here?"

"Not anymore. Come, Comisario. Have a cup of tea with me. Please."

Bengt didn't feel the least inclination for a cozy chat, but clearly Mendez had the right to a report. The thought of committing the day to paper for Sunne made him nauseous. He sank into the visitor's chair in Mendez's office, handed the weapons and the radio over, and closed his hands around his mug of tea before recounting Linares's and Luìz's visits.

He told Mendez about the article he'd found concerning the old computers and summed up the events in the warehouse: "He nearly collided with me at the door, his gun already in his hand. I should have parked the zorro further away. But he was too surprised to get off a good shot. And I couldn't risk a second. Everything happened very quickly. When the lean guy came toward me and reached for his gun, I already had his pal's in my hand. I had no idea the lean guy's gun was in the vehicle. I thought . . ." He fell silent. There was no excuse.

For a while, the capitán silently regarded his folded hands. "It's really not worth mentioning," he finally said. "But since I get the impression that you're in doubt, for the record: that was a clear case of self-defense." He looked at Bengt. "And you didn't have to tell me that Castillo was unarmed. I don't think we'll have to burden your office with that knowledge."

Bengt swallowed when Mendez paused.

"The decision is, of course, yours."

Tempting thought. But before he could think it through, Mendez continued. "I have no idea what happened between you and Rukow." He lifted both hands in a parrying gesture when Bengt opened his mouth. "And I don't want to know. In the interest of our investigation, however, I would appreciate it if you could postpone your differences until the case is closed." A minute smile deepened the sun marks in the corners of his eyes. "With all due respect."

Bengt stared into his mug. "You're perfectly right," he said quietly. "I'm just not sure . . . It would be easier if Alex could tell me exactly . . ." He shrugged. "But I'd really better talk that over with him."

"If he'd only talk to you? Believe me, I know what you mean. Rukow doesn't even talk to himself, but I'm sure you'll find a way." Mendez leaned back in his chair and looked out the window, lost in thought. "Hard to believe Luìz Rukow actually warned you. Must be the first time he's saved his son's life rather than making it as hard as possible."

Bengt felt the little hairs on his neck rise, shivered in the warm air. "Rukow? His son?" he managed, incredulous.

"Didn't you say Luìz—Coronel Rukow—brought the teniente's situation to your attention?" Mendez asked.

"Well, yes, but he's not . . . I thought . . . Alex told me he didn't have any family."

"Scarred face, gray hair, light green eyes?"

Bengt nodded.

"That's him. From what people are saying . . . But the teniente had best tell you that himself." Mendez stood up. "He went down the beach in the direction of the bay. You might still find him there."

Alex was sitting on a fallen tree trunk next to an old man. Smoking in silence, they were watching the sun sink toward the ocean. When Bengt stepped out from between the trees, the old man got up and left in the opposite direction down the beach. Alex didn't move. His arms rested on his knees, the cigarette glowing between his fingers and smoke drifting across his face.

Bengt hesitated. Then he screwed up his courage and sat down next to Alex. "I'm sorry. I had no right to say that."

The cigarette dropped to the ground. Alex got up and pushed some sand over it with his toes. He shoved his hands in his pockets and pulled them out again. "Who if not you?" he mumbled. "I guess I'm the one who should apologize. Again."

The sun touched the horizon and melted into its mirror image. "No need." Bengt's throat was tight. "I mean it. What I said . . ."

"At least you're still talking to me."

"And that won't change. I'd much rather have you yell at me than shrug and walk away without a word."

"That's sometimes . . ." Alex sat back down. "I'm not too good at talking."

That was probably the understatement of the century, but by now Bengt knew enough to swallow his sarcastic remark. "I know," he finally said, "that I drive you nuts when I constantly ask you what's going on with you or what's wrong. It's just that I don't know any other way to bridge differences or make connections. And I need connections. I'm not nearly as self-sufficient as you."

Alex stayed silent.

"For us, every life is a thread of unknown length," Bengt tried to explain. "With our birth the first knot is made, a first link with our family. Links, the weaving of knots, is the base of Skanian society—the striving to build a network, a fabric that holds us when we fall." He stared at the sand between his feet, breathed in the tangy scent of the ocean, waited for a reaction that never came.

He'd tried. You couldn't force anyone to talk. He could only explain it to the best of his ability. After that it was up to Alex. Except . . . His hands were shaking, and he folded them tightly. Except, of course, he could start by trusting Alex the way he was expecting Alex to trust him. He swallowed hard. "To tear a hole in that fabric, that's . . . I cut two threads today. Who knows how many knots will fall apart because of that, how many can't be woven anymore?"

"If you hadn't killed them, they'd have killed you. And I'd be dead, too."

"Probably." Bengt dared a quick glance at Alex's face, but his expression was impossible to read in the dusk. "The first word I ever learned in Esprus was 'Sorry.'"

"You apologize way too often."

A beetle ran across Bengt's left shoe, fell off the side, picked itself back up, and continued on its way. The sun disappeared behind the horizon. "I told you I worked with mining security."

"Two years."

"Mhmm. I didn't tell you why they kicked me out."

When Bengt didn't continue, Alex turned toward him. "Why?"

"I killed someone."

"What happened?"

"Isn't that enough?"

"Listen, Bengt, you don't have to tell me anything, but you didn't kill someone just like that. I don't believe that."

"Just like that." He paused. "There was a brawl, which was nothing unusual. Not exactly calm and collected, those miners. Fist fights like that weren't our business, the Santuarians took care of them. But this time, one of the combatants pulled a knife, and no one made a move to get between them. Or so I thought. I was already angry with Santuarian security, hated the way they worked, was convinced of their incompetence." He paused to collect his thoughts—and his courage.

"Today, I understand a lot of what seemed inexplicable back then. I was such a . . . In any case, I thought I had to do something. The one with the knife was too far away from me, so I grabbed the other one by the collar to pull him out of harm's way. He was lighter than I thought. Much lighter. His head collided with the support beam behind me." Bengt closed his eyes, but the image stayed. "If I'd thought for one minute rather than blindly jumping in, he'd probably be alive today."

"You don't know that. Knives aren't all that digestible. Did they find you guilty of some crime? Obviously not. You wouldn't be in ICE if they had, right?

"There was an investigation, but the commission concluded it was an accident, so it didn't even make it to court. Still, the mining company couldn't get rid of me fast enough, of course. They terminated my contract because of 'problems with authority and personal control.'" Bengt hastily shoved aside the images of the following year, when he'd completely lost his footing.

The tree vibrated slightly when Alex shifted his weight. "Sometimes, you just don't have time to carefully balance the arguments for and against. What's the alternative? We wouldn't act at all anymore, wouldn't give a shit about anyone. And, God knows, we have enough of that." His voice dropped to just above a whisper. "There are no perfect deeds, only perfect intentions."

They fell silent, but in the increasing darkness, the silence didn't seem embarrassing or oppressive to Bengt; the facelessness protected them from each other, made—probably for Alex, too—the closeness bearable.

"If you keep traveling in that direction," Alex held out his arm, pointing straight ahead across the water, "you'll eventually get to Jarðvegur. When I was a kid, I calculated it with a compass and a map." He laughed under his breath. "Both filched, of course."

"Why'd you do it? Calculate the direction, I mean."

"I wanted to know which way paradise was." After a while, he continued, a smile audible in his voice. "And you thought you were naive."

"Dreams can be anything, but they're never naive. Even if Jarðvegur, despite all its amenities, is hardly paradise."

"It wasn't anything tangible that made it paradise, but just the fact that it wasn't Santuario."

"Wasn't? Has that changed?"

Alex didn't answer for a while. "I applied for a job in the mines once," he finally said. "I would probably have been one of your incompetent security guards."

That stung, even though Bengt was sure Alex had aimed the barb at himself. "What kept you away?" he asked.

Again, Alex didn't answer. "You don't seem the least bit gay," he said instead, completely out of the blue.

The naive surprise in his voice made Bengt smile. "And what would seem gay to you?"

"No idea."

Bengt laughed. "Come on, you have to have an idea to say something like that."

"Well, yeah, but that was obviously way off."

"Is that a peace offering? I really wasn't going to—"

"I know. And I didn't really think that. You've . . . it was so fucking cold in there," he murmured, wrapping his arms around his body as if he was still freezing. "Thank you. And I'm sorry I can't tell you things you need to know," he said hesitantly. "If I find out . . . If I . . ." he breathed audibly. "I'll let you know." He paused. "How the hell did you find me, anyway?"

Careful! Returning to the minefield. Bengt stretched his legs. "Your father sent me."

Alex jumped to his feet. "My . . . who?"

"Luìz. He popped up at the hotel and told me you were in trouble and where to find you. At first, I thought it must be some kind of trap, especially after Linares's warning that—"

"Whoa, slow down. Andúja's secretary?"

For the second time that evening, Bengt summarized the events of the day while Alex drew lines in the sand with his toes. The rose-colored stripe above the horizon grew narrower, and above the trees the first stars came out.

"I give up," Alex said. "Why Kolya and Castillo? Who would send those two?"

"Andúja?"

"I don't think so. He'd send Luìz. And why does Luìz suddenly care what happens to me? Must've been a diversion or something."

"For what?"

"Or he just can't bear the thought of someone else taking away his toy."

The hatred in his voice made Bengt flinch. "It was him wasn't it? The reason your application wasn't accepted?"

"Very good."

"Still, isn't it possible that he wouldn't go so far as to actually kill you?"

"No." Hard. Certain. "He's never been afraid to kill anyone."

"Maybe not anyone else, but you're his son," Bengt said carefully.

For a heartbeat, he thought Alex would attack him. "Only biologically," the Santuarian hissed. "My real father was Manuel Vasquez, the man my mother was married to. Twenty-four years ago, Luìz cut his throat while he was asleep in his bed."

"Fuck, Alex, I . . . that . . . Madonna," Bengt whispered, unable to find a word in his own language that came even close to what he felt. He shook his head when Alex turned and started to walk down the beach. "Do me a favor and don't run away again. I'll shut up if that's what you want."

A chuckle reached his ears from out of the darkness. "Why don't you just give it up?"

"Not a chance."

"Skanian bullhead."

"If that's what it takes." Bengt stood up. "Alex, I accused Luìz of being the one who protects Soria to his face. He didn't deny it."

"What reason would he have to protect the clinic? He doesn't need it. He can send his people to the hospital."

"Maybe you should ask him. He seems to have motives you know nothing about. And I don't believe his warning was a distraction. That makes no sense."

"Which leaves us with a question: Who sent the two heavies?"

"That I can't answ— Shit, the radio!"

"Huh?"

"They had a two-way radio in the zorro. I'm an idiot. I wanted to check what frequency it was set to and forgot all about it."

"Well, we'd better get a move on then."

It was pitch black between the trees, but at least the heat of the day was receding. Bengt concentrated all his senses on not banging his face into the next tree. He wondered briefly how Alex could run around barefoot like that, and fast enough for Bengt to have a hard time keeping up.

There was still a light on in the office.

"Don't you have a home?" Alex asked when they found Mendez sitting behind his desk.

"I thought the two of you might be back. At least, if you'd remembered this." Mendez tapped his finger against the radio on his desk. He looked from Bengt to Alex. "You seem to have pissed off Vigo Andúja quite thoroughly."

"Vigo? The little shit sent the two goons?"

Mendez nodded. "I tried the radio. Listen." He pressed play on a small voice recorder in front of him. At first, they heard nothing but static, then Vigo's voice. "About time. Why did it take you so long?"

Pause. "Castillo? Everything okay there? Did you get the pig? Hola? Castillo? Shit!"

Bengt could almost see the thoughts chasing each other behind Alex's forehead.

"He made a big fool of himself with his public crying about Ramón's death," Alex said. "He must have tried to prove himself, show his father that he can do better."

"Why the elaborate setup, though? Why not just have you disappear? No offense." Mendez said.

"Maybe he wanted a body to show around? Unmarked, so he could stage an accident? I really don't know. He doesn't seem to be the sharpest knife in the drawer. Plus, he probably wanted to do this on his own and only had his bodyguards to fall back on." Alex shook his head. "I mean, not even Vigo could be stupid enough to think we could charge him with anything."

Bengt leaned against the doorframe and gave Alex a meaningful look. "Now we can."

For a moment, the Santuarian met his gaze, but then he shook his head. "Not tonight. I've had enough." He sank onto the edge of the desk. "I can't get those ship computers you mentioned out of my head. Someone told me today that Inés was an engineer or something like that. If that's true, there might be a connection."

"As far as I know," Mendez jumped in, "she studied communications engineering. She must have been pretty good, but, of course, her career was finished when she eloped with the gardener's son."

"You know who she is?" Bengt asked in surprise. Alex had half turned and was watching Mendez intently. Mendez held his gaze, his chin supported on steepled fingers. There was a form of communication going on here that shut Bengt out. He looked from one to the other and waited.

"Svoboda," Alex said, ending the silence. "You clued us in on that. You're involved with that group."

The capitán had obviously come to a decision. He nodded and leaned back. "Let's say I would welcome it if a few things changed around here," he said carefully. "I put out my feelers some time ago."

Alex lightly tapped his fist against his thigh. "I knew it," he whispered.

"Unfortunately, the results of your investigation make me think that Svoboda uses some methods that differ quite a bit from the ones they sell as their political program."

"And what political program would that be?" Bengt asked.

"Democracy is the word of the day. Of course, they want to break the familias's back. Everyone seems to have a different idea of how to go about that. Some as peacefully as possible, others . . . obviously less so. Unfortunately, experience forces us to be so suspicious . . . Not even within the organization will one faction let the other see its cards. If it's indeed Svoboda that's behind this, we're obviously dealing with the less peaceful faction."

Alex stood up and looked out the window into the night. His face was reflected in the pane. "That makes no sense. What kind of an advantage could they get from killing a few bums?"

"I had a lot of time to bust my head over that one today," Bengt interjected. "And I think you're asking the wrong question. You still think those people were meant to die."

Mendez was playing with a pencil. "Three 'accidents' with restrained victims?"

"Exactly. Consider, just for a moment, the possibility that one of those old computers resurfaced," Bengt said. "How much would the stored information be worth?"

"Databanks containing several libraries? Spaceship technology? Are you kidding?" Alex said.

Mendez nodded. "I'm pretty sure whatever technology they hold, it would be enough to break the familias's monopoly and thus, their stranglehold." He winked at Bengt. "I also imagine your people might be willing to move a few mountains to share in the information."

"Exactly. If we also imagine—just for the sake of argument—that kind of computer could indeed only be accessed by something as fantastical as a cortical connection, wouldn't someone still try to get at the data? Amateurish, for sure, and morally more than questionable, but imaginable, right?"

"If there were such a computer," Alex said thoughtfully. "But where would it have come from? People don't have something like that kicking around in their basement."

Bengt shrugged. "You'd be surprised what people hang on to."

"But why wait two centuries to dig it back out?"

"Maybe it had been forgotten? Whoever had it didn't know what it was?"

"And now it suddenly resurfaces? I can't imagine how anyone would be able to keep that a secret from the Securitas."

"I know it's not easy, but don't overestimate the Securitas," Mendez said. "Nobody is invincible."

"Amen," Alex commented dryly. "If I imagine that for two hundred years, someone's been sitting on information that could break the familias's collective back, I'm going to be sick." He turned to Mendez. "How well do you know Inés?"

The capitán hesitated. "Well," he admitted.

"Well enough to get her to work with us?"

"Depends on the circumstances. It's worth a try."

Bengt dug deeper. "How large is this organization?"

"Pretty large. And, no, I don't know anything that would help our investigation."

Bengt sighed. He could understand why the capitán wasn't more precise, but he didn't have to like it. He trusted Mendez, but that didn't make it any better.

Alex, who was leaning against the wall by the window, looked like death warmed over. He wouldn't go home before they were done here.

"I can't think anymore," Bengt said to Mendez. "And I still have a bit of driving to do. Can we postpone the rest 'til tomorrow?" From the corner of his eye, he saw Alex take a deep breath and his posture relax a little.

The capitán was also looking at his teniente. "We all belong in bed. Tomorrow's going to be a long day."

CHAPTER 13

Exhausted, Alex let the door close behind him. His ribs hurt with every breath, his leg with every step, and his heartbeat pounded the inside of his skull. He allowed himself the last of the painkillers Inés had given him. His thoughts jumped back and forth between speculations about ship computers, Mendez's involvement with Svoboda, the planned arrest of Vigo Andúja, and his conversation with Bengt. Standing in the middle of his living room, empty water glass in hand, he couldn't muster the energy to concentrate on any one of those thoughts in particular.

The cushions Bengt had slept on were still lying on the floor. Halfheartedly, Alex picked up the blanket to fold it away, then stopped and slumped onto the makeshift mattress. His eyes closed of their own accord; he just sank over on his side and buried his head in the pillow. The blanket still in his arm, the scent of suntan lotion in his nose, he slept until someone hammered on his door the next morning.

He started up, disoriented. Still holding onto the blanket, he opened the door.

Gijón, looking crisp and official.

"What time is it?" Alex asked.

"Seven thirty. Good morning, Teniente. The comisario called. You don't have to drive to Tierraroja. He's coming here to meet you at the comandatura at ten."

"And Vigo?" Alex had the feeling he was in a coma.

Gijón shrugged. "I don't know. Kazatin's been talking to him."

In that case, half the message was probably missing, anyway. "Vale, I'll be there at ten." He didn't even try to puzzle it out. Instead, he puttered about the house, made tea, showered, and straightened the living room. The only clean shirt in his closet was a uniform shirt. But today would be official anyway. He made a mental note to drop off his laundry on his way to the office.

At nine thirty, he entered the comandatura, not exactly at the top of his game, but way more alive than he'd been two hours earlier.

Mendez was already sitting behind his desk and threw him an inquisitive glance when he knocked on the doorframe. "When this is over, you're taking a couple of days off."

Alex propped himself up against the frame. "Why is Bengt coming here?"

"If Kazatin got it right, he managed to get an arrest warrant for Vigo issued at the crack of dawn and is going to bring the kid in. He seems to think it would be better for all involved if none of us were there." Mendez made a face, and Alex knew that wouldn't make any difference. Andúja would sic one of his killers on them the second he got wind of the arrest.

"The speed that Skanian is displaying makes me dizzy," Mendez said with a good dose of self-mockery. He was surprisingly at ease for someone who'd put everything on one card last night in front of his teniente and a Skanian official without knowing whether they would betray him or not.

Alex stuck his thumb in his pocket. "I hope we can clear up this mess without blowing the cover off the whole organization."

"That would be desirable not only for the organization. Our lives might depend on it. But that only works if Bengt plays along," Mendez said thoughtfully. "I offered to leave Castillo and Kolya out of my report."

Alex shook his head. "You won't get him like that. He'll have to be as convinced as we are that what he's doing is the right thing. I'll try to talk to him. We'll see."

As if on cue, they heard the motor of the approaching zorro. A little later, Vigo's voice, half fearful, half indignant, harping on about who he was, that he hadn't done anything, and what would happen to Bengt if he didn't let him go this instant. Judging from Bengt's expression as he walked through the door, the tirade had been going on for a while. The Skanian was steering the kid by his upper arm, and not gently. Alex was sure that his patience had been sorely tried. So all he said was, "My office," then went ahead to open the door for Bengt. When the Skanian passed him, Alex murmured, "You're in the perfect mood to play bad cop, just let me start."

Bengt acknowledged the ploy with a quick nod, then shoved the protesting Vigo onto a chair. Crossing his arms over his chest, he leaned against the wall where Vigo could see him, and stared at him from under drawn-together eyebrows. Alex sat behind his desk, started the recorder, and waited for Vigo to run out of steam.

"I don't even know why I'm here," Vigo pouted, crossing his legs. He plucked an invisible piece of lint off his pants and stole a covert glance at Bengt.

Alex crossed his arms on the desk and leaned forward. "Don't make it so hard for yourself, kid. We already know you gave Kolya and Castillo the order to kill me. Your father and brother must have given you hell over the thing with Ramón. That can't have been easy."

Vigo looked unsure, his lips pressed together belligerently, but his eyes held a question.

Suddenly, Bengt crashed his fist on the desk with such force that Alex feared for the elderly furniture's life. Vigo jumped nearly out of his skin and pulled his head between his shoulders when the Skanian thundered, "What's with all the questions? Why don't we just lock him up?"

Alex raised his hand in a calming gesture, not taking his eyes off Vigo. He watched the nervous movements, made an effort to keep the understanding in his voice. "Come on, kid, you only tried to make amends, right?"

"I really don't know what you're talking about. This is ridiculous."

Bengt closed his fist around Vigo's collar just under his chin. Then he effortlessly pulled him out of his chair and slammed him against the wall, feet dangling about half a meter above the floor. "Why don't you go get yourself a tea or something?" he flung at Alex over his shoulder.

Vigo's eyes grew wide, his hands clutching Bengt's wrist. When Alex stood up, desperation was plain on the kid's face. "Please!" His voice cracked. "Don't leave me alone with him. He's gonna kill me. You can't do this!"

Alex perched on the corner of his desk. "Give me a minute," he said to Bengt.

After a brief hesitation, Bengt simply let go. Vigo barely managed to keep his feet and stumbled back to his chair.

"Look," Alex said. "All we want is to find Ramón's murderer. Isn't that what you want as well?"

Vigo stared at his hands. "Yes," he said quietly.

"Then why the attack on me? It doesn't make any sense. One might think you didn't give a damn about Ramón."

"Never. I loved him," Vigo said with tears in his voice.

Bengt made a disgusted face.

"My father was so angry, and Santos, too," Vigo mumbled.

Alex replayed the recording Mendez had made the night before. Vigo's head came up when he heard his own voice. He looked at Alex aghast. "That was you?"

Alex nodded. "How did you know I'd be in Tierraroja?"

Vigo nervously kneaded his hands. He flinched when Bengt moved next to him. "You told your office that morning." He paused. Alex made a fist, and Bengt propped both arms on the desk right in front of Vigo's nose.

"Teniente Vilalba works for the Securitas," Vigo continued hastily. "He tells his capitán everything he hears."

"Shit." Alex leaned back in his chair. "I knew it. I should just listen to my gut."

"And that's how Luìz knew where you were, too," Bengt added.

"So then you sent the two clowns to wait for me?" Alex said to Vigo, who nodded mutely. "How much did you pay Juan, or was that Castillo's idea?"

"Who?"

"Never mind. I'm afraid you shot yourself in the foot, mi amigo."

Bengt straightened. "Vigo Andúja, I arrest you for incitement to murder."

Vigo looked thunderstruck. "My father will never let you get away with that," he whispered. Alex agreed, but Bengt would never just let the kid go. And Alex wasn't sure he'd try to convince him, even if he could. He saw his own thoughts reflected in Bengt's eyes, and lowered his head. "We have two drunk tanks in back. Keys are on the wall."

Bengt left, dragging Vigo with him. Now that the decision had been made, Alex felt weirdly relieved, as if none of this had anything to do with him anymore. In the back room, keys jingled, then the door clanged shut. He leaned his forehead against the window pane. Whatever would happen now, it was out of his hands.

"There'll be trouble," Bengt said behind him.

Alex shrugged without turning. Spilled milk.

"Would it make your life easier if we let him go?" The distaste was audible in Bengt's voice.

Alex was surprised and grateful he'd even contemplated the possibility, but knew he'd never stop questioning himself if they did. "Probably," he said slowly, then added, "Initially. In the long run, though, I doubt it would make any difference. It's not just Vigo. This whole case, Svoboda . . . we're raising way too much dust to stay under the radar. And Mendez is not going to let this one go." Then he surprised himself by adding, "And neither am I."

"Even if it brings Andúja down on you?"

Alex turned away from the window to look at Bengt. "A while ago Mendez told me this case was different, that it gives us a chance to change things. He might be right. In either case, I don't want to live like this anymore." He hadn't realized it before, but it was true. Having tasted the possibility of a life less miserable made it impossible to go back to simply enduring. "And since they won't let me leave, they'll have to get used to me pissing them off."

He looked at the door to the cells. "You asked me how I'd imagined gays," he said to change the topic. "Vigo Andúja is a classic example."

"Thanks a lot," Bengt said dryly.

Alex felt a smile tug on his mouth. "Well, I already conceded that you're different."

"Technically, I'm 'same,'" Bengt said, amusement in his voice. "The Skanian word for gay literally means 'same.' You're 'different.'" An answering smile crinkled the corners of his eyes, and Alex felt his throat grow tight. Was he now?

"We should go back to Tierraroja and talk to Inés," he said quickly.

Bengt nodded. "The sooner the better."

Alex took the recordings back to Mendez and warned him about Vilalba.

"Can't say I'm surprised." The capitán looked at Alex reflectively. "Until everyone's safely packed off, we should probably be careful what we tell Kazatin and Gijón. We know that Kazatin, at least, won't be able to keep his mouth shut in front of Vilalba. Once the Securitas knows Vilalba's cover is blown, they'll probably replace him anyway." He got up. "Well, we'll see. Let's go."

"We should take both cars, in case we'll have to bring someone back."

"Arrest someone, you mean? I'm sure the Comandatura One has cells, too."

"Yeah, but Bengt has to organize the transport to Jarðvegur, which will be much easier if he doesn't have to collect them from halfway across the island. And apart from that, I'll sleep better the farther any suspect is held from Tierraroja."

"Vale. Vamos." With that Mendez got in the zorro and started the engine.

"Who's driving?" Bengt asked.

"Let me drive, gives you more room for your knees." Alex waited for the dust to settle before he followed Mendez. Bengt turned the radio on and found a station with Son music; Alex looked at him in surprise.

"No?" Bengt asked.

"No, yeah, fine with me. I just didn't know you liked it. Never mind." Out of the corner of his eye, he saw Bengt's questioning look. Then the Skanian shrugged, leaned back, and pulled his hat over his face. With his throat stretched like that, Alex could see the line where the sun had started to tan his skin. Damn it. He swallowed and stared at the road. Bengt had assured him he'd keep his distance, and Alex believed him. With that, the problem should have been solved. So why did he still feel like he was walking on glass? Bengt's words echoed through his mind. *Yeah, scared of yourself.* He grabbed the wheel harder, tried to concentrate on the music, on the road, anything. On some level he realized that sooner or later he'd have to deal with the chaos that was tearing up his insides. But for now, he'd promised Mendez to talk to Bengt about Svoboda and Inés. Where to start? Again, he stole a sideways glance at the sleeping Skanian.

"Do you think Inés is going to talk?" Bengt suddenly asked from under his hat.

The question matched Alex's thoughts so exactly that he jumped, feeling caught. "Maybe, if it's worth it for her."

"Excuse me?" Bengt sat up and looked at him. "Are you planning to negotiate with murderers?"

Exactly the kind of reaction Alex had expected. "I'm sure a lot of good people stand behind the idea of Svoboda. If Inés is the woman I take her for, she'll be much more cooperative if she doesn't have to be afraid that the whole movement is going down the drain just because some of its supporters used unscrupulous methods."

Bengt was silent. The fingertips of his left hand drummed a staccato on his thigh.

"Besides, it might help to offer her immunity, or at least a mitigated sentence, depending on how deeply she's involved in the whole thing."

"Shit, Alex, justice is no bargaining matter."

"Whose justice? Yours? Mine? The Securitas's? The policía's? Santuario's or Jarðvegur's? Would you rather risk our investigations petering out without any results?"

"That's not the point. Does Mendez think the same way?"

"Anything else would surprise me. Come on, Bengt, you know how fucked up our system is. I'm far from believing that the end justifies every means, but is it really justice to destroy a good thing just to follow the rules?"

Bengt balled his hands to fists, the muscles in his jaws working silently. "Both alternatives are equally lousy."

Alex pulled up right behind Mendez's parked car, which sat in front of the café where Bengt had waited for Alex three days ago. Across the road, the clinic looked deserted today. No one was waiting on the stairs. The capitán came over. "I'd like to pick Inés up and talk to her here, rather than at the comandatura," he said. "Would you wait here for us?"

He pointed to the tables, which were empty at this time of day.

"Sure," Alex agreed before Bengt could say anything. He climbed out and entered the café while Bengt swore under his breath. In the end, though, the Skanian followed him.

"Don't try to manipulate me," he growled, sitting down across from Alex and barricading himself behind the menu.

"Bengt? Bengt!" Alex ripped the menu out of his hands. "You know I'm right."

"I don't know anything of the sort."

"Who's stonewalling now?"

Bengt threw him a glance that made Alex hold his breath. Then the Skanian groaned and buried his face in his hands. "I'm a cop, not a judge. Decisions like that shouldn't have to be made," he mumbled.

"In a perfect world? No. In this one, Svoboda could be the only chance we have left. At least listen to her with an open mind, talk to her, maybe you can—" He fell silent when the capitán came back to their table with Inés.

"Simón has told me why you're here and convinced me to talk to you," she began hesitantly.

Alex took a second before he realized she was talking about Mendez.

"But before this interview can begin, something has to be made perfectly clear."

Bengt stared rigidly at the table.

"As soon as the Securitas gets wind of Svoboda's existence, they will hunt and round up anyone connected with it. You'll have to give me your word that you'll investigate with the greatest discretion and not mention Svoboda in your reports." Her cheeks reddened. She stood, bracing herself on her crutches, waiting for their answer.

Mendez and Alex were both looking at Bengt, so Inés eventually addressed him. "The members of the organization have to be protected by every means possible from the tyranny of the patrones and the Securitas."

Alex could almost hear the seconds tick by, felt the tightening of his neck muscles. A waiter came and took their orders. Finally, Bengt looked up. "You have my word."

Mendez pulled out a chair for Inés, and after a long look at each of their faces, she sat. The waiter brought water and coffee. Inés's hands wandered over the table, her fingers folding and unfolding. "I'm glad it's over," she said. "But I'm afraid. What's going to happen to me?"

"That depends on what you did," Bengt answered.

Mendez covered her nervous fingers with his hand. "I'll do what I can to make this as easy as possible."

"You are, after all, helping us," Alex agreed. "You can be sure we'll reciprocate as far as the existing laws allow us to." He kicked Bengt in the shin under the table, and the Skanian flinched noticeably.

"According to Skanian law, Svoboda is not illegal, so mere membership is no crime," Bengt said.

She looked at him intently as if trying to read something in his eyes—a reassurance, a promise. Finally, she nodded at Mendez, who started the recording.

"I grew up in the familia Andúja . . . didn't question my world for a long time," she began slowly. "I don't think I need to bore you with what changed my mind. Just that it was a radical change. It made me see our whole society with different eyes, and that made me feel guilty for what I had so naturally accepted as my due in the past." She paused.

"A friend got me to work in Soria, where I met Dr. Martinez. He's a brilliant doctor as far as the medical side of his profession is concerned. Unfortunately he lacks emotions, compassion, love for his patients. His only passion is his hatred for the familias for what they did to him. Back then, we talked through many a night with hot heads about the cruel whims and injustices ordinary people have to live with. When I was recruited for Svoboda, I told him about it, and he was immediately hooked. It was his idea to recruit through the clinic as well." She gave Alex the tiniest of smiles that told him, *Don't think I don't recognize you.*

"But soon the organization grew so fast that its management became more and more difficult; we badly needed computers. About a year ago, we asked our members to bring us old or broken gadgets and computers they didn't need anymore, hoping we could build something useful with the parts."

So Bengt had been right about that.

"People brought us everything you can imagine: recording machines, radios, computers and computer parts, even telephones. It took a while to work through the stack and sort useful from useless. What was left was a black box the size of a small suitcase. We had no idea what to do with it. We finally managed to open it with brute force. It was the weirdest computer I've ever seen in my life. I was incredibly excited, was sure I was holding in my hands one of the high-performance computers my old professor used to tell me about, his voice full of awe. Until then, I'd always taken his stories to be the dreams of an old man. It was weeks before I found an input and an output sequence. But it wasn't possible to connect any known peripherals. Screens, printers, loudspeakers, nothing was compatible, and neither keyboard nor voice activated the system." This time Alex threw Bengt a quick glance and received the hint of a satisfied smile.

"I turned the library's entire computer archive upside down, with no result. It was so frustrating to think I might have all the knowledge of our ancestors in my hands without being able to access any of it." Her eyes glowed. "Imagine if we could break the energy monopoly of the familias, what that would mean for us."Dr. Martinez was even more impatient than I was, and started his own research. It was he who finally found a note in an ancient neurological thesis about a direct cortical connection. Just a mention, no manual or anything like that. I don't know what happened to all the documentation. Were the manuals destroyed? And what happened to the experts? No fresh blood?"

"It's not unlikely the documentation is actually part of the data you couldn't get at," Alex said resignedly.

"And it wouldn't be the only kind of learning that was neglected during the initial struggle of setting up the colony," Mendez added. "People were busy enough with mere survival."

"True. A gap of one generation is enough to lose very specialized knowledge like that. In any case, we calculated and discussed for days and nights without results. Finally, Dr. Martinez decided we wouldn't get anywhere without tests, and he asked me to leave the computer with him so he could start a testing sequence with animals. Now and again he'd come to me with more questions, or ask for explanations, suggestions." She closed her eyes; the blood had drained from her face. "A few days ago the coronel came to me."

"Coronel Rukow?" Bengt asked.

She nodded.

Alex stared at her in utter disbelief, felt as if someone had emptied a bucket of cold water over his head. Again, he met Bengt's eyes, broke the contact by turning to Inés. "So it's really him. Why? What does he get out of it?"

"Why does he help? When I was a child, he was working security in the house when someone threw a homemade bomb over the wall into the garden. That's how I got these." She pointed at her crutches. "Luìz Rukow never forgave himself for what he calls 'his failure' to protect me. Ever since then, he's been trying to make up for it."

"Luìz Rukow?" Alex couldn't grasp the concept, but Inés just nodded.

"He told me about the body you found at the beach and asked me if I knew anything about a surgery through the skull," Inés continued. "I was shocked, was sure Dr. Martinez was behind it. But I couldn't say that to the coronel. He might consider me his responsibility, but that cuts both ways."

Alex nodded. He knew the other way Luìz's "sense of responsibility" cut only too well.

"And anyway," Inés continued, "I wanted to talk to Dr. Martinez myself." She took a sip of water.

"Dr. Martinez assured me the man had volunteered, and he thought himself to be ready. He seemed quite affected by the man's death, assured me over and over he wouldn't let anyone talk him into that again. I believed him. Because I wanted to believe him," she whispered. "I didn't tell anyone, protected him to protect our project. And now Simón tells me you found two more bodies with the same injuries, one of them a child." She stared into space. "I can't believe he did that."

"Don't beat yourself up over Martinez," Mendez said. "Sounds to me like he was playing you."

Alex nodded. It fit with what he'd overheard at the soup kitchen. "He doesn't work in Soria because he cares, but because it gives him an angle. You said yourself he lacks emotion and hates the familias. He's probably still trying to get back at them for kicking him out. Or find himself a bargaining chip to regain something like his former position."

"And I helped him do it. Two people who'd still be alive if I hadn't kept my silence, three if I'd never let this cursed computer out of my hands. Are you going to arrest me for murder?" she asked Bengt frankly.

The Skanian shook his head. "It's doubtful a court would even hold you responsible for concealment, if you get a savvy defender. No,

I'm going to ask you to be a witness for the prosecution." He got up. "But we should take care of the 'good' doctor first."

Alex pushed his chair back as well, when a shadow suddenly darted toward the exit behind some planters. He took off in pursuit, but his foot caught in one of Inés crutches and it was all he could do to catch himself on the back of a chair. The pain in his leg and chest brought tears to his eyes. When he looked up, the shadow was gone. "I think that was Juan, the little rat," he said over his shoulder and limped into the street. He felt Bengt right behind him.

"Where'd the little shit go?"

"The clinic," Alex pressed out. He started to run, after a fashion, but Bengt had already shot past him. When he reached the top of the stairs, he saw the Skanian waving from one of the partitions.

Inside, Martinez was sitting on a chair, his left sleeve rolled up, the arm bent to his chest. "You're making a huge mistake," he said when Alex entered. Bengt held up an evidence bag with a syringe inside.

"I'm not going to prison," Martinez said calmly.

Bengt looked at the syringe. "I have no idea what this is," he said to Alex. "I wasn't quick enough. Is there another doctor here?"

Alex shook his head. He was turning to go look for help when Martinez toppled from his chair.

Bengt squatted next to him, feeling his pulse. "Forget it," he said quietly, then picked up the body and laid it on the cot. Alex gave him a sheet from one of the shelves, and Bengt used it to cover the body.

"About Luìz—" Alex started, but Bengt interrupted him.

"Never mind. Let's search the building."

They systematically combed every inch of the space. The cubicles held nothing but meds, dressings, patients, and nurses. Alex stopped one of them to tell him Martinez wouldn't be back and that they'd have to make do until someone else could be found. The nurse gave him a blank look, but Alex had neither time nor inclination for lengthy explanations. He left the man and followed Bengt to the back.

He couldn't get out of his head what Inés had said about Luìz, would have liked to talk about it with Bengt, could feel Bengt's presence on his skin, but the Skanian held him at arm's length.

Alex forced himself to focus on the search. The back was used to store supplies. They opened cupboards and crates, pulled out drawers.

"Looks like you were right about Luìz." Alex tried again. "It's just so hard to—"

"It's all right. Really. You don't have to explain." Bengt turned toward a door. He rattled the handle, then felt along the frame with both hands.

Alex could have kicked him. Weren't they supposed to play this game the other way around?

Bengt angrily banged his fist against the door, then stepped back and delivered a furious kick to the lock, which hadn't been made to withstand a full-on Skanian attack. It was dark inside. Alex felt around for a light switch, flipped it, and bathed the room in bright light. An operating table, an oscilloscope—where had Martinez found that?—a wheeled metal table with surgical instruments, a black box the size of a small suitcase. Suerte!

For a second, they grinned at each other like idiots, then Bengt turned serious again. "Try not to touch anything."

Really? Were they back at that point, now?

"I'll come back tomorrow with a crime scene unit." Bengt considered for a moment, rubbing the bridge of his nose. "We should take the computer, though, since we can't re-lock the door. I don't want it to disappear for another two hundred years."

He had clearly retreated into his own world. Alex made a fist in his pocket, then wrapped the box in a sheet and picked it up, though his ribs didn't like that one bit.

Bengt carried Martinez's body toward the stairs. Until now, they'd only attracted the occasional curious stare from a patient or nurse, but now people started to move closer together, and more joined them from outside. Alex couldn't make out their faces against the glare of the sun through the door. Bengt stopped.

With a murmured "Stay with me," Alex pushed past the Skanian. Nobody said anything, but the silence itself was aggressive. Slowly, Alex walked toward them, deliberately delivering himself within reach of their hands.

"Don't make it worse than it already is, vecinos." He talked in a low voice, never stopped moving toward the door, looked for familiar faces. "I can see how this must look to you, Xavier, but believe me, the last thing you want here is a riot. Please, Ena, do you want to serve yourselves up to the Securitas on a silver platter?" He knew Bengt was right behind him, could read his progress with the body in the way the crowd unwillingly parted left and right.

"I can only ask you to trust me, Nadya."

He didn't receive an answer from any of them, but they hesitantly opened a corridor for him and Bengt.

Down in the street, he packed the computer behind the seat of Mendez's zorro, where Inés was waiting patiently, while Bengt laid the body in the back.

"Martinez," Alex explained to Mendez, whose eyes had widened slightly at the sight of the body. "We were too late to stop him. He must have planned his 'exit' in advance. I'll drive Bengt to the hotel and see you in the office? We should get out of here pronto, before it gets ugly." He nodded toward the stairs, where the crowd was moving into the street. They were still undecided, but wouldn't stay like that forever.

Mendez slipped behind the wheel. "And Vilalba must have realized by now who's sitting in our cell. You be careful."

"Ditto."

Bengt had squeezed into his usual position in the other zorro without a word.

"You okay?" Alex asked him carefully.

"Sure." Avoiding eye contact.

Alex sighed and started the zorro. So much for *I need connections.* What the hell was going on here?

"Wait here," Bengt said when Alex stopped in front of the hotel. "I'm going back with you."

"Why, what—Bengt?" But the Skanian had vanished through the glass door without looking back. What the fuck? There was nothing left for him to do in Three. He should be organizing the transports and writing his damn report.

The white walls reflected the early afternoon light without mercy. Shaking his head, Alex parked the zorro in the shade and drifted into the lobby. He stopped in front of the hotel shop. Inés would need some things like a toothbrush and a towel.

He ran into Bengt with his purchases before he could stow them in the car. "For Inés," he said, a bit embarrassed.

Bengt raised an eyebrow, but didn't comment.

"Did you reach ICE?" Alex asked.

"Yup, I'm picking up Kvulf and one of our trace guys at the airport tomorrow morning at ten."

The first time Alex had seen the Skanian, it had been ten in the morning at the airfield in Cuevas. He had a hard time recalling his expectations and impressions from back then. Back then? That had been only ten days ago. He threw Bengt a sideways glance, would have loved to ask him what he wanted in Three, but the Skanian didn't owe him an explanation and wasn't very talkative in any case. He seemed lost in admiration of the dashboard as Alex steered the zorro back to the main road.

"Do you think Andúja will try to break his son out?" Bengt asked him.

"That's not really his style. He likes things a bit more covert. He'll probably try to scare one or all of us into letting Vigo go. I very much expect a visit from Luìz or Leonid, but if that doesn't work . . . I'm not sure." Alex shrugged. "We'll just have to be on our toes tonight."

Suddenly it seemed like a good idea to have the Skanian with them. A good idea, but not very good company. Alex missed the easy banter and silent agreement they'd shared more and more often these past days. "Something's eating you. Are you still sore about the compromise with Inés?"

"That would be my problem, not yours."

Alex gave it up, turned the radio on, and concentrated on the road. If the Skanian absolutely didn't want to talk, *bueno*. Alex had never had a problem with silence. He would've liked a cigarette, though.

They reached Peones around four. Alex parked the zorro in the usual place behind the comandatura.

"Are you or Mendez staying here tonight?" Bengt asked when they got out.

"I will for sure. And I don't think Mendez is going home either."

Bengt hesitated. "You said they'd try to intimidate us. That could easily mean someone showing up at your house again. With your permission, I'd like to spend the night there. I'd love to get my hands on anyone who might show up."

"Not a bad idea. You thinking of someone in particular?" Alex grinned, but Bengt's face stayed serious.

"I just hope you're reading the situation right," he said instead of answering.

"What the hell is wrong with you today? What choice do we have? I told you—"

"We're not very well armed, are we?"

"The two guns you took off Kolya and Castillo. And the comandatura has an old carbine. But it's probably safer just to use that as a club."

"And the Securitas is armed?"

"Often, not all of them." Alex looked intently at the Skanian. "But that's not it, is it? I really want to know what's going on in your head today."

Bengt looked back at him with the same intensity, then very deliberately laid both hands on his shoulders. Alex felt his body heat through the fabric of his shirt, despite the sun. Slowly, the Skanian ran both his thumbs up Alex's throat and along his jawline. "No," he said with conviction, "you don't."

A shiver raced down Alex's spine and across his shoulders as his body started to react in ways it shouldn't have. But before he could protest the intimacy of the touch, Bengt let him go, and walked down the road. Alex stared after him, his mind blank, his soft cotton shirt suddenly rough against his skin, his pants too tight for comfort.

Holy shit.

He mentally kicked himself and went inside the office where Mendez was already waiting for him.

"What's he doing here?" he asked Alex, nodding toward the window.

"Being part of the posse." He wondered how much Mendez had seen of their little exchange. Little? Fuck. He couldn't deal with this now.

He swallowed hard and continued. "He'll stand guard at my house in case someone pops up there again." Don't think. He gave Mendez his little package from the hotel shop. "I got a few things for Inés, but maybe you'd rather give them to her."

"Thanks." Mendez pointed to the empty desk at the entrance. "I sent Kazatin and Gijón home. Apparently Vilalba disappeared about two hours ago." He held up the package. "I installed her in the village, be right back."

Torn between relief and chaos, Alex started pacing, feeling like a cornered rat in the confined space. What the hell had Bengt been about, touching him like that? But that wasn't the point, was it? It had gone through him like lightning—that was the point. He'd never felt so alive. Or so turned on. It was all wrong. What he wanted, what Bengt wanted. Or did he even? Had that been a warning or an invitation? And what the hell of a difference did it make? Alex sure as fuck wasn't going to mention it again, was he? Or worse, act on it.

He was no closer to a decision when Mendez returned, rummaged through his desk, and triumphantly emerged holding half a bottle of Jerez up to the sunlight. "For special occasions," he grinned. "What do you think? Can't hurt, can it?"

Alex shook his head. "I don't think anything's going to happen while it's still daylight. Do we have cards or something?" He needed to stop thinking.

Mendez filled their tea mugs with two fingers of the golden liquid and pointed the bottle at a filing cabinet by the door. "There should be a suerte board down there somewhere in a box."

"Better than nothing." Alex set the box on the desk, where they fished for the cards and pieces.

Mendez raised his cup. "First names?"

"I'd be honored," Alex agreed. "Salud!" The Jerez was mild and dry and spread warmly through his body, relieving some of the tension. "That must have cost a fortune."

Mendez made an innocent face. "I didn't pay for it."

It was getting dark when they folded the board away. They hadn't mentioned it, but Mendez seemed as reluctant to turn the lights on as Alex was. The capitán leaned back in his chair and crossed his feet on the desk. "As soon as the Skanians are gone, you can forget that Svoboda exists."

"Hardly." Alex shook his head. He'd broken his own rules, gotten involved, would have Andúja breathing down his neck for the rest of his life. He needed Svoboda—the contacts, the cover. *As soon as the*

Skanians are gone . . . It suddenly hit him with brutal clarity. Bengt would be gone tomorrow. And Alex would be able to stop thinking about him—as soon as he managed to forget how it was not to be constantly on his guard, to trust someone who might pick fights with him but would never intentionally hurt him, someone to laugh with. As soon as he could stop wondering what it would be like to—

"Then you'll have to make a decision," Mendez said.

"I think I already have," Alex said hoarsely before he realized Mendez was still talking about Svoboda. He stood up and went over to the window, fighting to pull himself together. "Andrés made a remark a few days ago . . . How old is the organization?"

"The first small groups that helped each other and hid fugitives? Old. It started a long time ago. Certainly much longer ago than I first heard about them, and that's longer than you're old."

Your mother had many friends. Quite a lot of friends, Sasha. Never forget that. By now, Alex had come to doubt that Andrés had just been rambling when he'd said that. The old man was just following his own advice. *With words like that, Sasha, one has to be careful. Very careful. I remember your mother well.*

"I'm so blind."

"A fault confessed is half redressed. And now sit back down. Please. You're driving me nuts with your pacing."

Alex checked his watch. He hadn't been aware he'd been pacing, but the later it got without someone coming, the more claustrophobic the office seemed to him.

"How high is the probability that they'll really come here first rather than going to my house?" When Mendez didn't answer, Alex looked at him and met a curious gaze from those level gray eyes.

"Go on. I'll be fine here." The capitán nodded toward the door.

CHAPTER 14

Bengt felt Alex's eyes on his neck long after the Santuarian could possibly still see him. He buried his hands in his pockets and pulled his shoulders up. Why the hell had he thought he had to tear down Alex's walls? He'd promised him he'd leave him alone, keep his distance. Too late he'd started to realize that it hadn't been him keeping the distance, but Alex. Now that the Santuarian was opening up, Bengt suddenly couldn't hold the balance anymore, couldn't manage to walk that fine line between friendship and . . . desire? Love? He still felt Alex's shoulders in the palms of his hands, had deliberately let him know what he'd been keeping to himself until now. And he'd shocked Alex, though not as much as he had expected. He'd have to make it through one more day. Too long, and way too short.

He scanned the road, the underbrush, the driveway, still blocked by that tree. He walked around the house, checked the windows and doors, but so far no one seemed to have been here. Carefully, he entered the narrow hallway, searched the rooms. The usual Spartan cleanliness in the living room, the smell of herbs in the kitchen. He didn't find anything in the bath or the bedroom either. For endless seconds, he stood in the doorway, stared at the bed. He could have bounced a coin off the cover. Trying to get a grip on his unruly thoughts, he mentally kicked himself and settled into one of the armchairs in the living room. The creaking of beams adjusting to the sinking temperature was the only sound in the silent, viscous seconds, minutes.

This time tomorrow, he'd be home. No more shirts sticking to his skin. He'd have power available at any time, day or night. And Sunne, family, and of course Svenja, with whom he could talk about everything and nothing. He missed her counsel. He wondered what they'd do with the computer, didn't think the Skanian scientists had the knowledge to get at the data either. And it didn't belong to them, though for now it was evidence. Maybe it could be a joint effort to crack the thing. He sighed. First, the borders would have to fall.

Alex, who'd wanted so badly to leave Santuario. As soon as the annexation was through, he could—and have Andúja off his back. But it could be months until then.

In the opposite chair, he'd treated Alex's injuries only a couple of days ago. The memory of how beaten and helpless the Santuarian had been brought back rage that had lost nothing of its fierceness. He almost hoped Andúja would send someone, hoped it would be Leonid.

He jumped up, made another round through all the rooms. Nothing. In the kitchen, he put the kettle on, measured hibiscus into the tea sock. The scent mixed in his mind with that of the ocean and Alex. Shit, Bengt, pull yourself together. Why did Alex have to give up his reticence now? But he was probably just glad he'd be rid of Bengt tomorrow.

He sighed again, poured the water over the herbs, stared blindly into the steam for minutes before bringing the brew down to a drinkable temperature with cold water as he'd seen Alex do. Pot on the table, cup in hand, he resumed his seat in the living room, elbows on his knees. The evening sun painted the opposite wall red-gold. A piece of Son music ran on repeat in his head, his fingers drumming the rhythm against the mug, one foot holding the beat against the floorboards. Waiting. He leaned back, took a long pull of the lukewarm tea that quenched the thirst so much better than any ice-cold drink. Thinking of what his friends would say if he started serving them lukewarm tea in the summer made him smile. Would he be allowed to import some of the herbs? He'd miss so many things. Hibiscus, those little cubiertas, the music and the dancers—and yes, fuck, Alex. Especially Alex.

A sound from the driveway drew his eyes to the window. He put the mug down, came out of the chair in a crouch, and risked a glance. He didn't see anyone, but heard a sliding sound from the hallway—the front door? Then the doorknob moved. Bengt flattened his shoulders against the wall.

Someone pushed the door open, hesitated, stepped into the room. Securitas. Bengt lifted his folded hands for a blow to the neck, but at that moment the man whipped around. The blow connected with his shoulder. He went down, but managed to roll backward and be on his feet again before Bengt could cover the distance.

Leonid. Bengt could feel the smile on his face. He hadn't struck with full force, too conscious of how fragile these people could be.

But the Securitas seemed to have no problem absorbing the blow. He stood in a fighting crouch, arms held out. The surprise in his eyes gave way to recognition. He too smiled. "Bueno, much better than I expected." His fingertips twitched twice in a come on gesture.

Bengt lunged without hesitation. He was several inches taller and about twenty-five kilos heavier than the Santuarian. The attack sent both of them sprawling. Bengt heard the air being pressed out of Leonid's lungs, but before he could strike, the Securitas rammed his knee into Bengt's ribs. Now it was Bengt's turn to fight for air. This was fucking harder than he'd thought. Alex had taken this?

Bengt rammed his head forward at the precise time Leonid tried the same attack. Their skulls slammed together, and Bengt's vision dimmed. He rolled to the side to escape the next blow, but the Santuarian seemed equally stunned by the collision. They picked themselves up and started circling each other.

Leonid wiped the blood out of his face. A wild joy shone in his eyes. "It wouldn't have been half as interesting to beat Rukow up." He attacked while still talking, but this time Bengt didn't leave him even the hint of a chance. He powered every strike with the full force of the rage he'd saved up for this moment. He hardly felt the blows he received. The skin on his knuckles split under those he meted out. Again and again, he landed heavy punches on Leonid's head and body.

The Santuarian began to wheeze, his steps became uncertain, his attacks started to go into empty space. Finally, still with that wild joy in his eyes, Leonid lowered his head for a final bull attack into Bengt's solar plexus. Again, Bengt raised his folded hands, this time for the blow that would break Leonid's neck. A lightning succession of thoughts flashed through his head. At the last moment, he stepped aside and simply let the Santuarian run into the wall behind him. Leonid collapsed as if someone had thrown a switch.

Breathing heavily, Bengt fell into his chair. Unable to clear his thoughts, he reached for his mug. His hands shook so badly that the rest of the tea almost ended up on his pants. He emptied the mug and set it clattering back on the table. After a while, he managed to check on Leonid. He'd bloodied his skull, but didn't seem to have cracked it. He was breathing deeply and regularly. Bengt pulled the belt from the Securitas's pants, tied his hands in the front, and went to get a wet towel from the kitchen. He pushed the chair close to the unconscious Securitas and let the water drip on Leonid's face, waiting disinterestedly in the gathering dusk for him to come around.

A groan snapped him out of his reverie. Leonid struggled into a sitting position against the wall. Bengt threw him the towel, and Leonid pressed it to the bleeding spot on his head. Through narrow eyes, one of which was already swelling shut, he looked at Bengt. "It's not going to be very convincing if I tell you now that it would be better to let Vigo Andúja go, right?" he said with difficulty.

Bengt merely raised one eyebrow.

"'S true though. Better for Rukow anyway."

"Just be glad you're still alive," Bengt growled.

"I am, believe me. But even if you kill me, you won't be here tomorrow, and Andúja has a dozen people he can sic on Rukow."

"Like Luìz?"

Leonid shook his head, but stopped and grimaced with pain. "The coronel would never kill him. Rough him up, yes, but not kill."

"You call that roughing up?" Bengt was too spent for rage, but the expression lay like a rock in his stomach.

"He's still alive, isn't he?"

"No thanks to you two."

"Al contrario. Anyone else wouldn't have warned him half as often. The coronel had no choice but to discipline his son, who wouldn't stop breaking rank. It's his own fault if he constantly puts himself in the line of fire. How often do you think it saved his life that the coronel or I dealt with him?"

"Of course, nothing but love between you and Rukow."

"Listen, I've got nothing against him." Leonid grinned with an effort. "Kinda like him. The gnat has the balls of a bull. But that's the problem. The little shit never really stops fighting. He retreats and regroups, and then he's a pain in your ass again."

Bengt felt laughter bubble up in his throat. The situation was too absurd. Leonid, who was sitting propped against the wall, battered to a pulp, holding a towel to his head with bound hands and warning Bengt not to antagonize Andúja. Who had come here to finish Alex off and was now telling Bengt it was nothing but a brotherly correctional measure. He didn't seem to hold it against Bengt in the least that he'd been beaten up instead.

But what he'd said was no laughing matter. Alex was right; it wouldn't make any difference if they let Vigo go. As long as Alex was alive, he'd be a thorn in Andúja's side.

"If you care at all for Alex Rukow," Leonid said, "you should make sure Vigo gets home."

Bengt heaved himself out of the chair and crouched in front of the Santuarian. "If you care at all for your life, you should never forget how much you care for Alex Rukow."

"I won't be the one to kill him. And you won't be the one who can protect him."

In that, at least, Leonid was right. Bengt's fingers curled into fists again. There was nothing he could do except pray that Alex would last until the borders fell. Andúja did indeed have enough goons for his dirty work. Would Luìz try to protect his son in a pinch? And Leonid? If he let Leonid go . . .

"If I hear that anything has happened to Alex," Bengt said softly, "I'll take the next plane to Cuevas or Tierraroja and finish what I started tonight. I'll tear you apart piece by piece. If it's the last thing I do."

The Santuarian swallowed. "I'm not his babysitter. What do you want me to do? Play his bodyguard?"

"If necessary."

"That might lead to a slight conflict of interests."

"Your problem. But if Alex Rukow dies, that is going to be the biggest and last disaster of your life." Bengt released the belt around Leonid's wrists. "So the next time you show up here, think hard about your intentions, and before you take your eyes off Rukow, consider equally hard whether you can really afford to do that." He stood up. "And now piss off before I forget that I'll have a pile of paperwork to do if I break your neck."

Leonid looked at him searchingly, then pushed himself to his feet with a groan and saluted. "Pleasure making your acquaintance, Comisario," he said formally before leaving.

Bengt had the impression he actually meant it. He couldn't read the man, wasn't sure he'd done the right thing. He could at least have locked him up for breaking and entering. Or even attempted murder? That last one would be hard to prove, though.

Would it help or hurt Alex that he hadn't? And should that even make a difference? He groaned. How could something like truth or integrity exist in a system like this? How did one measure those values? And when had he started to doubt their absoluteness?

He poured the last cup of tea. His hands were stiffening by the minute. Surprised, he noticed his bruised knuckles, breathed in sharply when he realized with how little reflection he had thrown himself into the fight, how close he'd been to killing the Santuarian. Close, yes, but he hadn't. Despite blind rage. Wasn't that the point? He wasn't sure, but it wasn't a bad feeling to be free of guilt after a loss of control like that. He shook his head, which didn't clear his thoughts the least bit. It was a long drive to Tierraroja. He should get out of here.

He went to check the gash above his brows in the bathroom mirror, wryly remembered the day he'd seen Alex for the first time. His side hurt. He took his shirt off and frowned at the large mark Leonid's knee had left. Carefully, he cleaned the blood off his hands and face. There still had to be some of that aloe gel in the kitchen.

In the hallway, he almost collided with Alex, who let out a surprised hiss when he saw him.

Bengt raised a placatory hand. "It's not as bad as it looks."

"Should I see the other guy?" Alex asked skeptically.

"Absolutely. You'd have liked it."

"Leonid?"

Bengt nodded. "I'm hoping he won't bother you again."

His only answer was a disbelieving smile.

"What are you going to do until the annexation?"

The look Alex threw him said more loudly than words that Bengt wasn't playing with a full deck. *There won't be an annexation, you blockhead.* "Go into hiding, vanish into thin air—I'll think of something, don't worry."

"You'll have your chance. Soon. Until then, you have to keep your head down. And then you'll disappear from here."

"'Course."

Bengt gave it up. "You still got some of that aloe stuff?"

"In the kitchen." Alex led the way, dug the little jar out of the drawer and pulled up a chair.

Bengt sat and held out his hand. "I can do that."

"Hands off, you can't see a thing." Alex carefully turned Bengt's head towards the light, frowned, and gently applied the gel with his fingertips. "Looks like Luìz identified me as the weak link," he said wryly. "Well, at least Mendez will have a quiet night. Give me your hands."

"I can see those just fine."

For a moment, Alex looked as if he was going to argue, then he shrugged and handed over the jar. The usual evening shadow covered his chin and made his jaw look carved in the lamplight. Bengt rubbed gel on his knuckles and the contusion on his side and got up.

Alex was leaning against the doorframe and didn't take his eyes off Bengt. "You . . . will be glad to get back home tomorrow."

"Haven't thought about it," Bengt lied noncommittally. He took a step to leave the kitchen, but Alex didn't move out of his way.

"My shirt's still in the bathroom," Bengt finally said.

"I'll get it. Why don't you take your time and finish your tea?"

In the living room, the tea had gone cold. When Alex came back, Bengt held out his hand for the shirt. "Time I got back to the hotel."

"Mhmmm." Alex ignored him and dropped into the chair. "What's going to happen now?"

What the fuck? "You know what. I'll pick up my colleagues at the airport tomorrow, we'll process the crime scene, or what's left of it, come here, bring the dead and the living to Cuevas, pack them all into the plane, and then we're gone." That sounded desperately final.

Alex stared at him, the balled-up shirt in his hands, until Bengt didn't know where to look anymore. "I'd really better go."

The Santuarian absentmindedly rubbed his chin. "Don't you ever have to shave?" he asked disjointedly.

"No, not for a wh— What in the world does that have to do with anything?"

"No idea. Something I'd been wondering. Handy."

"Yeah, well . . . Alex, I—"

"Want me to make more tea?"

Bengt sighed. If it hadn't been so ludicrous, he could have sworn the Santuarian was trying to stall him. "No, thanks. Really. Listen, it's already—"

"That pattern on your arm, does that have any special meaning?"

"Excuse me?" Ludicrous or not, that was hard to explain away. He looked at his upper arm. "It's a Fletta. Those patterns are traditional. Symbols of what I told you about, knots, connections, that stuff? Most people get one around puberty, some sort of initiation I guess." His thoughts were elsewhere. Surprised and breathless by the possibility that Alex might indeed want him to stay, he touched the brand. "Come here."

Alex hesitated.

"Well?"

The Santuarian got up and came closer.

"Give me your hand." Bengt took Alex's fingers and traced the brand with their tips, watching him intently.

A shudder ran through the Santuarian's body, but he didn't pull back, left his hand on Bengt's arm when Bengt let him go, moved his thumb over the pattern, stood heart-stoppingly close, eyes huge and dark. Bengt swallowed hard, wanted so badly to return just this little touch, but knew he wouldn't be able to stop if he started. Finally, he raised his other hand and let his fingertips glide slowly, tentatively, over Alex's five-o'clock shadow, waiting for the unavoidable reaction—embarrassment, panic, anger. But there was nothing, only curious expectancy. "Did I miss something?" Bengt asked hoarsely.

There was uncertainty in Alex's eyes, but he didn't move. "I can't repair my wall as fast as you tear it down," he murmured.

Bengt breathed in sharply. Was that an invitation? Could it be anything else? Still incredulous, wary, all senses ready to recognize denial or defense, he lowered his head, kissed the point under Alex's ear where the jawbone ended, traced the line to the chin with his lips, kissed the corner of his mouth.

Alex's head followed the movement. Bengt licked over Alex's half-open lips, his teeth, when the Santuarian suddenly wrapped his arms around Bengt's neck and kissed him back.

As if the wall he'd torn down had been a dam, the flood now swept Bengt away in a wild torrent as unexpected as it was irresistible.

CHAPTER 15

Alex's world shrank to the tiny section of it that was Bengt, on whom he concentrated with every nerve ending. He didn't know what he wanted or had expected; he only knew what he didn't want—for Bengt to leave. When the Skanian took his fingers to move them across the brand, desire shot through him all the way to his toes.

He felt like he was standing at a chasm high above a raging firestorm. Every fiber in his body screamed at him to pull back, not to give in to temptation, not to let go. And every fiber in his body hungered to do just that, to give himself up, to spread his arms wide and fly.

He might have taken the step back if it hadn't been for those unbearably light kisses. Those merest hints of a touch on his skin awakened a lust that denied control. Suddenly he couldn't bear their teasing any longer, wrapped his arms around Bengt's neck and pulled him closer, caught those fleeting kisses, lips and tongue, could hear his own intake of breath.

Bengt's hands under his shirt, on his skin, the downy touch of Bengt's chest against his own. The threat of losing himself in the hunger that tore through his body. What the hell was he doing?

Bengt's embrace grew tighter. His hands wandered down Alex's back into his pants, closed around his ass. Touches like sparks on his skin. How could he possibly pull away from that? Alex felt the sound in his throat without hearing it, moved his lips across Bengt's chin, along his collarbone, rested his forehead against his shoulder, buried his face in the silky down on his chest.

He felt Bengt strip the pants off both their hips without ever taking his lips off Alex's body. The places Bengt touched with tongue and lips burned. Then the soft down was against his back. Hands caressed his chest, his belly, lips on his neck. He let his head fall back against Bengt's shoulder, felt the trembling tension run through the Skanian's body, his own becoming unbearable. Fast breathing. Harder, more urgent movement. Bengt's cock against his ass. Hands on his shoulders pushing him forward, the back of the armchair against his thighs.

Panic cut through him like a knife. "No!"

Bengt let him go. "Easy." He sounded as breathless as Alex. "We can stop anytime. This only goes as far as you want." He stood so close that Alex could feel the heat coming off his skin.

Alex was soaked in sweat, tense to the point of snapping. The fear in his head did nothing to diminish his desire. He cursed his disappointment with the interruption. How could he want this? How not? He wanted so badly to just be able to switch off thought, surrender to the seduction.

Bengt caressed his neck with his fingertips, but stayed where he was. Maybe it *was* possible to relinquish control. He could do this, with Bengt he could. Give himself up and fly. He closed his eyes, let himself be pulled in by the touch.

Bengt's arms. Bengt's hands on his thighs, arms, chest. Lips and tongue on neck and shoulders, the need for more. "Don't stop."

Time does.

There's only now. Nothing exists but a hand on his belly, tracing his groin, everywhere except where he wants it, avoiding the direct contact until Alex pleads. Kisses on his shoulders, his neck, the hand that finally closes around his cock, only to let go again when he moans. This time he hears the frustrated sound he makes, bites his lips. Bengt's soft, deep chuckle behind him. The down at his back, his ass, his legs driving him wild.

He slumps against the back of the chair, bracing himself on its arms. Bengt's sharp inhalation of breath, the smell of aloe. Tentative, gliding fingers, their pressure becoming more insistent, pain that flashes through his body like deliverance, merging with his arousal to mindless ecstasy. No thought of holding back, just the plunge into the flames that singe his skin and burn his fear. Deep probing that carries him to the brink of completion and back. The impatient attempt to bring himself relief, but Bengt holds him effortlessly. He squirms in Bengt's hold, at the same time trying to escape and to feel the man behind him closer, the fingers deeper, until Bengt finally resumes his grip around Alex's cock. Madonna! He pushes into the new touch, and back against Bengt and those fingers, back and forth, faster and faster until the flames at the bottom of the chasm engulf him, and what he was, what is left of him, shatters in the inferno.

Darkness surrounded him. For a moment he had no body, saw, heard, felt nothing, was nothing. Then his senses returned one by one. The creak of a beam. Bengt's deep breathing at his back. Arms around his shoulders. He lay on the rug, nestled full length against Bengt's body. Replete lassitude in his limbs, he stretched his muscles, sat up, felt for the lamp on the table and lit it. He watched the sleeping Skanian next to him, his mind carefully approaching what he had done, circling it, touching it. But there was nothing except this languid contentment of satisfied desire, as if the rules had changed or the world wasn't the same anymore.

Tentatively, savoring this new feeling, he passed his hand over the hard muscles on Bengt's chest, laid it against his smooth cheek, traced the lips with his thumb, followed with his own lips.

Bengt mumbled something Alex couldn't understand, then, waking, pulled him close, kissed him, taking his time, newly kindling the lust Alex had thought satisfied. Suddenly, there was no trace of languor, only the hope that this tantalizing game might never end.

He felt a smile on his lips, heard Bengt moan. Spurred on by Bengt's arousal, he stretched Bengt's arm above his head and traced the outer contours of his pecs with the tip of his tongue. Bengt groaned and turned on his back, pulling Alex along in his arm.

Alex stretched out on top of him, heard Bengt's sharp intake of breath, kissed his collarbone and the hollow at his throat, playfully bit his nipple, felt him grow hard underneath him, stoking his own arousal. He covered the muscular belly with kisses, played his tongue around the navel, down the treasure trail underneath, making Bengt hold his breath. Took the skin on the inner thigh between his teeth, sucked on it, kissed the spot, licked the salt off. He, too, took his time.

He woke when Bengt sat up. The first shimmer of light outlined the transom of the window darkly against the sky. Please, don't let the day start. Stop time again.

Bengt smiled at him with the same satisfaction Alex had felt so warmly only a few hours ago. Alex tried to recapture that feeling, but it eluded him. That had been last night. Now it was morning, the last day. He swallowed hard, stood up, and walked over to the window, cooling his face against the glass, desperately trying to lock away yesterday somewhere he'd be able to find it when he needed to—when Bengt was gone.

"Alex? You okay?"

"Fine."

Silence.

"Please don't."

"What?"

"Stonewall."

"Madrios, Bengt, what the hell do you want to hear? That it breaks my heart that you're leaving?" Alex prepared a smile before he turned. "Don't worry, I'll survive."

A crease had appeared between Bengt's brows. "The annexation won't take forever. And then you're coming to Jarðvegur." Pleading. "You know I can't stay here. I can't take those meds forever. And I need my family."

"I know."

"You'll come?"

"I will." There would be no annexation.

"I love you." Softly, hesitantly, almost a question.

Alex flinched. "Oh, for the love of . . . come on, Bengt, no lines. Please!"

Bengt closed his eyes, his cheek muscles jumping briefly before he looked at Alex again. "I swear, my report will light a fire under everyone's butt. Sunne is going to bombard the Þing. I'm going to rally everyone I know to bombard the Þing. Hell, we'll involve the media. Anything. The annexation. Will. Go. Through," he finished, stressing every word.

"Right."

"You can already start growing your hair; you look ridiculous." He had such a confident smile on his lips that Alex almost believed it, almost gave in to the temptation of imagining a life far from here, a life with Bengt in it . . .

He shook his head. Don't go there. But that was so infinitely hard with Bengt sitting on his rug, buck naked, and smiling as if it weren't morning, as if time didn't exist.

"I'll be in the shower." Why did the Skanian have to make this so fucking hard?

Alex gasped under the cold water and flinched when pain flashed through his chest. He'd completely forgotten about his ribs. Why hadn't he just let Bengt go home last night? Would it have been easier then? Maybe. Would he do it again? Think of something else.

He'd best go directly to the comandatura to relieve Mendez and close his report.

He made tea while Bengt took his shower, avoided touching him during breakfast, felt Bengt's looks, which he didn't dare to return, afraid his brittle control would shatter like glass.

When Bengt finally drove to the airport, he breathed a bit easier, was almost relieved. Still, it was difficult to concentrate, keep it real, plan the day. Who was he? Gay? Or not? He had no clue, and no inclination to pursue the question. He felt sealed off, as if there were no world outside these rooms. And yet, he knew the world would catch up with him only too soon. During these last few days, he had broken its most compelling taboos. That could not remain unpunished.

Stepping out onto the porch, he was therefore not surprised to see Luìz's zorro parked in the road. The thought of how quickly the coronel would answer his question, whether he was gay or not, brought an evil grin to his lips. But why would he let Luìz stick him with any labels?

The coronel stepped over the tree trunk and strolled up the driveway, while Alex waited and searched for cracks in the granite of his face.

"Your friend provided Leonid with a couple of sick days. I suppose you'll plead temporary insanity?"

Alex didn't answer, felt for the fear inside him and found only a shadow of it.

"The patrón is quite worried about his son," Luìz continued. There were shadows under his eyes, and he looked even more gaunt than usual. Surely the patrón was more than just worried. He must have lit quite the fire under his coronel's ass.

"He won't get Bengt to release his son," Alex said. "Did he send you to avenge the hammering Leonid took?"

"He sent me to kill you."

That came out so quietly, so completely flat that it took a few seconds to sink in. "What's your plan? Shoot me on the porch?" And why not? No hiding, no eternal running, and he wouldn't have to say good-bye to Bengt.

"You'll have to disappear."

"Excuse me?"

"Am I mumbling?"

"What . . . Why are you telling me that? And where do you think I'd go? Somewhere Andúja can't find me? Where's that supposed to be?" It wouldn't be easy, that much was certain.

Luìz's shoulders drooped. "I could have told him you'd cleared out." Something like exhaustion showed in his face.

Alex crowed inwardly. Luìz didn't know. He had no idea how to escape Andúja. And if Bengt was right? If he really didn't want to kill Alex? How far would Luìz go? If he knew what had happened here last night? No question.

"Why don't we just get it over with," Alex said, tense.

Luìz's eyes narrowed, a crease appearing between his brows. "Get it over with? You're my son."

The old hatred took the edge off Alex's surprise. "That's a point we'll never agree on."

"It's not negotiable. Family's not something you choose."

"Family? You don't have the faintest idea what that is, family. You slit the throat of the man who was my father from ear to ear because he had something you will never have. And what did it get you? You're nobody's husband, and no more anyone's father than you'd be if you'd left us all in peace."

Luìz froze. "You're my responsibility. I would never kill you."

Alex shrugged, felt safer despite his doubt. "Tough luck. What do you want to do? Ignore a direct order?"

"You want to argue about that out here?"

"Why not?"

Alex could see the thoughts chasing each other behind Luìz's eyes. His fingers drummed against his thigh, curled into a fist, opened again. Alex couldn't remember ever having seen him so undecided. It was inconceivable that there should be something the coronel was not prepared to do.

Then a decision showed in those icy eyes. "Your mother should have drowned you at birth. That would have saved both of us a lifetime of trouble."

"A lamentable lack of foresight." Alex could feel how tense Luìz was; he hummed with suppressed energy.

The coronel acknowledged the cynical comeback with a cold smile. "Indeed. I wish you'd gone to the mines in Jarðvegur instead of the policía. Why did you change your mind? You seem to have such a connection with Skanians."

"Why did *I* change my—" Rage exploded in Alex's chest and reduced any rational thought to ashes. "You contemptible chilito," he started, saw Luìz grin, swallowed the rest, and lunged off the porch. He managed to grab Luìz's shoulders, paid for the lack of cover with a blow to the solar plexus that made him gasp for air and reminded him of his ribs, but not before he registered with satisfaction the crunch of Luìz's nose breaking against his forehead. The pain of the impact nearly blinded him. He jerked up his knee, connected with something soft and, when Luìz yelled and jackknifed, brought the knee up again, connecting hard with Luìz's jaw. The coronel's head whipped back, and he instinctively tried to step away, but Alex hooked his foot behind Luìz's calf, sending him sprawling ass first in the dirt. Alex kicked him hard, then again—he didn't care where. Luìz managed to get a grip on his gun, but Alex's boot catapulted it onto the porch, where it clattered across the boards. Again and again, he kicked the prone body.

Only when Luìz curled up into a fetal position and protectively brought his arms up around his head did he stop. It wasn't like the coronel not to defend himself. If getting kicked to a pulp was his plan, it wasn't going to work. Breathing hard, Alex tried to get a grip on his fury. "You're a piece of shit, Luìz. You want me to kill you to spare you Andúja's wrath."

Luìz didn't move. Not until Alex turned and went to pick up the gun did he take his arms down. Alex shoved the gun into the back of his pants and walked down the drive.

When he passed Luìz, the coronel sat up and wiped the blood off his face. "You could at least leave me the gun." And when Alex ignored him, "Alex! Do you really want to see what Andúja is going to leave of me?"

Alex stopped. "You're assuming I give a shit about what happens to you."

Luìz chuckled. "You're so much more my son than you think. You heed the law only when it suits you."

"What law? Do you want me to lock Andúja up? For what? There's no such thing as preventive arrest." And yet the remark stung. Alex grimaced. "If I shoot you with your own gun, no one will even believe it was self-defense."

Luìz stared at him.

Alex shrugged impatiently. "What did you expect? That I'd defend your life?"

"Just leave me the gun."

Alex hesitated. Luìz had earned every pain and every humiliation Andúja could inflict upon him. A bullet seemed too quick and easy to pay for everything he'd done. But where did justice end and revenge begin? He hated Luìz for the decision he was forcing Alex to make. Longed to defeat him with the very laws he'd trampled underfoot all his life. But if he arrested Luìz for breaking and entering or for assault, and locked him in the drunk tank, the Comandatura Three wouldn't survive the day. Apart from that, despite everything, he really didn't want to serve Luìz to Andúja on a silver platter. But other than that, there was nothing he could do. Except . . . A thought flashed through his mind, so beyond impossible, almost blasphemous. He stared at Luìz, who was still sitting on the ground holding his balls, considered his idea, circled it, looked for a weakness, then carefully accepted the possibility that he now had the solution that had eluded him for so long.

"Luìz Rukow, you're under arrest for the murder of Manuel Vasquez."

Luìz looked at him, incredulous. "*You* are arresting *me*? For something that happened over twenty years ago? And how are you going to prove that?"

"I don't have to. You're going to sign a confession and disappear behind bars in Jarðvegur for the next thirty years, because that is your only chance to escape the patrón."

Luìz stared at him. "He's going to kill you."

"He's planning that anyway. Get up."

"Forget it. I'm not going to jail."

"You don't have a choice."

"Do you seriously believe you could prevent me from just walking out of here?"

"To go where, exactly?"

"And what rock are *you* going to crawl under?"

Alex smiled tiredly. "Don't even try, Coronel. That only works once. The difference between us is that I at least have a chance. You have nothing. You may have subordinates, but their loyalties lie with Andúja first. The second the patrón brands you a traitor with a snap of his fingers, they'll tear your uniform to pieces and feed you naked to the wolves. Go, if you want. Be interesting to see how far you get."

"Give me the gun."

"Andúja or the can, that's all that's on offer today. What's it gonna be?"

Luìz stared at him, visibly searching for a way out. Finally, he dragged himself to his feet. Alex automatically took a step back, which Luìz noted with a wolfish grin.

"We could fight for the gun."

"We did. You lost." Alex didn't bother cuffing him, but clicked the magazine out of the gun and flipped the bullets one by one into the underbrush as the two of them walked east toward the comandatura.

He was almost surprised that the road looked the same as always. He still had this skewed feeling that the world had shifted, become alien, broken. Broken rules.

For a while, Luìz walked silently beside him, only occasionally throwing him a sideways glance. "Do you seriously believe you have a chance?" he finally asked.

Did he? At least he had friends, as incredible as that sounded. What else had Andrés tried to tell him in his cryptic way? And Bengt . . . was someone he should forget as soon as possible. But there was also Mendez, who had his own security net. Yes, he had a chance, however small it might be. *Chingate,* Luìz. He smiled contentedly. "That's none of your fucking business."

Gijón sat at his desk and jumped up, terrified, when he saw Luìz. But Alex was in a hurry and, for once, ignored the kid, taking Luìz directly into his office. Confession, report, and then get the hell out as soon as Bengt's zorro came down the road. He didn't have much time. Couldn't face seeing him again. Not to say good-bye. Gijón could do the official handover of the prisoners.

Mendez stuck his head in the door; startled at the sight of Luìz, he raised an inquiring eyebrow.

"Long story," was all Alex said.

Mendez's brows crept higher, and Alex sighed. The capitán was holding him up. Bengt wouldn't be gone forever. "He killed my . . . my mother's husband. He's going to Jarðvegur with the others. I'm just taking his confession."

"His . . . confession."

"Go home, Simón. Sleep a couple of hours. I'll stay until ICE takes the hot merchandise off our hands. I'll see you later. Or tomorrow."

Mendez blinked tiredly. Alex took it as a sign of his trust that he said no more than, "I hope I'll be able to make more sense of this after I've read your report," before he disappeared.

After Luìz had signed his confession, Alex locked him in the cell next to Vigo. It was getting crowded in the tiny comandatura, but it wouldn't be for long. Then he sat down at his typewriter, inserted a blank sheet of paper, and stared at it. How to explain what had happened since his last report?

What finally helped him was the dry, official language that allowed him the necessary distance. When he was finished, he locked away Luìz's gun, copied all the papers for ICE, collected them in a folder, piled his keys on top, and handed everything to the rurale.

The sound of a motor brought him to the door, where he nervously watched the cloud of dust coming closer. Without a doubt Bengt and the Skanian cavalry. The zorro was bursting at the seams. Alex turned and melted into the thick underbrush that grew alongside the path to the beach. If he walked along the water, he wouldn't run into Bengt's arms. The sooner he started to remove the Skanian from his life, the better. The sea was deep blue and smooth as glass, a perfect day for swimming. Automatically, his gaze wandered across the water in the direction of the mainland. Forget it, Alex.

At home, he didn't know what to do with himself, cleaned up a bit, constantly checked his watch—the hands didn't seem to be moving at all—and finally decided to take that swim, despite his ribs. Armed with a towel, he opened the door and collided with Bengt's chest.

"I didn't want to leave without saying good-bye," the Skanian said.

Alex barely swallowed a curse. Both zorros were parked at the end of the drive, Gijón at the wheel of one, the backseat of which held Inés and Dr. Kvulf. In the other, Luìz and Vigo were being guarded by a Skanian Alex had never seen before. "You couldn't find a bigger audience?" he snapped.

"Can I come in for a second?"

Alex hesitated, but couldn't bring himself to slam the door in Bengt's face. He stepped back into the living room, threw the towel onto one of the chairs, and stood undecided in the middle of the room. Finally, he leaned against the wall and shoved his hands in his pockets. "Keep it brief," he said before Bengt could open his lips. "I have to go back."

Bengt stood in the door as if he'd walked into a wall. "Every time I think I finally understand you . . ."

Alex pressed his shoulders against the wall and curled his fingers into fists.

The Skanian pinched the bridge of his nose, tried twice to say something. "You'll come as soon as you can?" was the only thing he finally got out.

Oh, Bengt, you dreamer. "On the first plane." And now get the hell out of here.

Bengt looked like he was waiting for something. An embrace? A kiss? Alex couldn't have moved if he'd tried.

In the end, Bengt just nodded, turned without another word, and left. Motors started up outside, then slowly faded.

Silence. Alex's legs gave out, and with a dry sound in his throat, he slid down the wall, wrapped his arms around his knees, and stared at the door.

EPILOGUE

THE BORDERS HAVE FALLEN

pas. Hentavik - After long and difficult negotiations, the Þing has finally granted Santuarians visa entry to Jarðvegur. The Herald has repeatedly reported about the shocking revelations in ICE's press releases these past months. These prompted the government to establish an embassy in Tierraroja, the island's capital, in order to support the adoption of democratic principles and ensure that none of those willing to depart are refused a visa.

This morning, an official protest from the patrones, the oligarchy ruling the island, reached the Þing. However, according to our sources, Simón Mendez, leader of the opposition party "Svoboda," welcomed the decision in no uncertain terms and expressed his hope that the annexation would soon be followed by democratic elections and a Santuarian seat in the Þing.

Opinions in the streets of Hentavik are divided. But the majority seem to be looking forward to meeting the visitors from Santuario with curiosity and an open mind.

Alex fell silent and slowly folded the page he'd been translating for Xavier. The fire had almost burned down, and Alex kicked a log back in, restarting the flames and sending a shower of sparks into the night sky. Open borders and visa entry. Just like Bengt had predicted. The naive, absurdly hopeful and so very magnetic bastard had been right.

Mendez would know more about the details. Alex had to find a way to meet with him again. No, he *would* find a way. He wasn't out of the woods just yet, but visa entry . . . Magic words.

"*Es cierto*?" Xavier asked.

"It's their paper. Why would they lie about it?"

Xavier grabbed the page and unfolded it, staring at the words he couldn't read. "Holy hell."

"Or rather, a way out of it," Alex said. That, and a way toward a huge cop who talked too much, who didn't know how to eat cubiertas, and whose eyes were too blue.

"You gonna leave, then?"

"You can bet your skinny fugitive ass I am."

ACKNOWLEDGMENTS

I owe a big thank you to my beta readers, Elizabeth and Margaret, and to Y, always and for everything, but especially for learning to kick my butt.

ABOUT THE AUTHOR

G.B. Gordon worked as a packer, landscaper, waiter, and coach before going back to school to major in linguistics and, at 35, switch to less backbreaking monetary pursuits like translating, editing, and writing. Having lived in various parts of the world, Gordon is now happily ensconced in suburban Ontario with the best of all husbands. *Santuario* is G.B. Gordon's first published work, but many more stories are just waiting to hit the keyboard.

Gordon online:
Website and blog: gordon.kontext.ca
Twitter: twitter.com/gb_gordon
Goodreads: www.goodreads.com/author/show/367361.G_B_Gordon

Enjoy this book?
Find more romantic suspense at
RiptidePublishing.com

Historic haunting with flair.

www.riptidepublishing.com/titles/
gravedigger's-brawl
ISBN: 978-1-937551-63-6

Serving ghosts with the Guinness.

www.riptidepublishing.com/titles/
gleams-remoter-world
ISBN: 978-1-937551-67-4

Printed in Germany
by Amazon Distribution
GmbH, Leipzig